"I don't know if Carla is going to show up at all, or when, if she does. And you can't just hang around. Either play or leave."

I should just leave. I wouldn't be able to talk to Johnny if I was at the table anyway. But maybe one of the other players could give me some info on him. Or when there were breaks in the game. Or after, if I lasted until the game broke up.

A tingle ran down my spine. A different feeling than Johnny's leering had caused. This was a competitive juice flowing through my body. A juice different from a Hummer, but no less compelling.

Suddenly, I *wanted* to be able to last until the game broke up. Even though the other players had probably started with twenty thousand each and I only had ten. Even more of a challenge. And with players I didn't know?

Yeah, I wanted this.

I told myself all the things I'd said to Monty in the car. It wasn't about me. Not about playing. It was all about getting information that might help Niall's parents breathe a little easier about their son. That they were safe in their Topeka home.

But I'd be lying to myself if I said that was the only reason.

I wanted to beat these guys with less time and less money.

"Then I guess I'm playing," I said. I took the cash out of my pocket and handed it over. Johnny gave me a stack of chips. Noticeably smaller than most of the stacks in front of the players at the table.

"Good luck," he said. There was a snideness in his voice that told me he didn't really wish me well. I only wished he was at the table too so I could beat his ass and take his money.

I tapped my horseshoe pendant three times and made my way over to the table.

For Niall, I told myself as I took my seat.

"Liar," JoJo's voice said in my head.

AGAINST THE GRAIN

♣ ♦ ♥ ♠

Anna Dawson Book Five

MARA JACOBS

Published by Mara Jacobs
©Copyright 2021 Copper Country Press, LLC

ISBN: 978-1-940993-08-9

For more information on the author and her works, please
see www.marajacobs.com

To my nephews—Jake, Kyle, Tyler, and Tanner.
You're all Good Boys!

One

I LOOKED DOWN THE INDOOR HALLWAY OF THE HOTEL, checking for security cameras, but there were none. Not surprising at this fleabag place.

Putting my shopping bag down on the ground, I hiked my short skirt up and my small top down. After a quick adjustment of my wig, I picked up the bag and knocked on the door.

"Who is it?" came a voice from behind the door. Immediately. Like he was waiting for me.

I was more convinced that I was doing the right thing, even though putting on these clothes after so long had me nearly hyperventilating.

"JoJo," I answered, hating the name. Hating everything about being here.

And yet, in a way, knowing this was exactly where I needed to be.

The door opened and a young man, lanky and pale, stepped into the hallway, looking both ways, seeing if I was alone.

"Just me, man," I said, and started walking into his room.

The stench of BO and old food hit me, and it was all I could do not to gag. Trying to breathe with my mouth—and none too deeply at that—I put down my bag on a rickety table and pulled out the bottle of Maker's Mark that I'd bought on the way here.

"Johnny said you were cool, man. Shut the damn door and

act like it," I said to the kid, who seemed startled but followed my directions.

He had dark blond hair that looked brown due to not having been washed—or combed—for days. His cheeks had a sparse growth, though it seemed he would never have a full beard, if the odd patches were any indication. He was wearing skinny jeans and a ratty tee that was really just filthy instead of a thoughtfully distressed look. If you'd cleaned him up, he could have been in the latest boy band. But not like this. His feet were bare and it was the sight of them—narrow, pale, toes curling into the stained carpet with nervousness—that somehow gave me the courage to go through with this.

I had done this sort of thing before. But never *this* thing.

Relaxing a little, he walked deeper into the room, eyeing the bottle of bourbon.

"What's your name, boy?" I asked.

"Niall," he said, nodding at the bottle.

"Glasses?" I said. He went into the tiny bathroom and came out with one filthy drinking glass.

I took it from him and turned my back to him as I made a show of pouring him a drink. Niall made it easy, moving over to the only chair in the room and sitting down. His leg immediately began to jiggle. I could hear the soft tapping of his heel as I dumped the contents of a baggie I'd hidden in my waistband into his drink. After swishing the powder around in the amber liquid with my finger until it dissolved, I turned around and brought the glass to him, holding the bottle in my other hand.

"Drink this and let's talk for a bit, yeah?" I said. He nodded, taking the glass from me.

Whatever manners his mother had taught him had not totally gone down the toilet, because when he realized I only held the bottle, he offered the glass to me, but I shook my head.

"It's okay, Niall. This works for me." I took a healthy swig straight from the bottle, letting the booze burn down my throat, willing myself not to cough.

He followed suit, drinking from the glass. I moved to the bed, sitting down, hoping I wouldn't have to delouse myself from the nasty bedspread.

"Okay, here's the thing—" he started.

I held up a hand. "Plenty of time for that, Niall. I'm here to help, like Johnny told you. Let's just get to know each other a little bit first, yeah?"

He blinked a few times, like he was trying to focus on me. Maybe he was. Maybe he just couldn't believe that I wasn't already harassing him for the money he owed.

His focus sharpened, and though there was clearly suspicion in his eyes, he sat back in the chair and took another deep drink from the glass.

"How long you been in Vegas?" I asked him, then took another drink directly from the bottle, letting all of the liquid return out of my mouth, only imbibing a little bit.

"A year," he said. "A long fucking year."

I nodded, tipping the bottle toward him in a mock toast. "I hear that."

"You?"

I thought about how much of my real story to tell him. Or how much JoJo?

But really, it was all the same, wasn't it?

"Thirteen years. I came out as soon as I turned twenty-one." Same as him.

"Same as me," he said.

"Yeah," I said. "Almost like twins."

We eyed each other warily while he continued to drink and I faked it.

"Have *any* luck?" I asked. "In the long fucking year?"

A spark flashed in his eyes, and something caught in my throat.

I knew that flash. I'd had that flash. It was what I called a

Hummer—when everything is going right and you know you can't lose.

I missed that flash.

And yet look where that flash had gotten Niall. Where it had gotten me.

"Yeah," he said. "At first," he added, his head starting to drop. I wasn't sure if it was from the drug or the shame he no doubt felt.

Both could quickly drag you under.

"But then not so much?" I said, waiting to see if his head dropped further from the drugs starting to kick in.

Not quite yet. His head bobbed back up, but I was glad to see his eyes were already glassy. Good. I wanted to get this whole charade over with fast. This should have been the one JoJo mission I was actually proud of, but I wasn't.

Because I could so easily have been Niall.

Hell, I *was* Niall.

But I'd been given a chance to climb out of my own hellhole. Been given that chance by Ben Lowenstein and the Corporation.

"Not so much, no," he said, before following my lead and drinking deep. The glass was nearly empty, and I knew I wouldn't need to make small talk much longer.

"And thus, Johnny," I said.

Niall nodded, letting out a breath that was part scoff, part disgust. Of him or Johnny, I wasn't sure, but if I was betting, I'd lay money on self-disgust for Niall.

Maybe not. Maybe he hadn't sunk there yet. Maybe he was still blaming others, the horses, the cards, whatever had taken him to this point.

I recognized that, too.

"Fucking Johnny Aces," he said.

I shrugged. Supposedly JoJo was tight with this Johnny Aces. That was the story that was told to Niall. "He's just doing his job," I said. "Nobody put a gun to your head to make you take the money."

Another scoffing sound, like it was all out of his control. Yeah, maybe Niall wasn't quite there yet. I had a sinking feeling that this might not be the last I saw of Niall in Las Vegas.

I hoped not. For him. For us all.

"You would say that. He sent you here to negotiate terms for that bitch. What else are you gonna say?"

A chill ran down my spine. *That bitch*? The information I was given was that Niall was afraid of a guy named Johnny who was going to do him some major bodily harm unless Niall came up with the money he owed.

I'd assumed the money was owed to Johnny, but was he just the muscle? Did Niall actually owe a woman?

Another shiver ran through me, all over this time, when I thought about who that woman probably was.

"Carla," I said. If I was wrong, Niall was bound to be suspicious, perhaps even bolt, but I knew I wasn't wrong.

"Yeah, Carla," he said, confirming my thought.

Shit. She was not going to take too kindly to JoJo's interference in her business.

If she found out.

Knowing that what I'd come here for was even more important to accomplish, I let Niall rant about Carla for a few moments until his words started to slur and his neck bobbed like his head was too heavy to hold.

"Niall?" I said, interrupting him.

"Yeah?" he said, his head coming up. His eyes were really fuzzy now, but I thought he could still process what I was saying.

"If you had it to do over again, would you?"

"Huh?"

I leaned forward, my knees almost touching his in the small room. "If you could have a do-over, a clean slate, would you take it?"

"Whatta ya mean?"

"If you could turn back time and never come to Vegas. If you could just be a kid at college again, or go back home to Topeka, would you?"

His eyes narrowed—he'd caught that I'd known where he was from. Information I shouldn't have had. It wasn't a slip on my part—I knew he was only going to be conscious for a few more minutes, if that.

"Would you, Niall?"

He thought about it. That alone made me even surer that I'd probably be seeing Niall again. Or maybe nobody would ever see him again.

If he had really hit rock bottom, he wouldn't have even hesitated. Niall wasn't there yet, but maybe in his case he wouldn't have to be.

Maybe he wouldn't have to have his foot broken and be taken in by a retired oddsmaker for his life to change.

"I guess," he said with little conviction. "Hey, how'd you know I was from…"

"Topeka" never left his mouth because he slumped forward, and I reached out to catch him. His body weight took me off the bed, but I broke his short fall from the chair and lugged his slight body to the bed, depositing first his torso, then swinging his legs up.

I made sure his breathing was regular, that his pulse was steady, and that he was in a comfortable position—my standard operating procedure when dousing people with knockout drugs.

I then rinsed out the baggie I'd used and tucked it back into my waistband. I soaked the glass he'd drunk from in the sink, tossing in the bar of soap that was still in its wrapper.

Niall had bigger things to worry about than personal hygiene.

Mainly owing major money to Carla Rossetti.

Satisfied that Niall would survive meeting JoJo, I took out a burner phone and sent a text.

Then I sat down and waited, not wanting to leave Niall alone in case something went haywire with the pickup.

I really didn't want to be here when the door was knocked, not sure if it would be Johnny or the man I'd just texted, but I stayed in the chair, my hand on the phone.

I traced along the flip phone, opening it and shutting it, not truly believing I had the need for one again.

But it was different this time.

Yeah, I'd told myself that before. But this time I really meant it.

(Yeah, I'd said that before, too.)

There was one short rap on the door. Then two more quickly together. Then one last one.

Was that some kind of code that Johnny had set up with Niall? Or was that just a weird kind of knock for me?

Quietly I made my way to the door and looked out the peephole. Relaxing, I opened the door to Monty Westerfield.

Intervention Man, if he was a superhero. Which he was kind of becoming.

Monty Westerfield dealt with addiction recovery, in particular gambling. Tall and lanky, almost the same body type as Niall. But Monty was way more put together. And there was no smell. He wore glasses and had floppy, light brown hair, but not overly long. He typically wore business casual when I saw him for therapy. Khakis and a golf shirt or long-sleeved shirt. Tonight, he was dressed in jeans and a retro Kinks tee. Trying to blend in.

I stepped back and let him in. "What was with that knock? Was I supposed to know that code or something?"

"Didn't we talk about it? I swear we talked about that." He walked past me and went right to Niall.

"We didn't talk about any secret knock," I said.

He put his hands on his hips as he looked down at Niall. Monty, at twenty-seven, was only five years older than Niall, and just as thin and pale.

But Monty didn't have the haunted look of a man being chased.

Monty pulled out his phone—not a burner—and tapped, then put it to his ear. "We're here. Bring in the chair. Room two-fifty-seven." He disconnected and looked at me. "Thanks."

I nodded and moved to the table, grabbing the bottle of bourbon, lighter now than when I'd arrived. "I'm going to take off," I said.

"Don't you want to stay? I'm sure his parents would want to thank you. They haven't been able to get anywhere near him without him taking off."

I shook my head. "That's okay." I very much did not want to meet Niall's parents, in from Topeka to pluck their son from the cesspool into which he'd sunk.

No doubt they would remind me of my parents back in Wisconsin, oblivious to the knowledge that they could have gotten a call many times years ago like the one Niall's parents had received about their child in peril.

"Okay. I'll talk to you soon?" he asked, and I nodded.

I walked from the room and down the hall, turning at the corner to see what had to be Niall's parents approaching, pushing an empty wheelchair.

I kept my head down and was grateful I'd already turned the corner so they wouldn't know that I'd just come from the room that held their son.

I passed them, squeezing against the wall to let them pass with the chair, not making eye contact. Trying to look like just some hooker strolling through a flophouse hallway.

A few steps past them I heard, "Excuse me," from Niall's mother. I willed myself to keep going, but I turned around. The polite Midwesterner in me wouldn't allow otherwise.

She left her husband with the chair and walked the few steps back to me.

"Are you… Umm… Did you?"

I nodded once, but didn't say anything.

She was in her early fifties, with soft brown hair cut short. She was wearing beige slacks and a dark blue blouse. Total mom material. My heart hurt thinking about my own mom.

Tears pooled in her eyes, but she tried to blink them back. Reaching out, she clasped my wrist. "Thank you," she whispered. "I don't know how to thank you enough."

I patted her hand with mine. "It's okay," I said. "I'm glad I could help."

"We've been so frantic. Trying to get him to see us. Then he runs again. We love him. I don't know why he'd run from us."

I did, but it would take too long to explain it to this nice woman. I was only beginning to be able to explain it to myself.

"Take care of him," I said, and took my hand from hers.

She released my arm. "Bless you," she said, then turned to join her husband, who gave me a nod.

"Yes," he said. "God bless you, whoever you are."

I acknowledged his words, then turned and made my way out of the hotel.

Whoever you are.

That was just it… Who was I?

Two

❖

IF I WASN'T EXACTLY SURE WHO I WAS, IT WAS BECAUSE the past eight months had turned my life completely upside down.

Not that it was that great nine months ago. Or for the thirteen years previous to that.

That was when I came to Vegas from Wisconsin, freshly twenty-one and armed with the hubris and delusions that can only truly belong to the young.

And to the stupid.

I had ups and downs those first three years, winning some, losing a little more. I got into some trouble and met Vince Santini, a local loan shark who also ran private high-stakes poker games.

His team consisted of enforcer Paulie Gonads, who had inflicted a most painful punishment upon my foot when I couldn't pay Vince, and Carla Rossetti, who was Vince's bookkeeper and pretty much ran the poker games.

That was when I met Ben Lowenstein—both of us in physical therapy. Him with a bum hip and me with a mangled foot.

Ben knew Paulie Gonads' handiwork right away and called me on it. I told him my situation.

And to my everlasting gratitude, Ben paid off Vince, buying

me some time, and moved me in with him. He said it was a good move for him, as he was slowing down and would need help around the house.

But let's face it, he was throwing me a lifeline, and I grabbed it with both hands.

Vince, not liking my foot being demolished any more than I did, came up with a way for me to pay off my next debt. (Because of course there was a next debt—I mentioned the degenerate gambler part, right?)

As I knew how a lot of people "worked off their debt," the plan he came up with sounded doable to me.

I'm a degenerate gambler—of *course* his plan was one I jumped at.

So I became JoJo, and over the course of the next eight years or so, I would *disable* a star player on a college basketball team that was heavily favored. Typically this caused the team to not cover the point spread—but usually still win, so no *real* harm, right?—and Vince would win his bet.

I did say *typically*, right?

Yeah, there were some atypical times in there, too.

That was how Raymond Joseph came to live with Ben and me.

A junior point guard from Central Iowa, he was one of the players that I'd roofied to get a poor performance out of him.

But then I got into some serious debt and needed Raymond's actual involvement. Which I procured only because he was desperate for money to get his sister into a good rehab facility.

And it worked for a bit, until it didn't and Jack Schiller and I swooped into Chicago, when Raymond was sent home in disgrace (and under investigation), and brought him home with me to Vegas.

Which brings me to Jack Schiller. It should be an easy recap because I'd only known him since February, but there was nothing easy about Jack Schiller.

A homicide detective for Las Vegas Metro, he came into our lives investigating when Danny O'Hern, one of Ben's breakfast buddies, was murdered.

And he kind of just…stayed.

Jack and I had been on, off, on, off, all through his drinking (which was currently not at all) and my gambling (ditto) and then finding out that Jack was actually Ben's biological son. News that made them both very happy, but awkward as hell around the house when Jack and I were in an "off" period.

But things had turned a corner, sort of, in the late spring, when I met Monty Westerfield.

Lorelei Samuels, who had joined our household six years ago as basically house manager, took her role seriously and arranged periodic interventions to try to help with my gambling. None really took, but poor Monty didn't give up.

He had formed a new type of support group, based on different techniques for us degenerate gamblers. And wanted me in it.

So I joined Monty's group, GREET—Gambling Recovery through Emotional Exchange Treatment. The theory was to find the emotional reasons why you gambled, through discussion, therapy, exercise, meditation, and other resources, then re-channel those emotions to a healthier lifestyle.

Yeah, I thought the same thing the first time I heard about it. Total bullshit.

But it had been going pretty well. I liked my support group, and was liking the program enough to become a silent partner in Monty's counseling business.

Until I woke up in bed with a member of the group with a bullet in his head. Caused by another member of the group.

So for now, I worked just with Monty—no group therapy.

Vince and I dabbled with idea of dating—again while Jack and I were off—but that didn't work out. And then it *really* didn't work when he tried to kill me and Carla saved me by getting Vince off me. Literally *off* me. And plunging to his death from the balcony of his high-rise apartment. Paulie Gonads had been killed before that, so just Carla remained of that unholy trinity. She took over the games, and she and I reached an uneasy alliance. I stayed out of her way; she stayed out of mine.

Still, she saved my life, so there was that.

Let's see, what else?

So yeah, life was going pretty well. Jack had spent the summer at my place recovering from being shot. He'd started out not speaking to me and in the wing of the house where Ben and Lorelei had their rooms.

But eventually we not only spoke, but much more, and now he spent his nights on the side of the house where Raymond and I had our rooms.

And he wasn't sleeping with Raymond.

All of these events played like a movie montage in my brain as I left Monty, Niall, and Niall's parent at the hotel.

I changed out of my JoJo garb in my car, which was not easy in a Porsche 911, then I put the duffel bag in the trunk in the front. I didn't even want it in the car with me, such was my disdain for all things JoJo.

I drove around for a while, not wanting to go straight home. In the past, I'd look for a poker game that might still be going on, but I was still not gambling, so that was out. Though poker had never really been the problem. Still, I just drove around Vegas, even a little out into the desert, before turning around and heading back to my house.

I was surprised to see lights on in the dining room as I walked to the front door. Too early for Ben to be up for breakfast. Or for Lor to be up, even if she was taking an early dance class.

Raymond Joseph was sitting at the dining room table, a mug of coffee in front of him, stuffing a few notebooks into a backpack.

"Aw, first day of school," I said. "Wait, let me get a camera, and make a sign for you to hold up saying what grade you're in."

He held up a sign, but it was a middle finger. I laughed and joined him at the table. "Nervous?"

He scoffed, but his heart wasn't in it. He was nervous, though he'd never admit it.

Raymond Joseph was a twenty-two-year-old Black man from the South Side of Chicago. He'd been a point guard for the Central Iowa basketball team and a year away from graduating with a good degree and hopes of going on to become a physical therapist when his basketball days were over. He was a great college player, but too small to make it in the pros, so those days would probably come sooner rather than later.

His life had been planned and was on track. Until he met me.

Until he met JoJo.

He'd been living with Ben, Lorelei, and me since the spring, when he was asked to leave Central Iowa and Chicago became too dangerous for him. He'd gotten rid of his recognizable braids, gone bald all summer, and now had just the shortest bit of hair growing in as he started his senior year at UNLV.

It wasn't the life he wanted, what he'd planned, but it was better than being in jail—or dead—which had been a couple of the options we'd escaped.

I pulled a sheet of paper my way. His class list. "Heavy stuff," I said.

He took the piece of paper back from me and looked it over. "Yeah, it is. But no point in taking basket-weaving, right? Crunch time. Let's get this shit done."

"You never took basket-weaving at CIU," I said.

"How would you know— Oh, yeah, you knew all about your boys before you made your move, didn't you?"

"Geez, you make it sound so creepy." He did some kind of grunt/scoff/harrumph, and I sighed. "Yeah, okay, it probably was creepy. But it was just research. Had to pick the right people.

You should be flattered."

"Oh, I am. So flattered. Right when I should be packing for classes in Dubuque, I'm here in Vegas, where I am lying low, don't know anybody, living with a—"

"Careful, now," I said.

"I was going to say an octogenarian, a showgirl, and a…"

"Yeah, that's the one I'm afraid of."

He zipped up his backpack, put it on the floor, and took a sip of coffee. "I guess I'll let you fill in your own blank," he said once he'd swallowed.

"That's even more terrifying," I said.

"Ain't that the truth," he said, then leaned back in his chair, cradling his mug in his hand. He was ready, but early. Yeah, nervous.

"So, you wanna talk about where you've been all night?" he asked.

I thought about Niall's parents, so frightened for their kid. Raymond's mother, Mahalia, had been just as concerned about her son. Did me helping Niall cancel out what I'd done to Raymond? Nope. Not even close. Still, it felt good to not have to run to the shower when I got home to wash JoJo and guilt off me.

"Not really," I said. He nodded and took another sip of coffee. "I mean, I wasn't playing cards or anything."

I was twelve years older than Raymond, owned the home he lived in, and was paying for him to finish up his degree. But right then, I felt like a teenager explaining to their father why they broke curfew.

I hated that feeling. Normally I would bristle against it, but I was getting better at recognizing it and acknowledging it.

Not so good at getting over it.

"I wasn't asking if you played cards. None of my business," he said.

I nodded and let out a deep breath. "I know. Reflex."

"I get it."

"Actually," I said, "I do want to ask you something. I came across a name tonight I wasn't familiar with, and I thought maybe you were."

"This is your town, not mine," he said. "I haven't done shit since I got here."

"I know, but this name might be connected with Carla. And since you've been working some of her games, and I haven't been to one in a while—"

"What's the name?" Raymond said.

"Johnny Aces."

"Jesus, what is it with this town and stupid nicknames?"

He wasn't wrong. Still. "There are a lot of stupid nicknames in sports, too."

"Touché."

"Well?"

He sat back up in his seat, setting the mug on the table and resting his elbows there, looking across the table at me. "Yeah, I've met him. He's come into a couple of Carla's games in the last month. New on the scene, from what I can tell."

"He's a player?"

He shook his head. "No. He's *with* Carla. Not sure how. Maybe her new muscle."

"Because you wouldn't be?"

Carla Rossetti had recruited Raymond to work the door at her private, high-stakes poker games. She figured that a young Black man might feel intimidating to old, rich white dudes who wanted to maybe get an extension on the money she'd just lent them. All he'd have to do was stand there in a very expensive suit, glowering. She wasn't wrong. It worked.

Still, beyond that, she'd occasionally need someone to do actual intimidation. More than just standing and glowering.

Raymond had—smartly, in my estimation—declined that job offer.

"Probably. I think she thought I'd come around once I got a taste of some money. But he showed up about a week after I told her I'd have to cut back to weekend games once classes started."

"He worked the door with you?"

"No. Maybe on nights I wasn't doing it, I'm not sure. But the few times I saw him, he came in, said a few things to Carla, nodded to me, looked over at the players, then left. Why are you asking about him?"

I weighed telling him about Niall, but figured it was best if he had no knowledge. "I think I might have done something that would piss off this Johnny Aces," I said. He knew right away that was as much as I was going to tell him, and why. He'd seen my brand of protection before. That was why he was attending UNLV this morning and not Central Iowa.

"If you're pissing off Johnny Aces, there's a good chance you're pissing off Carla, too," he said, summing up the conclusion I was also coming to.

"I'm guessing that's the way I'm leaning."

He took a quick look at his watch and put his mug down. "You two are on good terms, though, right? Would it be something she'd overlook? If you talked to her about it?"

"Maybe," I said. "Good terms, though? I guess. I mean, I don't owe her any money. But I'm not playing her games anymore, and she's not happy about that."

"Why?"

I shrugged. "I was a bit of a draw for her when she took over Vince's games after he died. Like collateral or something."

"An endorsement for her?"

"Something like that. But from what you said, it looks like she's getting players at her table, so maybe she doesn't care anymore if my butt is one of the ones in the chairs."

Raymond rose from his seat, pushed in his chair, and grabbed his backpack. He started to reach for his now-empty mug, but I waved a hand at it. "I'll get it. I'm heading to the kitchen anyway."

"Thanks," he said, swinging a strap over one shoulder, securing the backpack in place. He took a deep breath. "Here goes nothing."

"Oh!" I said, remembering something. "Hang on." I got up from the table and went over to the long credenza where Lor usually set up brunch. I slid one of the drawers open, pulled out a box, and brought it to Raymond. "Here. Just something I got you for today."

He looked at the brightly colored pencil box. Like the kind you'd get for a second grader. "Are you kidding me?"

"I know it's stupid. And I know Lor got you set up with a laptop and the real stuff you'd need, but I…"

He opened up the cheap plastic and rooted around inside, seeing the pencils with basketballs on them, the mechanical pencils and lead, eraser, sharpener. A smile crept across his face. He had a great smile, all sparkling white teeth. "Nah, this is cool. Thanks." He pulled out the one expensive item I'd purchased for him: a beautiful Montblanc pen. "This isn't usually in a kid's pencil box."

"No, not usually."

"It's too nice for everyday use," he said, holding it out to me.

"Then use it for special occasions," I said, refusing his outstretched hand.

"Thank you. Really."

"You're welcome. Like I said, it's kind of—"

"No. I mean it. Thank you. For all of it."

He meant more than the pencil box. And yes, getting him here, paying for school, a car, and everything he'd need was a lot. But I'd taken a lot from him.

"You know, Raymond, sometimes we mess up in life. And sometimes our mess-ups fall on other people. I'm sorry my messing up fell on you. I can only hope that—"

"Stop. Just stop. Yeah, you started the ball in motion. Or JoJo did. But I took the pass and made the drive to the basket on my own. We both messed up. Big time. But DeeDee and my mom are in a good place. And I'm starting my senior year of college. And you seem in a good place. So, I figure this is where it's supposed to be, you know?"

I didn't, not really. He was better at letting shit go than I was. All I could see was what would have been his final year of college basketball gone, his reputation sketchy at best, and having to start all over at a school he didn't know in a town that wasn't his.

"Yeah, I guess," I said.

He stuffed the pencil box in his backpack and threw it back over his shoulder. "New beginnings start today, Anna," he said.

"Okay, Raymond," I said. I felt like I should hug him or something, but we just stood there until he nodded and left the dining room and then the house.

I sat back down and thought about Raymond's new life until it was time to wake up Ben for breakfast.

Three

❖

I ATE A HUGE BREAKFAST. MUST HAVE BEEN THE
adrenaline coming down after the Niall rescue. It reminded me
of eating a big breakfast after having played poker all night.
The feeling was both comforting and unnerving. I'd missed the
rushes of adrenaline now and then. It was something I had been
working on with my support group.

My now-defunct support group.

Murder had a way of hampering open dialogue.

"Geez, you put away a ton this morning," Jimmy said as I
handed my empty plates—yes, plural—to Grace, our waitress.

"Jimmy!" Ben said.

"What? She didn't? Gus, you see the food that Anna went
through this morning?"

Gus smiled. "Kind of like old times, hey, kid?"

"I was just thinking that," I said.

Jimmy Mancino, Gus Morgan, and Ben Lowenstein
were the three remaining members of a group nicknamed the
Corporation. All were retired oddsmakers. In their heyday, they
ran some of the tightest odds on the Strip. Now in their eighties,
they met each morning for breakfast. Since Ben and I lived
together (not in *that* way) and he was no longer able to drive due
to a bad hip, I had become part of the breakfast bunch years ago.

We had dwindled in size, but not in spirit.

With our plates cleared and our coffee cups replenished, we turned to the important part of the mornings: the Observation of the Odds.

The boys pulled out the daily odds sheets that they'd gotten from various casinos before coming to Arizona Charlie's for breakfast. Ben, having come straight from home with me, only had the one we'd swung by and picked up from Charlie's book room on our way through the casino to the Sourdough Café.

Normally, I'd have grabbed my own copy and we'd all discuss the various point spreads and favorites of the day's upcoming games. Where we thought the odds were off, if we had any inside scoop, and where we were going to lay our money.

But times weren't normal.

Now, I didn't grab my own sheets. Instead, I pulled a journal from my bag when the guys spread the sheets out on the table in front of them. I had a bunch of things going on in my journal, but today I pulled out a piece of paper that Lor had given me and I'd tucked between the pages.

How to become a licensed private investigator in the state of Nevada.

My to-do list, as it were.

It was daunting, which was why it had become wrinkled, with spots of coffee and Diet Coke, and what I surmised was dried egg yolk on one of the corners. It wasn't the first time I'd pulled this list out after breakfast.

The first half of the page was a bullet-pointed list done by Lorelei:

Be 21 years of age.

Check.

Be a U.S. citizen.

Double check.

No felony convictions or conviction involving crimes of moral turpitude or the illegal possession of a dangerous weapon.

Convictions? No. Arrests? No. Suspicions? Probably, but

that wasn't disqualifying.

Be able to pass a background investigation through the FBI and the Department of Nevada Public Safety.

I was pretty sure my JoJo activity was deeply buried. Raymond Joseph living with me might be a red flag. But by the time I had the next requirement out of the way, Raymond would have graduated from UNLV and probably moved to Atlanta to be near his family.

Have at least 5 years of investigative experience totaling 10,000 hours.

Yeah, that was the stickler.

A bachelor's degree in political science would equal 18 months or 3,000 hours.

Lor even put an asterisk note in that she would look to see what it would take for me to finish up my long-ago-abandoned college degree and switch it to a poly-sci major. Hey, maybe I'd be getting my own back-to-school pencil box in the future.

Once you had the qualifications in, you applied for your license and took an exam.

I didn't know what I'd been thinking when I asked Lor to do the research on this for me. The thrill of finding killers—and, okay, sometimes they found me first—was the closest I'd come to a Hummer that in any way resembled the kind I'd get when sports betting.

I'd asked Jack about getting in some of my required hours with him, but he'd given me a hard no. "It'd be the finish of us, and you know it," he'd said.

He was undoubtedly right. We'd toyed with the idea of teaming up once I got my license—and maybe we still would—but that was something different than him being teacher to my student.

Not a power dynamic I wanted to introduce into our relationship. Which, even on its best days, was built on a foundation of shared addictions and bad habits. Not to mention disregarded felonies.

He'd looked at Lor's list and then scrawled two lines on the bottom of the page.

Pass a handgun safety class and target-shooting test.

Take (and pass!) a self-defense course.

"If you get those two things covered, I'll ask Frank to pass on the name of some of the better PIs in the area who might take you on," he'd said when he handed the sheet of paper back to me. "I haven't been here long enough to know any of them myself."

I could have just looked up the names of private investigators in the area. (Or Lor could have.) But I knew Jack's partner at Metro would have the inside scoop on who was good, and would maybe even put in a good word for me.

So, until I got some of his prerequisites out of the way, Jack was figuratively out of the picture for it all. And literally for the next five days, as he'd taken his son, Casey, back to Portland after a last week with us in Vegas before school started. Jack would stay through the weekend and see Casey to school with his ex, Lisa, and her new husband, Brett, Jack's former partner on the Portland police force.

I folded up the piece of paper, careful not to add any new food stains to it, and put it back in my journal. Further back than I'd placed it yesterday.

I didn't realize the sigh I let out was physical and not internal until each of the boys looked up from their papers and first glanced at me, and then at each other.

Ben—darling, sensitive Ben—was the first to fold up his betting sheets and try to get them out of view. "We can do this anytime, no need to do it now. Hannah, dear, more coffee?"

"What? No, I'm good." I watched as Gus took his cue from Ben and folded his sheets up too, putting them in the inside breast pocket of his dapper houndstooth plaid sport coat. "You guys don't need to stop on my account." Gus' hand froze, ready to pull his sheets back out. Ben looked skeptical. Jimmy hadn't bothered to clear his area, even for show.

"Truly. I wasn't sighing about betting. It was something else." I didn't elaborate. Ben had heard Lor and me talking about the investigator stuff, but I hadn't really discussed it much with him or the others.

A safety net in case I didn't go through with it.

Gus slowly eased his bet sheets out of his pocket, watching me as he did, as if the sight of the long white sheets might make me spontaneously combust.

At times, he'd have been right.

I waved for Gus to finish. "I mean it. I'm good. You guys have been talking bets all summer and it hasn't bothered me." Three sets of eyes narrowed on me. "Much," I added.

"Yeah, but this is different," Jimmy said. He still hadn't moved his sheets, and now laid a protective hand across them, as if my combustion might spray ash on them.

Anna's Ashes. Ha.

"Why is it any different?" I asked.

They looked at each other, then at me. "Seriously?" Jimmy asked.

"Yeah. Why is today any different than what you've been doing all summer? Hell, since I've known you."

"NFL, Hannah, dear," Ben said. Gently, like he was telling me someone had cancer. He even reached out to touch my arm.

Oh. Right. The first weekend of pro football. College football had begun last weekend, but I had been deeply involved with Casey and Jack, even having Lor bring Ben to breakfast a couple of mornings when we'd taken Casey to the Grand Canyon.

And now the first weekend when both college and pro would be in full swing. Sure, there were some cupcake pairings in college this early, but still probably some good matchups. Besides, the point spread accounted for the cupcake scheduling.

"It's okay. I can cope with football season. I mean, there's no way to avoid it, is there?" I didn't really mean for that last bit to sound like a question, but it came out that way. As if I was indeed asking for direction on how to avoid the next five months of weekends. And Monday nights. And Thursday nights.

I ran a finger down the leather cover of my journal, wishing I hadn't put the list Lor had given me away. It was daunting, yes. But could it be more daunting than a looming NFL betting season beginning in Vegas for the first time since I'd stopped gambling?

It hadn't been easy. Monty could tell you how hard it was for me not to sports bet since the night that I'd woken up with a dead body a few months ago. But it had been made easier by the fact that the only season that I typically bet on currently being played was baseball. The Yankees were on every day at our house, but it didn't invoke that hunger in me that betting other sports did.

Football, though, was the Mecca of sports betting in Vegas.

And a personal favorite of mine, having grown up in Wisconsin and being a cheesehead-wearing Packers fan from the time I was five.

"No, dear, you can't avoid it. But that doesn't mean we have to—"

"It's okay, Ben. Really. I'm good."

His brown eyes—so like those of his son Jack—looked at me with concern.

"You know what? Why don't you take off? I'll drive Ben home," Jimmy said.

"What?" both Ben and I said, looking to Jimmy.

"Yeah, sure," he said, waving his big hand at me. "Get out of here. Go do something on that list of yours. I'll get Ben home safe. It'll give me a chance to see what leftovers Lorelei has in that huge fridge of hers."

Technically that huge fridge was mine, but Jimmy was right:

all things kitchen at *Chez Dawson* belonged to Lorelei Samuels.

I didn't correct Jimmy. And I didn't question how much he knew about my list. I just nodded, threw money on the table, declaring this morning's breakfast my treat—over objections from Ben and Gus, but not Jimmy—and got the hell out of there.

I got in my Lexus SUV that I drove when I had Ben with me, and wondered where I could go that would make me forget about all those delicious point spreads, over/unders, and parlays that were out there for the taking.

And then I knew where to go.

Four

❖❖

I GUESS I SHOULDN'T HAVE BEEN SURPRISED TO FIND the shooting range open before most people had eaten their breakfast. This was Las Vegas, after all.

The owner, Buddy, a man who looked not unlike a billy goat, with a shock of white hair standing at the top of his head and off the bottom of his chin, got me set up with a Colt 1911 after questioning me about my preferences (none) and my experience (almost none, except for that one time). He seemed shocked when I told him I'd grown up in a hunting family but we didn't have handguns.

I rented my space and the gun. Bought the ammo. Got the tutorial from Buddy, and shot for a half-hour with him behind me. He was patient and guided me, and I thought again how Jack was probably right about not being my mentor for any of this. No way would I have taken his guidance as easily as I did a stranger's. Weird, but one of those relationship things.

A few more customers trickled in, and Buddy left me to my own devices. I probably looked safe enough. I hoped I was.

I knew people liked shooting ranges because of the power they felt when holding a gun. When shooting a gun. I didn't feel any of that. I felt vulnerable more than powerful. And as I remembered the other time I'd shot at a target—a human being whom I loved dearly—I became overwhelmed with guilt.

I had done what I'd had to. It didn't make me feel any better.

I shot until my bullets were gone. I'd done okay for a beginner, or at least that was what I told myself. It would take many more visits before I could check that item off my list, but at least I'd taken first steps today.

I left my little carrel and went to the long table that ran the length of the range behind the shooters. There were others shooting now, so I left my earmuffs on while I cleaned up my area and put the gun back in its plastic case.

I made my way out of the glassed-in range area and back to the shop area, where Buddy was behind the counter helping a man who had brought his own assault rifle.

This was so not the place for me, but I'd need to adjust if I was going to see this through.

"They make it look so easy on TV and movies, don't they?" said someone to my left. I turned to see a woman looking at a display of holsters. A woman I'd only seen once before in my life. At the reading of Vince Santini's will.

"Cassandra Hall?" I said.

She nodded. It wasn't exactly a smile she offered, but her tone had been friendly. "Hi, Anna."

"You know who I am?" I said. Which was kind of stupid, because though we'd only met the one time, I certainly remembered her. But she'd made quite an impression on me, mainly because she'd been a secret to me.

She wore her white-blond hair (natural, not bottle, if I was guessing) in a chin-length bob. She was dressed similar to the other time I'd seen her, in a tasteful navy blazer, white silk tee underneath, expensive jeans that looked tailored to fit her, and the most beautiful suede boots.

I was a bit of a betrayal to my gender by typically not giving a shit about shoes. But even I had a case of boot envy looking at hers.

"I know who you are, Anna," she answered. "And you

remember me too, I see."

I nodded. "What are you doing here?" I said. I hadn't dressed purposely for the shooting range, since I hadn't known I'd be coming, and I had no idea what one wore to a shooting-range session anyway. But she looked way too professional to be here for target practice. Even in jeans.

"Same thing as you, I imagine," she said, nodding toward the range from where I'd just come.

"You're shooting?" I said, stating the obvious.

"I had a little time between meetings and was on this side of town," she said, with a graceful shrug of one shoulder. Like that was how anybody would kill time between meetings—blasting holes in paper silhouettes of bad guys.

"Oh, okay, well, I'll let you get to it, then," I said. I took a few steps away from her. I would have loved to ask her some questions, but didn't feel it was my place. Will readings aren't like a doctor's office waiting room meeting, where you feel you need to keep confidentiality or anything, but still, it felt a little weird to talk about where and how we'd met before.

"Listen, Anna," she said, and I turned around quickly. The look on her face mirrored what I was feeling inside: curiosity, trepidation, and a little embarrassment. "I'd rather kill time with a cup of coffee if you'd join me?"

"I'd like that," I said.

She nodded and moved toward the door. "Not shooting today, Buddy. See you soon," she said with a wave to the owner.

"Sure thing, Cassie," Buddy said. He gave a chin nod to me, and I returned it before walking out into the morning sun.

"There's a place in the next plaza over that has a great homemade cinnamon roll," Cassandra said. She pointed down the street, and I saw the sign for Koffee Klatch.

"Sounds good," I said. I didn't mention that I'd already had a giant breakfast. I could just toy with the cinnamon roll.

Yeah, right.

She got in her car—an older silver Toyota 4Runner—and I got in the Lexus, and we drove, weaving through the parking lots of the plazas next to the gun range. There were parking spots next to each other. Neither of us said a word as we walked into Koffee Klatch and were seated. I didn't bother with a menu, and nor did Cassandra. She ordered coffee and a roll, and I asked for the same.

"I'm glad I ran into you," she said after the waitress had poured us our coffee and left. She doctored hers with cream only, while I took a sip of mine black.

"You are?" I said.

"Yes. I meant to look you up not long after...we met."

"At Vince's will reading," I said. Might as well get it out on the table.

She put her cup down after savoring the taste. "Right. Yes."

A day several months ago in which Cassandra walked away a very rich woman. And yet still drove a car six or seven years old, if I had to guess. Interesting.

"Why were you going to look me up?" I asked.

Our cinnamon rolls were delivered, and they indeed looked incredible. I should have just had mine wrapped up and brought it home for somebody, but instead I lifted my fork and put my napkin on my lap.

"In some of the things Vince left for me was a note about you," she said. Interesting.

"He mentioned you in the letter he left for me," I said.

This seemed to surprise her, though she would have made a good poker player, as it was hard to read. "Oh? What did he say?"

I thought about the ethics, or even advisability of letting her know what Vince had said, then figured it didn't matter. "He said that if you ever came to me and needed help that I should help if I could. That you were...good people." I couldn't remember the exact wording Vince had used in his letter to me about Cassandra. Mostly I remembered the feeling of "what could have been" that he had for he and I.

Thoughts that I hadn't had until I'd read his letter.

Thoughts I still didn't have often. Until I'd seen Cassandra Hall at the shooting range.

"Well, that's nice to hear, I suppose," she said. "Actually, he said much the same to me about you. That if you needed help, you could be trusted." She waved a hand, fingernails bare of polish, but well maintained. The wave seemed to encompass my worthiness as a person. I guess I passed whatever her litmus test was. Maybe it only needed a vouch from Vince Santini.

Truthfully, even after the way it ended, Vince's word held a lot of sway with me as well.

"And you were going to look me up to let me know that? That if I needed help to come to you?" I said. She was a better person than me. I guess I should have looked her up after Vince's letter mentioning that she might someday need help. Honestly, it hadn't occurred to me. And let's face it, she wasn't going to need help financially after the windfall she'd received.

I wasn't sure what more I could have offered her. One person lying low in my household was probably enough.

"That, and something else. Obviously I never got around to it, so I'm glad to see you're doing okay."

I took another sip and thought about the intervening months since the will reading. A lot of shit had gone down. But none that Cassandra Hall would have been likely to help me with.

"Although you were just at a shooting range, for what appeared to be a first time, so maybe things aren't all right after all?"

"I was just learning to shoot," I said. "No other reason. Things are good right now." That was all true.

"Glad to hear it," she said.

"You said there was something else?"

She chewed on a bite of her cinnamon roll, then wiped her mouth off and sat back in the booth. "Yes. I'm not sure you'll be able to answer this. Or if you *will* answer this if you can."

Interesting.

"Marvin gave an envelope to Raymond Joseph that day," she said.

"Yes."

"Am I correct in assuming you know the contents of that envelope?"

I tried to run through the scenarios in my head. What could hurt Raymond if Cassandra knew what had been in that envelope? Would he be in danger from her? Did she know of Raymond's point shaving?

"I know the contents, yes," I said, figuring that was as far as I'd take it. It might be good for her to know that someone other than Raymond was privy to whatever she thought might be in that envelope.

"Okay. And am I also correct in assuming that the envelope contained pictures and reports on two federal investigators?"

Okay, what the hell was going on? It had obviously been too long since I'd played poker, because by the amused expression on Cassandra's face, I'd just telegraphed my thoughts on my own.

"I thought you were some hotshot poker player," she said, voicing my concern that my poker face was no more.

"Out of practice," I said. She laughed. It was a nice sound, rich and throaty, with no hint of giggle. I got the impression that Cassandra Hall was not a giggler. "Yes, you're right, that's what was in the envelope," I added.

She nodded and dabbed her napkin on her mouth again, then tossed it on her plate. "That's what I thought. I'm glad I ran into you, Anna." She took two tens from her wallet and laid them on the table. I started to object, but she held up a hand. Not much differently than I just had at breakfast with the boys. "I want you to know—or I guess let Raymond know—

that if he ever needs the originals of that material, or additional material on either of those gentlemen, to let me know. Although I imagine he has the best of the lot already."

I was dumbfounded, but tried to hang on to any last vestige of calm and cool. "I'll let him know that. Can I ask how you knew what was in that envelope?"

She dug in her wallet and came out with a business card that she slid across the table to me, facedown. "I was the one who gathered the information."

She stood from the booth, slipping her wallet back into her small purse, then tapped her finger on the downward-facing business card. "If either you or Raymond need anything—*anything*—please contact me. I owe that much to Vince."

She left the coffee shop, her cinnamon roll nearly intact except for a few missing bites. Mine had only a few bites left. Turning the card over, I had a strange feeling that my life was about to change.

It was the closest I'd felt to a Hummer in a long time.

The card was tastefully embossed, silver lettering on cream linen.

Cassandra Hall, Private Investigator.

Five

❖❖

I HUNG UP MY PHONE AFTER TALKING TO JACK IN Portland. We'd tried to do some dirty talk, him alone in his hotel room, me in my bedroom at home. (The door safely locked in case Ben or Lor were still up and wanted to see if I was.) But it didn't work. I couldn't stop my embarrassed laughter. He was not amused.

So, instead of phone sex, we just chatted about our days since he'd left. He'd delivered Casey back to Lisa and Brett's house yesterday, and today he'd killed the day having lunch with an old friend from the Portland police force. Tomorrow being Saturday, he'd take Casey again for the day, then spend Sunday on his own. (Probably watching football, but we successfully skirted that subject altogether.) Monday he'd join Lisa taking Casey to school, then catch a flight back to Vegas.

I didn't tell him about meeting Cassandra Hall yesterday morning. I didn't know why. Probably because I was unsure myself if I'd contact her again. She could be the answer to my issue of hours accumulated working on investigations. Even grunt work in her office would probably count. I could take an unpaid internship or something, if she wasn't looking for an official hire.

I grabbed my journal off the bedside table and made a note to check into how specific the guidelines for hours completed would be.

But the main reason I didn't tell Jack about Cassandra was that I had to determine how serious I was about this all myself, before I could truly get other people involved.

I mean, let's face it, I had never really held a job as an adult. I'd put in loads of hours on poker tables, learning, getting better, making myself into one of the best players in the world. (Or so it said in my online bio on the poker sites—I wasn't just tooting my own horn.)

But I'd done that on my time, when I'd wanted to. The drive was there, but on my terms.

The drive was there to follow the thought of taking my sleuthing to the "show," but for how long? Would it replace the need to be a great poker player? Or was it just something I fell into because dead bodies kept falling into me?

Three to five years of someone else's time was a lot to ask if this was just something I thought I wanted to do because I couldn't gamble anymore.

Yeah, best to sort my own shit out first, before involving some professional like Cassandra Hall.

And until I had that sorted, no need to spring it on Jack.

My phone buzzed, and I half expected it to be Jack wanting to give the phone sex thing another go. But no, it was a text from Raymond.

Working a game for Carla. Johnny Aces is sitting in for her. Looks like he'll be here a while.

It was ten at night. I was in bed, albeit still dressed in sweats and a tee. (Hadn't even gotten as far as undressing on the phone with Jack before I started laughing.)

Which casino? What room? Is there a spot at the table?

Raymond texted back with the suite number at the Venetian where tonight's game was being played. He didn't mention whether there was a spot at the table or not.

Is there a spot at the table? No intention of playing. But if I show up, I'll need to have a reason why.

A pause. Not even the bubble pause.

Yeah, there's a chair open.

On my way.

In a jewelry box on my dresser, I rummaged until I found a key card for the Venetian. It wouldn't get me into any room, but it would get me past the security guards at the elevator banks. I traded in my sweats for one of my many pairs of cargo pants, pulled a nicer top over my tee, grabbed my sneakers, keys, and phone, and left my room.

Ben and Lor were still up and in the home theater watching a movie when I poked my head in to let them know I was heading out. Understandably, they both looked pensive at the news.

"I'm going to hang with Raymond," I said. Not a lie. Not the whole truth.

"Isn't he working a game for Carla tonight?" Lor asked. No accusation, no baiting. But concern. Definitely concern.

"Yeah, he is." They exchanged glances. God, I hated that it'd come to this. They weren't sure I was telling the truth, even though I'd never actually lied to them while I was gambling. While I was JoJo. But they also didn't want to ask me more. To put me in a bad position. A position to maybe finally lie to them.

"There's somebody I'd like to meet. To talk to for a friend. Raymond let me know he's at the same suite he is. Right now. I'm just going to see if I can—I'm not sure what exactly."

"You're going to get intel. To investigate!" Lor said happily. She, more than anyone, I thought, was invested in the idea of me turning my propensity for falling in a pile of shit into a positive.

"Maybe. I guess," I said.

All trepidation from their faces was gone. In its place was something akin to...pride?

Shit, that was almost harder to handle than the shame I usually felt around the people I loved.

"You'll be careful?" Ben asked.

"I will."

He nodded, Lor wished me luck, and I left them to finish their movie. I was about to head for the front door, but made a detour into the office and went to my cigar box to see what kind of cash was on hand. Ten thousand. More than I would have guessed. I hadn't played in months. The last time I'd sports bet, I'd been a huge winner.

And went to bed with a man who would never wake up again.

I'd told Lor to take the winnings and invest it in the counseling center I was helping Monty get off the ground. She must have kept some of the winnings out to have some ready cash. It wasn't cash for household expenses, she would have kept that someplace separate.

Even though I had no intention of playing in the game, I put the wad of money in my pants side pocket and left the house.

On the drive to the Strip, I called Monty.

"Are you okay?" he asked when answering. Ben and Lor weren't the only two who worried about my nocturnal outings.

"I'm good. I just felt I should let you know that I'm heading to a poker game."

A pause. Just like Raymond texting. "Where are you? I'll come and we can talk. We can—"

"It's not like that, Monty." I explained the situation to him. "I'll just see if I can talk to Johnny Aces, find out if he's aware of Niall leaving town. Is he going after him? Is Carla involved? I'm not really sure what."

"I don't like this," he said.

"It'll be fine. I won't be alone with him. Raymond will be there, as well as other card players. Do we even know how much Niall owed him?"

"Why? Are you planning on paying off his debts? That's not how recovery works, Anna. You can't just bail everyone out. That will only enable them to gamble again."

"I know that." Oh, did I know that. JoJo had done me no favors by paying off my debts so that I could once again bet.

But then again, she'd kept me from having more than just a sore foot when it rained. I had two working kneecaps and both my thumbs thanks to her.

"And no, I wasn't going to pay off his debt." That was exactly what I thought I might do. "But the amount he owes would be a direct indication of how badly this Johnny guy and/or Carla, if she's involved, want to track Niall down." Okay, so I'd just thought of that angle. Didn't mean it wasn't true.

"But there must be other ways than to go to this card game," Monty said.

"Better ways, surely, but probably not a better opportunity," I said.

"Are you sure you don't want me to meet you there?"

I was at the light at the Strip. A block from the Venetian. It'd been a while since I'd been down here. Jack and I had taken Casey to see the gardens at the Bellagio when he'd been in town once over the summer. That'd been early August, the visit before when he'd just been here and Jack had taken him back for school.

"I'm good," I told Monty. "Really. Poker was never the problem. It was always more of a job than—"

"But it's a trigger. That's what I'm worried about."

He was right. And he probably hadn't even put it together that it was the first big football weekend of the year. "I'll make sure I go straight back to the parking deck once I leave the suite. Won't even go down to the casino."

There was a pause while I heard him rummaging. "What casino? What room will you be in?"

I told him. "But you can't be there, Monty. It'll be weird enough me showing up and not playing. But if you show up too, a couple of days after Niall splits, it will seem really suspicious." I didn't know anything about this Johnny Aces, but if Carla showed up, or even if he told her I'd shown up, but didn't play cards, she'd rightfully think something was fishy.

Even using Raymond as an excuse, as I planned to do, would send up a flag to Carla. I'd never just stopped into a game he was working before.

"I want you to call me as soon as you leave the room, and I'll stay on the phone with you until you're in your car," Monty said.

"That's not necessary. Plus it could be really late. I may need to stick around for a while to get this guy to even talk to me."

"I don't care how late it is. What, you think I'm going to be able to peacefully sleep now that I know where you're heading?"

"Right. Yeah. Sorry, I should never have—"

"No. I'm glad you called. It's fine. Just call me when you leave the room, okay?"

"Okay."

"Promise me," he said.

"I promise, Monty."

There was a short pause, which I didn't fill trying to convince him. He sighed and said goodbye and hung up just as I was entering the parking deck at the Venetian.

Intel. Investigating. Helping Niall. Not poker.

All things I told myself as I parked and made my way through the parking deck and into the hotel.

All things I'd try to remember for the next half-hour or so.

Or maybe longer.

Six

I HAD TO HAND IT TO CARLA: JOHNNY ACES WAS exactly what you wanted your enforcer to look like. Whereas Paulie Gonads had that old-school *Sopranos* vibe to him, Johnny was definitely of the new wave of goons. Brawny, powerful but squat, with his hair in a crew cut that was longer on top. The haircut was a cross between military and white supremacist. A neck tattoo—a pair of aces, which felt a little too on the nose to me—peeked out of the top of his buttoned-up dress shirt and tie. He looked uncomfortable in the suit he wore. The suit looked equally uncomfortable to be worn by him.

Raymond introduced us. Raymond, whose tailored suit fit him like a glove. Who looked comfortable in his own skin, even though he wasn't exactly happy about being the doorman/intimidator. Though he didn't need to worry about the latter with Johnny in the room.

"Carla said you might turn up at a game sooner or later," he said to me.

We were in the far end of the large suite, not too far from the door. I could see the table of players, not recognizing any of them. In one of the corners were a self-serve bar and a table with some sandwiches, power bars, and bottles of water. Whatever you needed to make sure you could play through the night.

"She did?" I said. Huh. I hadn't played at a game in months.

But apparently Carla thought it was just a matter of time before I showed up? Well, I guess the odds would have been good to take that bet. And here I was, after all. Although not for those reasons.

"Actually, I didn't come to play. I wanted to talk to Carla about something," I said.

"So talk to me about it," Johnny said. He gave Raymond a dismissive nod to return to the door. Raymond glanced at me, and I gave him a nod. He left us, making a slow walk around the suite, then once again took up his post by the door.

"Listen," I said to Johnny. "No offense, but I don't know you from Adam. You might work for Carla now, but—"

"With."

"What?"

He folded his arms in front of his chest, pulling on the seams of his suit jacket. If I'd walked behind him, I wouldn't have been surprised to see the thing split right up the back, Hulk-style.

"Okay. *With*. Again, I haven't seen Carla in a couple of months, so if she's made some, uh, organizational changes, I'm unaware."

"Lot can happen in a few months," he said.

He looked me up and down, and it made my skin chill, but I summoned up my latent poker skills and didn't let it show.

"Don't I know it," I said. "You should have seen my life just nine months ago."

"What? Did ya have a baby or something?" This time I couldn't quite hide the revulsion when he took a longer stare at my body. The baby-making and baby-feeding parts in particular.

"Hardly," I said. In a way, though, I had given birth. Birth to a new way of living my life. One without as much collateral damage. One where I gave back where I could because I'd hurt others without them even knowing it.

Which brought me back to the reason I was here—finding

out if Johnny was aware of Niall's flight and if he was going to try to track him down, or write the debt off.

And just how big of a debt was it?

"Well, this is personal with Carla, not really business. Is she going to show tonight? I can just hang out and wait for her." I motioned to the large sitting area with its inviting couches and chairs.

"I don't think so," he said.

"Why not?"

"Players don't need to see you sitting around, not playing. I'm sure most of them know who you are."

Maybe. Maybe not. "So why would that matter, even if they did?"

"You not playing? Just sitting there? They don't need to feel self-conscious about you being in the room."

"But being at the table would make them feel less so?"

He grimaced a little. Or maybe that was his version of a smile? "Well, then they'd get a chance to win your money. And say they'd played against a pro."

"I'm not playing. But I'd like to wait and see if Carla shows up." My voice was firm, as if I laid down the law to hood enforcers all the time.

Bluffing, if you will.

He called me.

"I don't know if Carla is going to show up at all, or when, if she does. And you can't just hang around. Either play or leave."

I should just leave. I wouldn't be able to talk to Johnny if I was at the table anyway. But maybe one of the other players could give me some info on him. Or when there were breaks in the game. Or after, if I lasted until the game broke up.

A tingle ran down my spine. A different feeling than Johnny's leering had caused. This was a competitive juice flowing through my body. A juice different from a Hummer, but no less compelling.

Suddenly, I *wanted* to be able to last until the game broke up. Even though the other players had probably started with twenty thousand each and I only had ten. Even more of a challenge. And with players I didn't know?

Yeah, I wanted this.

I told myself all the things I'd said to Monty in the car. It wasn't about me. Not about playing. It was all about getting information that might help Niall's parents breathe a little easier about their son. That they were safe in their Topeka home.

But I'd be lying to myself if I said that was the only reason.

I wanted to beat these guys with less time and less money.

"Then I guess I'm playing," I said. I took the cash out of my pocket and handed it over. Johnny gave me a stack of chips. Noticeably smaller than most of the stacks in front of the players at the table.

"Good luck," he said. There was a snideness in his voice that told me he didn't really wish me well. I only wished he was at the table too so I could beat his ass and take his money.

I tapped my horseshoe pendant three times and made my way over to the table.

For Niall, I told myself as I took my seat.

"Liar," JoJo's voice said in my head.

Seven

❖

RIDING A BIKE. MUSCLE MEMORY. WHATEVER YOU WANT to call it, I was back in the groove. I hit great cards. I made it work when I didn't. I pulled off a monster bluff. And folded when I smelled one directed at me, much to the chagrin of my opponents.

I was on fire. God, it felt so good. The only thing that would feel better would be taking my winnings down to the sports book and seeing what games—

No! Absolutely not!

I looked at the time display on my phone. Four in the morning. A glance at my chips showed I was up about forty thousand dollars.

I wanted the game to end. I wanted the game to never end.

It'd give me a chance to talk to Johnny if the game ended soon. I'd already knocked out two of the five other players. One had left immediately after busting out. The other sat over in the comfy-looking living room area (where I'd wanted to wait, but Johnny said no!) looking like he wanted to pull more money out of his pocket and get back in.

I knew there was no more money in his pocket. Because he'd have had it on the table in a second if there were.

This I knew firsthand.

No, what he'd spent the last hour torturing himself over

was whether he should borrow money from Carla/Johnny to get back in the game, or to cut his losses and go home to lick his wounds.

I never caught his name. Nor those of the other players. Some had recognized me, though; I could tell by their expressions when I took my seat.

One of the men who didn't know me from the poker world had a different expression. An expression I knew well from my early days of playing.

A woman? Really? Even here? Well, okay, I'm happy to take her money. Easy pickings.

He was the player I knocked out first.

The one who had immediately left the room.

I did pick up from chatter that one of the players was affiliated with the visiting NFL team that would play the Raiders on Sunday. From the looks of him, he was probably a GM or some other high-ranking front-office guy.

Definitely not a player. Too little. Too old.

That was why people played in backroom games when there was a perfectly good poker room fifteen stories down in the casino.

Up here, what happened in Vegas actually *did* stay in Vegas.

I looked at everyone's chip stack. People were bleeding. Everyone seemed down except the NFL guy and me.

If I took him out, the game would either break up right away or limp along for a few more hands.

Yes, they could pull more money out of their wallets. Or borrow more money, as Johnny doubtlessly hoped they would.

But they didn't look like they wanted to keep on. They'd all pack it in if NFL guy went down.

Okay, buddy, let's see what kind of strategy you preach to your team. Slow and cautious, running game for four yards a carry? Or Hail Marys on first down?

A half-hour later, I'd completed three Hail Marys in a row

and his running-game ass was running out the door.

"I don't know if that was the gutsiest playing I ever saw or the dumbest," the man to my immediate right said. He still had some chips left, but like I thought, he and the other players were gathering them up, calling it a night. Morning, actually.

"Probably both," I said.

"It's like she just wanted it over and done with," the man in the number one seat said.

"That too," I said.

There were looks of both admiration and exasperation from all the remaining players. Johnny, getting a wave from the dealer, brought chip racks over, and we started stacking our chips in them. Well, I did. The others had so few chips that they could carry them in one hand over to Johnny's table to get their cash.

Raymond moved from the door, nearer to the table. No one expected any kind of smash-and-grab from this caliber of player, but Raymond's presence would deter them from even thinking about it. Or bitching about losing.

Either it worked or this was not a bitching group, because all the men got cash for their pittance of chips and left the suite while I stalled with racking my chips.

The guy on the couch finally realized the decision on whether or not to borrow money had been taken from him. I wasn't sure if it was relief or disappointment on his face. I knew the expression, though. Had lived it a million times.

But not tonight. Tonight I was a big winner. A glance at my rack told me I had won nearly eighty thousand off my ten K starting cash.

I tried to do mindful tricks. Be present. Emotional check-in. All the shit Monty had taught us.

But all that ran through my mind were the thoughts that I used to have after a big win. *JoJo won't have to come out and play for a while. What games can I bet on?*

I reached for my filled racks, but my hands shook, so I

wiped them on my pants and took a couple of deep breaths, trying to breathe my thoughts away.

JoJo was dead. She would never need to come out again. Except for something like helping Niall the other night.

And yes, there were games to bet. Many, many glorious college and pro games. But that wasn't where this money would go.

No. I'd give it to Lor as soon as I got home. Ask her what should be done with it. Something fast, so it wouldn't be sitting in my cigar box all weekend.

The dealer had gone to the restroom after the game broke up, and now emerged changed from her outfit of black pants and crisp white shirt.

She'd let her hair down and was wearing a black tee, torn jeans, and red Chucks. She was rolling her neck and doing some stretches with her arms.

I knew how she felt.

Johnny came and took my racks, swearing a little under his breath at the size of my winnings. No doubt Carla had mentioned trying to get me into debt if I ever showed up to play.

"Give five to the dealer," I said as he took my racks back to his table.

"Five hundred to the dealer. Got it," he said.

"No. Five *thousand*," I said.

Johnny stopped in his tracks and turned back to me. "Are you shitting me?"

"I'm not. Five K to the dealer. Do I need to do it myself?"

Meaning would he skim off the dealer's tip?

There was a soft "Fuck you" under his breath, but he turned and walked back to his table.

The dealer made her way back to the table where I still sat. She looked around the suite, and when she saw that I was the only player left, she said, "That was some ballsy playing."

"Thanks," I said. She was about Monty's age, I guessed,

maybe younger. "You're a good dealer. Kept the game moving."

She laughed. "I think you did that all on your own. Nobody wanted to get in the Black Widow's way."

So she knew my public persona. "You play?" I asked. A lot of the dealers I'd met were really good poker players themselves. But also a good share stayed away from the tables altogether. They knew the cards could be fickle, no matter how skilled a player you were.

"A little," she said. "Some of the smaller daily tournaments around town. Cash game now and then." She waved an arm to include the poker table setup and luxurious suite. "Nothing on this level."

"Game's the same at any level," I said. "You learn a lot at those smaller tournaments and cash games."

"That's what I'm trying to do. Learn."

I was just about to offer to play at one of them with her, maybe offer some advice after watching her play. Mentor a young woman player, pay it forward. And then I remembered I didn't play poker anymore.

I nodded at the table. "What's your takeaway from tonight?"

"What do you mean?"

"Who, in your opinion from observing, were the best players? Who got lucky? Who should have won but didn't? Who didn't belong at the table? Any kind of impressions?"

I thought for a minute that maybe she didn't have a bead on the game like I thought she might. She was staring at the empty table. I was just about to tell her to forget it when—

"Number one chair was a good player, but in over his head. And he knew it. When you joined in, that confirmed it to him. He was too cautious, didn't want to make a mistake. Couldn't pull the trigger when he needed to."

I nodded. She picked up a little steam in her summation.

"Second chair was maybe a better player than we saw. He got shit cards and just couldn't find a way to make them work.

Frustration got the best of him."

Another nod from me. A smile from her.

"Three seat was your main competition. But he wanted it too badly. Went after you when he thought you were bluffing."

"I wasn't bluffing," I said.

"Not that hand, no. But three hands later? With the three clubs on the flop? You had nothing, right?"

I'd pulled in a monster pot on that hand. "Right. Nothing."

She rattled off her opinions of the other players, and they matched up with mine. I rose from my seat, pushed in the chair, and stretched, working out some kinks in my neck that I hadn't kinked in a long time.

I hadn't missed the torture to my body that all-night games brought on.

Who was I kidding? I'd missed it all, even the aches and pains.

Johnny came over with two white envelopes in his hand. He handed one to the dealer. "Nice job, Kaitlyn," he said.

"Thanks for the opportunity, Johnny," she said. She took a quick look inside her envelope and held it out to him. "I think you gave me the wrong one. There's—"

"A good night of tips for you," he said.

"Seriously? Wow," she said. She dropped the envelope into her bag.

"Mostly from our benevolent winner right here," Johnny said, handing me the other envelope with my winnings in it.

His eyes were daring me to count it in front of him, but I just folded the envelope (which was difficult due to its thickness) and put it in one of the zippered pockets of my cargo pants.

"I… Thank you…really," Kaitlyn said to me.

"You earned it," I said. "Keep playing. You've got the reading of players part down cold."

A blush rose up her face, and she nodded once more and left the suite, waving to Raymond across the room as she did.

The door hadn't even closed behind her fully before it swung open again and Carla came into the room. Her eyes darted across the suite, taking in Raymond cleaning up the food area, and landed on me.

"Johnny says you wanna talk. So, talk."

Eight

❖❖

"YOU NEED TO STICK AROUND HERE, OR CAN WE GO somewhere?" I asked Carla.

"Give me a second to talk to Johnny, grab the books. You wanna wait here?"

I didn't. I wanted to get out of this room and take my winnings down to the sports book. It was five in the morning, probably nobody even at the counter yet. But I could look at the board, with all its colorful lights and delicious point spreads.

"Meet you at the Coffee Bean by the parking deck?" I said. It was at the opposite end, and on a different floor, than the book room at the Venetian. And it would no doubt be open.

"Yeah. Fine. Get me a latte, would you? And one of those scone things if they got 'em."

I nodded, waved to Raymond, left the room, and took the elevator down to the parking-deck floor. I weaved through the walkway to come out by the food court, all closed down, and around the corner to the Coffee Bean, which was open.

They only had a couple of tables, being a mostly get-and-go type of place, but I made my order and sat at a table, waiting for Carla.

But it was Monty Westerfield, not Carla, who planted himself in the chair across from me.

"What are you doing here?" I said.

"You didn't call me when you finished. I started to worry."

"Oh. I ended up playing. Johnny wouldn't let me wait for Carla, and he was giving nothing away."

Monty look startled, and I barreled on, trying to reassure him. "One-time deal, no biggie. I was trying to stay in the room the only way I could. It's not going to trigger anything. I promise." I didn't bother mentioning my desire to be one floor down and in the book room. I was at the Coffee Bean—that was good enough.

"Yeah, but you still should have called when you finished. Even more so if you were playing."

"I just finished," I said.

"My God, that was a long time," he said. I laughed at the look on his face. Whatever gambling issues Monty may have had in the past (didn't know/didn't want to know), it obviously didn't entail playing poker for hours, or days, on end.

"Actually, it broke up a little earlier than those games usually do."

"Why'd it break up earlier?" he asked.

I gave a half shoulder lift. "I don't know. I guess I was ready for it to break up." Yeah, a flex of sorts. Whatever. It felt damn good to have controlled that game like I had.

"So, the game actually ended? You didn't just…"

"Lose? No, I won. Big, actually."

"Oh, okay." He seemed surprised. I would have guessed that he would have done some digging into my past. I was all over the internet as a successful professional player. The compulsive sports gambling bit wasn't mentioned in those online bios, though. And that was what I worked on with Monty.

"I'm a pretty good player," I said, a tad defensively.

"Yeah, no. Of course. Sorry. I just…" He shook his head, not sure what he was going to say. Just as well—I probably didn't want to hear it. "Anyway. What about Johnny? Did you talk to him? Or Carla? Is there… I don't know. Do you think Niall is in danger?"

"I wasn't able to get into it. Not with Johnny. But Carla showed at the end. She's meeting me here any minute."

"Should I get out of here, then?"

I didn't know what the harm would be in Monty meeting Carla, but it just seemed like a bad idea, so I nodded. "Yeah, I guess. Probably."

"Okay." He got up from his chair and pushed it in. "And you're okay? No need to keep gambling?"

I thought I had my poker face still on, but something must have shown up in my expression, because he leaned forward, across nearly the entire small, café-style table.

"Anna? How are you really feeling?"

"Like I have a pocketful of cash and sixty-five college football games are just hours away from starting."

"Yes. It's a hard time. Several clients have brought that up this week. The beginning of football season. So, a little shaky?"

"A little, yeah."

"Maybe I should stick around for a while? Make sure you're good after you talk to Carla? I'd like to hear what she has to say anyway. I'll take a walk around the canal area and circle back. Stay here after she leaves, yeah?"

I didn't really want a babysitter. It felt like a step backward. But the envelope in my pocket seemed to be growing heavier and heavier. "If you don't mind, that would be great. I'd appreciate it."

He straightened. His hair was mussed up, like he'd been tugging at it all night while I'd been at the table. He was wearing jeans and a Tulane hoodie. It made me wonder who Tulane was playing today and what the spread would be. I took a shaky breath and nodded that I was okay. Monty studied me, hesitant to leave. "I'm okay," I said. He left.

The barista called my name, and I got Carla's latte and scone and my coffee and brought them to the table just as Carla came around the corner.

"Thanks," she said after she took a deep drink from her cup. Breaking her scone in half, she offered some to me, but I shook my head. It wouldn't be too long from now and Lorelei would be serving the bagels and lox that arrived weekly from the place Ben grew up with in New York.

"So? What's up?" she said. "Johnny said you were the big winner. Congrats."

"Thanks," I said. "How long has Johnny been with you? This is the first I met him."

"You should play more often," she said. She eyed me over the edge of her cup as she took a drink. When I didn't make a comment about my lack of playing, she said, "I've been using Johnny a couple of months. Why?"

How to play it? Bluff? Bet big and hope to scare her? Or lay my cards on the table? I chose the latter. "His name was brought up to me the other day and I was curious about him. So, I asked Raymond to let me know when he saw him again."

"So you didn't need to talk to me at all? You playing was just so you could, what? Check out Johnny?"

"Partly. I did want to talk to you, too. Sorry if I made you get out of bed to come down here."

"I haven't been to bed yet," she said. She sounded tired. I looked at her more closely. She had changed her image a little since Vince had died and she'd started running games on her own. Better clothes, lost a little weight, taking it to the next level. But this morning she looked like, well, maybe she was in over her head.

I decided to pull back a little. "Are you doing okay, Carla?" I was genuinely concerned. Carla and I had never been besties; it was always a business relationship. But we had gone through something traumatic together earlier in the year that I felt allowed me to cross over into caring.

"I'm okay. Thanks," she said. "It's just a lot, you know?"

I didn't. Not really. I wasn't sure what went into hosting backroom poker games with the intention that players would go into debt with you at an exorbitant interest rate, with physical punishment offered up as repayment incentive.

"Yeah, I'm sure it's a lot." It was the best I could offer up. She nodded, accepting my lame attempt at commiseration.

"I thought I knew everything about Vince's business. But there was stuff even I didn't know about. Fires that *still* need putting out, you know?"

"Sure," I said, not really sure at all. Or at least hoping the fire-putting-out was just an analogy.

But it did make me think of something. "Hey, did you ever work with Cassandra Hall? I mean, did you know she worked with Vince?"

"Cassandra Hall? The woman who got everything of Vince's?" The bitterness in her voice was almost visible, shooting from her mouth like a dragon's fire.

"Uh-huh. Her. Do you know about her and Vince's relationship?"

She narrowed her eyes at me. "What relationship? You mean were they fucking? Why else would she get all his money?"

That wasn't what I'd meant, but it made sense. Except that Vince and I had gone on a couple of dates. Had considered starting a relationship of some kind before the shit had hit the fan with Raymond in Iowa.

And Vince just didn't seem the two-timing type.

Murderous loan shark, sure. But a cheater? Not really, no.

"What about her?" Carla asked, pulling me back on track.

"I ran into her the other day. And it made me wonder about her. That's all."

Carla studied me, then took a sip of her coffee. She knew she'd never be able to read me if I didn't want her to.

Not that there was much to read about the whole Vince/Cassandra thing. Or at least not from me.

"I'd never seen or heard of her before the will reading," Carla said, confirming what I'd learned that day long ago in Vince's lawyer's office. "So I assumed she was a woman Vince felt it best to keep secret. I have enough of his known shit to deal with. I don't need to go turning over any rocks looking for more."

"Right. Sure."

"Anything about her I *should* know?" she asked.

"No. I don't think so. Like I said, I ran into her and it made me wonder. Nothing more than that."

She finished her scone—even the half she'd offered to me. "So, what's really going on, Anna? Why are we here?"

"Niall," I said. And waited.

Carla, even though she'd spent the last several years standing sentry at high-stakes poker games, could never have been a good player. No poker face whatsoever.

"What do you know about him?" she asked.

"I know he's in trouble with Johnny Aces. And I wanted to know if that trouble extended to you as well."

"And what if it does?" she asked.

"Then hopefully we can come to some kind of agreement."

"Agreement? Or restitution?"

"That depends on the size of the restitution," I said.

She sat back in her chair, looking a little less tired than she had a few moments ago. "What have you gotten yourself mixed up in, Anna?"

"I'm not sure. I guess that's what I'm trying to find out."

"Leave Niall alone. I would consider it a favor to me if you did."

"Yeah, well, that might not be so easy."

We'd had tense conversations, Carla and me. Over loans, vig, repayment plans. But she'd always had Paulie for backup. And Vince as the final word. This was now just the two of us. And it wasn't my debt I was trying to wriggle out of.

We were both in uncharted waters with each other.

"Well, I'm sorry about Niall. I really am. Seemed like a good kid. But you know as well as anyone how easily the wheels can come off even the best people."

I wasn't sure if she meant I was a "best" person, or that my wheels had come off. A case could be made for—and against—both.

And then I replayed her words in my head. What exactly was she sorry for?

No more laying my cards on the table. Close to the vest time.

"Well, it's a shame. You hate to see it," I said.

"Yeah, it is. And you know, it's never personal."

"And yet my foot aches when it rains."

A present from Vince, administered by Paulie, reported on by Carla.

"Not personal, either," she said. I nodded. "And you know, it's not like it's good for business for us when something like Niall happens. It's a lost revenue stream. That's never good. We like return customers. And now…"

Was she talking about Niall in terms of disappearance? Or demise?

"Right. And not only a non-repeat customer, but a write-off for the, what? What was he into you for?"

"A hundred. With the motor running."

Okay, time to tip my hand. Maybe not the best strategy, but maybe I could shake her into admitting something. "But Topeka's a long way to go for collection. And who knows if he's even there anymore. He might have gone into a facility or something."

Yeah, not a poker player, Carla. Her surprise was evident. "Topeka? What the fuck is he doing in Topeka?"

"That's where he's from," I said.

That wasn't what she'd meant.

"What the hell is going on, Anna?"

Down the hallway, behind Carla, Johnny Aces was leaving the hotel area, making his way to the parking deck. He didn't look over our way, and I did nothing to get his attention.

"I helped a friend help Niall. I didn't know at the time that he was involved with you."

"Would that have stopped you?" She asked the one question I didn't have an answer for.

"I'm not sure," I said.

"Fair enough. What exactly did you do for this friend?"

"I helped get Niall to his parents to get him some help. I assume out of Vegas."

"You saw him yourself? Niall?"

I nodded.

Her body tensed, one hand actually fisting. Definitely a shitty poker player. "When?"

"Two nights ago," I said.

"That motherfucker," she said low and to herself. "I gotta go." She quickly got out of her seat, causing the wrought-iron café chair to harshly scrape across the tile floor.

"Carla, wait. I just—"

She cut me off with her glare. "I can't talk about this right now. Not with you. Thank you for letting me know what happened."

"You're welcome," I said. It was more of a question. I wasn't really sure what she was thanking me for.

She quickly left the Coffee Bean, hitting a few buttons on her phone and raising it to her ear as she walked down the hallway that led back to the hotel room elevators.

I assumed she was calling Johnny, unaware that he had just left in the other direction. I didn't bother to stop her.

"You okay?" Monty said, coming up from behind me, making me jump. "Sorry," he added.

"It's okay," I said.

He had his phone out in his hand, like maybe he'd just been

on it. "Um, I know I said I'd stick around and make sure you're good, but…" He held up his phone, confirming my thought.

"Yeah, I'm good. If you need to go."

"I do. But I can—"

"Go. I'm fine. I'm just going to finish my coffee and go home. No side trips."

"You're sure?"

"I'm sure. Thanks for being here."

He looked toward the parking-deck hallway. "Okay. I've really got to go. Call me later today if you want."

He was gone before I could even answer him. I said a silent prayer for whoever needed Monty Westerfield's help at five in the morning.

I guess that included me.

Raymond came down the hallway next. Like Johnny, he didn't even look in the direction of the Coffee Bean. I was going to yell out to him, but let it go. He looked tired, and he'd just feel like he had to join me here at my table when he could be heading home and to bed.

A few minutes later, as I gathered up the trash from the table and walked around the corner to the garbage can, I saw Carla walking quickly from the hotel hallway around the corner to the parking deck. She must have gone up to the room and found it empty.

She was still—or again?—on her phone. I couldn't hear what she was saying, but she sounded as angry as she had when she hurriedly left our table.

I took my time with the trash, letting Carla get a head start on me. I didn't want to meet up with her in the parking-deck elevator area. Not in the mood she was currently in.

Giving Johnny, Monty, Raymond, and Carla time to have gotten to their cars and out of the deck, I went to the deck and to my Porsche.

I drove home thousands richer, and yet I felt like I'd lost.

Nine

❖❖

I DIDN'T BOTHER GOING TO SLEEP WHEN I GOT HOME. It would only be a couple of hours before Ben would be up, the boys over, and Lor serving bagels, as happened most Saturdays. I went to my room and took a long, hot shower, wishing Jack were there to scrub my back. And other places.

The man was good in the shower.

I put on clean clothes, though it was really pajamas I wanted to wear. I flicked on the television in the sitting area of my room while I got dressed. *College GameDay* was on ESPN. We got the show ungodly early on West Coast time. They were in Madison, not too far from the small town where I'd grown up. My dad and uncles had had season tickets to Badgers games for as long as I could remember. Each one of us kids got to go to one game a year with him.

The nostalgia hit me hard. I sat down on the large ottoman to put on my socks, watching as the sea of red cheered behind the ESPN guys.

And even though Monty had warned me that playing poker might be a trigger, I was still shocked at how powerful the need to bet the Wisconsin game devoured me.

Washed through me like a wave of nausea. My heart started to race and I bent over while sitting, my face nearly touching the floor.

I looked at the time. I had a pocketful of cash and about an hour before Ben would be up, the bagels out, and the coffee hot.

I could be at the Red Rock book room in fifteen minutes.

In Nevada, you could now open online accounts with your favorite sports book account, making bets from your phone. As long as your phone was in Nevada. I'd heard stories about cars pulled over at the state border, drivers and passengers making a bunch of bets on their phones, then turning around and heading back to California, Arizona, or Utah. But that wasn't an option for me. I didn't have that app on my phone. And my Apple account was held by Lorelei so that I couldn't download any apps without her doing it for me.

That was all done with moments just like this one in mind. Keeping the temptation at bay.

I tried everything Monty had worked with us on in therapy. Deep breathing. Visualization. Making plans to do something else. I was about thirty seconds into trying meditation when the thought of all that money won out.

The Hummer started to zing through my veins. The Badgers! And Lions! And Tigers (LSU, in this case)! Oh my!

I grabbed my shoes and put them on, having to steady my hands to tie the laces. My body was alive for the first time in months. Well, okay, it came alive during sex with Jack, but this was altogether different.

And yes, better.

Sorry, Jack. (And every other man, for that matter.)

After snagging the cash from my win, I made for the door to my room, happy that I'd put clothes on after my shower instead of PJs like I'd considered.

That thought made my step slow, just the tiniest bit. Did I know this would happen all along? Was that *why* I'd put clothes on?

Did I know this was the inevitable outcome when I walked into that suite at the Venetian?

Or further back than that? When the boys pulled out their sheets and I escaped to the shooting range?

My hand hovered at the doorknob. I could just stay here. In this room. Turn *GameDay* the hell off and crawl back into bed. Not come out until Monday morning when all those beautiful games were over with.

Monday Night Football, JoJo's voice whispered in my ear.

The Hummer zinged, and I pulled open my door and stepped into the hallway.

Only to see Raymond coming toward me, his head down, furiously clicking on his phone. When he heard me—or sensed me—he looked up and froze. So did I.

His glance took in my shoes on, jacket on, and car keys dangling from my hand. Puzzlement briefly crossed his face, but turned to realization. He knew. Of course he knew.

Raymond lifted his hands out to his sides, like he was nearing a cornered animal and wanted to show that there was nothing to fear. I nearly laughed at the idea, but the sound surely would have lodged in my tightening throat.

His phone vibrated, and he took a glance at it, but kept his hand out at his side.

Moving a step away from his bedroom door, he maneuvered to the middle of the hallway. The message was clear: *You're going to have to go through me.*

I understood why Carla wanted Raymond on the door at her games. I knew he'd never hurt me, and yet right now, he scared the shit out of me.

Or maybe it was something else that was making my heart pound so loudly that he could probably hear it from his doorway. Shame.

His phone vibrated again, and he took another look, his brow furrowing as he saw whatever message had come in.

"I have to take this," he said. "But then let's do something." His intention was clear: he wasn't letting me out of the house.

And like that, the Hummer started to die. The need, the craving, to make a bet subsided enough that I nodded to him. "I'm good. Do what you need to. I'm going back to my room." I chin-nodded to the door behind me.

He didn't want to trust me. He *didn't* trust me. Could I blame him? Nope.

I walked down the hallway and held out my keys to him. "Really. I'm okay. Take care of your call."

He took the keys and curled them tightly in his fist. That action alone felt like a punch in the gut. But again, I couldn't blame him.

"Give me ten minutes and I'll come hang with you," he said.

"No need."

"I'll be there," he said firmly. I nodded and went back to my room.

Once inside, I quickly kicked off my shoes, letting them fly across the room. Peeling off my jacket and tossing it across a chair used up all the physical strength I had, and I suddenly felt deeply exhausted.

The bed was even too far away, so I went to one of the chairs in the sitting nook and crawled onto it, shimmying the large ottoman up to create a makeshift chaise. I curled up in the fetal position, hoping I'd be asleep before Raymond finished up with whatever (or whomever) he was dealing with.

I tried to focus my thoughts on something other than all those glorious bets I'd *almost* made.

Stupid Raymond.

Why was he even just coming home when he left the Venetian well before I did?

He probably went for something to eat. Damn. Another minute of French toast (or whatever) and I'd have made it out of the house without anyone knowing.

And then what?

I'd have a lovely, silky pile of bet slips in my hand by now. *And then what?*

Shit.

"You decent?" Raymond said from behind my door, which I'd left ajar.

Not really. "Yeah," I said.

Coming in, he took in my position, snagged a throw from the back of the other chair, and laid it over me. Then he lowered himself into the other chair and stretched his legs out in front of him, crossing them at the ankle. He was still in his suit pants and dress shirt, but had left the jacket and tie in his room.

Still, he looked older than his twenty-two years. Older, and much, much more tired than a twenty-two-year-old should be.

And not just from the long night he'd worked.

"Wanna talk about it?" he said.

"Not really."

"Got it."

"You take care of what you needed to?" I asked.

"Maybe. Kind of. Yeah, I guess. For now."

I didn't pry, and he didn't offer up any more. We just sat in silence until we heard Lor and Ben in the kitchen.

Ten

❖❖

I SWAM. AND THEN SWAM. AND THEN I'D FLOP ON A chaise longue, exhausted. And when I had the strength to move, I swam some more.

Lorelei brought me lunch to the pool and sat and ate with me.

Ben came out and offered to sit with me, but I told him to go back in and enjoy the games.

Raymond came out to check on me a couple of times, but I just lifted a weary thumbs-up as I turned to do another lap.

It wasn't nonstop laps. At times I'd flop onto my back and just stare up at the flawless blue sky and let the sun beat down on me while I tried not to think about all the different games being played.

My phone dinged while I was eating lunch with Lor. A text from Monty asking if I was okay. If I wanted him to come over. I told him I was fine, and he wasn't needed. Lor said I should invite him over for dinner, so I did.

"Maybe you should take my phone in with you," I said when she was clearing up our plates and loading them onto the tray she'd brought out.

Alarm was on her face and the tray froze in her hands. "Are you able to bet on your phone? I purposely made—"

"No. Not bet. But I can check scores."

She relaxed. Slightly. "And even that is…"

I shrugged. "It doesn't help."

"Yeah, of course. Give me your phone."

Even though it was my idea, it was with reluctant fingers that I placed my phone on the tray.

"Want me to bring it if somebody calls or texts?" she asked.

"No. Jack's with Casey today, and I'm guessing they'll call to FaceTime with Ben later. Monty just checked in. Anybody else I'd want to hear from is sitting in there watching football."

She nodded, opened her mouth as if to say something, but didn't. "Dinner's at seven," she said.

"Need any help with it?" I asked. Yes, I was so desperate for distraction that I'd even offer up my meager culinary skills.

Lor had the good graces to quickly cover her look of horror. "No need. It's covered. But if you need—"

"I'll be fine. I'll stay out of your way. Promise."

"I really have no idea how hard this weekend might be for you, Jo. I wish I knew how you felt."

I wasn't sure how I felt, so there was no way I could describe it to Lorelei.

"Lost," I said, the word tumbling from my mouth, surprising myself. I guess I *did* know how I felt.

"Oh, Jo," she said, starting to put the tray down on the table. The pity in her voice nearly broke me.

"I'm fine. Really," I said. I motioned with my hand for her to pick the tray back up, which she did. "Nothing a few more laps won't kill." I rose from the table, took the few steps to the edge of the pool, and dove in.

I swam the length of the pool underwater. When I finally came up, Lor had left.

I swam some more.

♠ ♥ ♦ ♣

THE DINNER TABLE WAS FULL. Jimmy and Gus, who I assumed had been in our home theater all day with Ben and Raymond, had stayed for dinner. Monty had joined us. And Lorelei had outdone herself with a prime rib that was so tender and flavorful that there was absolute silence at the table as we all devoured it.

When the table had been cleared by Raymond, Monty, and me, and coffee and dessert served, the boys started pulling out their notebooks and bet sheets like they did after breakfast.

Raymond joined in, but all his info was on his phone. Old school meets new school.

"What's happening right now?" Monty asked.

"They're comparing how they did for the day," I explained. At Monty's confused look, I added, "Betting."

"Oh. Should you and I, I don't know, go watch a movie or something?" he asked. Lor nodded, indicating she'd join us if I wanted to leave the table.

But I didn't. I really didn't. I desperately wanted to know how each of them had done betting the day's games.

"No, it's okay. I want to hear."

"Are you sure, Hannah? We can do this some other time," Ben said.

"How'd you make out, Ben?" I asked, ignoring his suggestion. "Up or down?"

Ben didn't actually bet on any of the games. He'd given it up years ago, I suspected for the same reasons I had now. But he was an oddsmaker at heart, and he studied every game and wrote down his predictions in his little notebook. It was as much a critique of the odds that the casinos set as a guess of the outcome.

"I did very well today. As always, they botched the smaller conferences, and I was able to sneak in there for a few wins."

Gus and Jimmy nodded as they studied their own papers. "That service most of them are using now don't know shit about the MAC and the Sun Belt," Jimmy said, naming two conferences that probably didn't see as much action as teams in the SEC, Big Ten, and the other power conferences. "They were way off in six of those games."

I scooched my chair closer to Jimmy, and he shared his lists with me. Jimmy, unlike Ben, *did* put actual money on the games. I didn't know how much—that was like asking someone their weight or age—but I'd guess it was a few thousand every weekend. Maybe more. I knew that he'd dropped ten thousand on one of Raymond's rigged games last spring, so he wasn't afraid to put down a chunk if the situation arose.

Jimmy, old-school stat keeper that he was, had written down the final score next to the projected spread and over/under of every game.

Who needed a phone for scores when I had Jimmy's crib sheets?

"You had a good day," I said, looking over his info. He'd circled the team that he'd placed a bet on.

"I did okay," he said.

He'd done more than okay, but I just nodded and continued to look at the final scores. Typically I'd file all that info away to be used throughout the season. But now the numbers swam at me, refusing to come into focus, not allowing my memory to latch on to them.

That was probably for the best. It would only torture me next week.

And the weeks after that.

"My big win of the day was the tip you gave me," Jimmy said to Raymond.

I looked up. Gus was doing a finger-gun thing at Raymond. "I made out on that one too. Thanks."

"Yep," Raymond said.

"What game?" I asked. Jimmy pointed with a meaty finger to his sheets. "Ohio State and Coastal Carolina?" I said. Jimmy had circled Coastal Carolina. They were getting thirty points against perennial powerhouse OSU. I still would have taken Ohio State. Easily.

I looked to Raymond, who shrugged. "I have a buddy who plays basketball at Ohio State. He texted me last night. He was at a party where a bunch of the football team was. He said they were all pretty hammered. For whatever reason, they weren't staying in the hotel they normally do the night before a game. I'm guessing they figured they'd have no problem with Coastal Carolina. Even with hangovers, they'd beat 'em by twenty."

But the spread was thirty.

Gus, Jimmy, Ben, and I all froze, startling Raymond.

"What?" Lor said. "What just happened?"

Jimmy leaned across the table, his finger now pointed at Raymond and not on his winning bet circled on paper. "Kid. Do you know how valuable information like that is?"

He didn't. You could tell. But when he looked around and saw Ben, Gus, Jimmy, and me staring at him, he quickly got it.

"I've got a lot of friends," he said, the meaning behind the words clear.

I sat back in my chair, a moan escaping me like I'd just been sucker-punched.

In a way, I had.

This valuable source, this inside track to several college campuses and their goings-on, lived in my house. Had a bedroom *one door down from mine.* And I wasn't betting.

God—or who/whatever—had a wicked sense of humor.

Eleven

❖❖

I SWAM AGAIN ON SUNDAY EVEN THOUGH MY BODY WAS exhausted from the day before. If only my brain would give out like my backstroke did.

It was a little easier than Saturday. I didn't fool myself into thinking that it was because I was in any way stronger. It was only because there were so many fewer NFL games being played than college.

But still so many bets to be made.

I didn't go back in the pool after Lorelei joined me outside for lunch, but instead showered up and tried to take a nap. Exhausted as I was, I still couldn't fall asleep. Finally, I got out of bed, only to lock my door, pull the blinds extra tight, and snag my phone.

"Hey," Jack said when he answered my call. "I didn't expect to hear from you today."

He and Casey had FaceTimed with Ben and me last night, and we'd said we'd see each other on Monday when he got back to Vegas.

"I know. But I thought maybe we could try again."

There was a pause from him. I'd almost started to rescind my offer when he said, "I guess I thought we *were* trying again. Did I have it wrong?"

"What? Oh. Yeah, we are. I meant, try the other again."

"Wha— Ohhh. Yeah? Not going to break out in laughter this time?" he asked.

"I promise nothing, but I'm willing to give it a try if you are."

His voice lowered and sounded throatier when he said, "Oh, Johanna, I definitely am."

It wasn't a Hummer, but it was definitely a good feeling.

"Feel better?" Jack said when he heard my breathing return to normal. I wasn't the only one who had been out of breath.

"I guess so," I said. "Wait, what do you mean?"

He chuckled, his voice even lower and throatier than before. Who knew I'd be good at phone sex?

"Oh, Johanna, I don't even have to see you to see your tell."

If I wasn't so sated and languid, I would have been pissed off, but I only laughed.

"I guess you could say the last couple of days have had me on edge."

"Want to talk about it?" he said.

"I thought we just did," I said. He laughed. God, what a lovely sound, made all the more precious by its rarity.

"I suppose I should feel used," he said.

"Do you mind?"

"Not in the least—you have my full permission to use me to take the edge off anytime."

"I'll keep that in mind," I said. I snuggled deeper into my bedding, wishing Jack were with me in body as well as spirit. And voice.

"Is it because of football?" Jack asked.

I let out a deep sigh. "Yeah."

"Shitty weekend for me to be away. Sorry."

"Not your fault. Anyway, I have to do this on my own. You can't babysit me."

"No, but I can be a distraction. I think we've just proven

that," he said.

I smiled even though he couldn't see me. If he was right about knowing my tell, he knew it anyway. "Well, there is *Monday Night Football* to get through tomorrow. What time does your flight get in?"

"Around noon, but I'm going to go straight to the station. Make my case again."

Jack still hadn't been allowed on active duty since he'd been shot a few months ago. They were letting him do limited hours on desk duty—working on cold cases—which may have been more torturous to him than not being involved at all.

I'd learned my lesson about telling him to give it time, so I just said, "Okay. So I'll see you after that?"

"Yeah. I need to stop by my apartment too. Pick up mail, get some stuff."

There was a pause, neither of us willing to say what should have been an easy thing to bring up.

He didn't want to push it, and I didn't want to jinx it.

Jack had only been at his apartment sporadically since he'd been released from the hospital, and never to spend the night. He'd moved into the guest room to recuperate, and then into mine after that, though most of his stuff was still in the guest room where he stayed when Casey visited.

What the hell—I wasn't betting anymore, so no need to worry about jinxes, right? "So, is it time to let your apartment go?" I said, being the first one to jump from the high dive.

"It's certainly time to have the conversation about it," he said.

I released a breath. "Okay," I said.

"Okay?"

"Yeah. I'd like that. To have the conversation."

"Me too," he said.

"Tomorrow night?"

"Done. Want anything from Portland?"

"Only you," I said, then cringed. *Sappy, Anna, so sappy.*

"Wow. You did need to take the edge off," he said. He laughed again, and I stopped chiding myself. Jack got it.

Jack got me.

We said our goodbyes, and I finally was able to get a nap.

When I woke up, the games were over, with only the Sunday night game to be played.

I could handle that, so I went out into the house in search of my family.

Ben had seen enough football for the day, so he and I watched a gangster movie.

I went to bed having made it through the first football weekend with not making a bet.

Only sixteen more to go.

Plus playoffs.

And the Super Bowl.

Piece of cake.

Twelve

❖❖

MONDAY AFTER BREAKFAST, THE BOYS PULLED OUT THE line sheets for the coming Saturday's college games, scanning the early spreads for any signs of weakness.

I asked Jimmy to drive Ben home again and went back to the shooting range. Buddy remembered me from last week and got me set up with a Colt 1911 again. I did a little better. By better, I mean that it didn't scare me quite so much, and I didn't jump at the recoil quite so blatantly.

I half expected Cassandra Hall to be there, but she wasn't. When I finished, I thanked Buddy and drove home.

I sat with Lorelei in our shared office and went over some household things that she had questions about. I was about to hand over the money I'd made playing poker on Friday, but something had me just putting it in my cigar box instead.

I told myself it was to keep it liquid in case the whole Niall thing was unfinished and I could help the situation with a pile of cash. I even kind of believed myself.

When Lor went off to start dinner (I offered to help; she wisely declined my offer), I found Raymond just back from classes at the dining room table, so I sat with him.

His backpack was on the floor beside his feet and a book and notebook were on the table in front of him, though it looked like he hadn't started studying yet.

"Okay if I do this here?" he said. "I'm afraid I'll fall asleep if I do it in my room."

"Of course," I said. "Can I bring you anything? Water? Pop? Energy drink?"

He smiled, but shook his head. "Nah, I'm good. Thanks. You really have energy drinks?"

I shrugged. "Lor and I thought it might be a good idea to stock up now that we have a college kid in the house."

"Might be more useful to the eighty-plus and the one who's up all night playing poker."

I sat across the table from him. "You know, even when I was playing, I never liked those things. Never really needed them."

"Adrenaline do it for you?"

I shrugged. "I guess."

He nodded. "I get that. I never needed to get up for a game. Never needed the pep talk from the coach."

"Just wanted to win," I said, summing up how we'd both felt when we were doing what we loved to do. At what we were most talented.

At what we had given up.

"Liking your classes?" I asked, trying to get our thoughts from where they'd been headed.

"Yeah, I guess," he said. "Three of the four are interesting. Good profs. One's so-so, but manageable."

"That's good. And you're not overdoing it with other stuff?"

He knew I meant Carla's games and anything to do with that world.

"She hasn't called since the Friday night game, so that's all good. Plus the money I won on the Coastal Carolina game is more than I'd make with her in weeks, so I'm going to turn her down from now on."

"Look, if it's about the money, I've told you—"

"It's not the money. Not *just* the money. I don't take charity. We've had this conversation before, Anna."

"I know, Raymond," I said, trying to sound as stern as he did. He rolled his eyes at me. "Anyway, I'm glad you're able to turn her down."

"Yeah, well, like I said, she hasn't called since Friday, so I think I've been replaced full-time by Johnny Aces anyway."

"That might be just as well," I said.

"Yep. It's all good."

"Johnny Aces," I said, doing the eye rolling myself this time. "What a douche."

"Total douche."

"Like, which do you think came first, the tattoo or the nickname?" I said.

"Oh, the tattoo. He only did the tattoo to *get* the nickname, I guarantee you."

We both laughed, thinking about the absurdity of Johnny and his straight-out-of-Central-Casting appearance.

"Johnny Aces. Dude's seen too many movies," Raymond said.

"What about Johnny Aces?" Jack called from the doorway. I hadn't even heard him come in.

"Hey there," I said, warmth in my voice as I took him in. Yeah, the phone was good, but having Jack Schiller in my house—in the flesh—was so much better.

"What about Johnny Aces?" he repeated. I started to rise from my seat, but he stopped me with a hand. He walked into the dining room, standing at the head of the table, looking from me to Raymond and back again. "Johnny Aces?"

"Just some guy Raymond and I both know. Sort of. He's like a bad caricature of every lowlife in every Vegas movie."

"I know who he is," Jack said.

Well, sure, that made sense. Jack was police. Mostly homicide, but that didn't mean he didn't know who the neighborhood bad guys were.

"Well then, you know how ridiculous he is," I said. I looked over at Raymond for confirmation, but he was studying Jack, seeing something before I did. I looked back to Jack. "How do you know him?"

"I know *of* him because I was just at the station."

A tingle went through my body, rushing up my spine and lodging at the base of my neck. Not a good Hummer-type feeling, but one that felt like a fight-or-flight moment was coming on.

"And he was there?" I asked softly. I knew what the answer was. The way I knew when a player at the table was about to make a big bluff.

Only Jack wouldn't be bluffing.

"Not at the station, no. But a topic of conversation, yes. He was at the morgue."

Yep, I saw that coming like someone was about to push all in.

"Johnny Aces was murdered," Jack said, confirming my suspicion.

"When?" Raymond asked Jack. He looked at me with meaning, and I sighed, knowing what Jack was going to say next.

"Medical examiner thinks between four and six in the morning on Saturday."

Yep. Would have bet the farm on that time frame.

Shit.

"Shit," Raymond said.

"Shit," Jack said, pulling out a chair and taking a seat. His stare moved from Raymond to me. "Okay. What have the two of you gotten yourselves mixed up in?" I started to balk, but he stopped me by adding, "Again."

Yeah, guess I couldn't really argue with that.

Thirteen

❖

WE TOLD HIM ABOUT FRIDAY NIGHT/SATURDAY morning. He even went to his room to get his little detective notebook before we gave him our account of the night.

And he recorded it with his phone. Leaving no stone unturned, Detective Jack Schiller.

When we were done, he went to his room to call Frank Botz, his regular partner, to brief him.

"Do *not* contact Carla or Monty about this," he warned us before leaving to fill in Frank.

"Do you think we're going to be suspects?" Raymond asked.

I sighed. "Probably. I'm getting kind of used to it."

"Well, *I'm* not. And I can't have this kind of spotlight on me. *Neither* of us can," he said.

I tried to wave away his concern with a nonchalant hand in the air, but it thunked on the table when it landed, causing me to flinch. "It'll be fine. Jack won't let that happen. Johnny Aces has nothing to do with JoJo and her goings-on. Or you and basketball."

"Jack can't protect you if he's sitting on the bench," he said.

That was true.

And yet I knew Jack would try to help if he could. Not interfere in an ongoing murder investigation. He was too good of a cop for that. But he knew when things like past indiscretions would only muddy waters and when they would be an integral part of the investigation.

I was pretty sure he did.

I hoped he did.

"Okay, let's go," Jack said, entering the room like I'd conjured him with my thoughts.

"Where?" I said, already rising from the table. Raymond, I noticed, stayed in his chair.

"Both of you," Jack said to Raymond.

"Where?" Raymond said.

"To the station. Frank will take your official statements there."

"And then that will be it?" I said. "We help give the timeline of when Johnny left the Venetian and then he can start the investigation from there?"

"Something like that," Jack said. He motioned at Raymond, who reluctantly got up from his seat, shoved his things in his backpack, and left it all on his empty chair.

"I'll tell Lor we'll be a little late for dinner," I said.

"I've already told her that we wouldn't be back until late," Jack said.

"Did you at least say hello to your father?" I asked.

His stern look softened. "I said a quick hello to Ben, yes. Ready to go? Need a purse or anything?"

"Have you ever seen me carry a purse?" I said.

He snorted, but stood back and let me lead the way.

"I'll drive," I said, snagging my keys from the bowl in the foyer where I'd left them after getting home from the shooting range.

"I'll meet you there. I have shit to do after," Raymond said.

I expected Jack to balk, but he didn't. So instead of the Lexus, I headed to my Porsche, and Jack got in beside me.

Jack used my phone to text the address of the station to Raymond, and he pulled out of the driveway first.

I started to put the car into gear, but Jack's hand stilled over mine on the gearshift. "Wait," he said softly.

He used my hand to put the car into neutral and then pulled up the parking brake. I took my feet off the clutch and brake pedal and turned to him.

His hand curled around mine on the shift and clasped it. With his other hand, he reached up and placed a finger on my horseshoe necklace. His skin was rough and warm.

"Hey," he whispered just before he leaned forward and kissed me.

Much, much better than on the phone.

"I missed you," he said when we finally broke apart.

"Me too," I said. He leaned his forehead on mine for a second or two, and I breathed deeply, loving the scent of him.

A low grunt of dissatisfaction came from his throat, and he sat away from me, facing forward in his seat.

"Okay. Drive. It's going to take me that long to switch to cop mode."

I smiled, liking the thought that boyfriend mode was hard for him to shake.

As I drove, the smile faded, because I knew that when we walked through the doors of the station, Cop Jack would be the one escorting me in for questioning.

"Feels a little like déjà vu, hey?" Carla said to me when I saw her at the police station. We were in the lobby of Metro headquarters. I was done with my interview and had decided to wait for Raymond, even though he had his own car. Carla had just gotten off the elevator from upstairs, apparently done with her interview as well.

"What?" I said.

She waved a hand around the building. "You know. Like

after Lion LaGasse was killed. Me and you here."

"Oh. Right," I said. It hadn't been that long ago, but it felt like a lifetime. Carla had just started running games herself after Vince's death. I'd gotten a big name to play in one to give her some credibility. And then he'd been murdered by another one of the players.

An accident. Kind of.

And now another man had been killed after one of her games.

"Might put a damper on things for a while," I said.

She shrugged. "Maybe. Maybe not. We'll see. A lot of the players didn't even know Johnny. Only dealt with me. Only saw me or Raymond at the games. It might not even make a blip. Certainly won't get the attention of a Lion LaGasse."

Not even a blip. Nothing to slow down the draw of high-stakes backroom poker games.

"So, what'd you tell 'em?" Carla said, a nod of her chin toward the elevators and the floor where we'd been questioned. Separately, of course.

"I told them the truth. The chronology of events. When I saw Johnny leave for the parking deck. When—"

"You saw him leave?"

I nodded. "Yeah. While you and I were talking."

"You didn't say anything at the time."

"Should I have?"

She sat down on one of the chairs that were against the wall of the long hallway. I sat next to her. I could see her putting pieces into her mind, twisting them this way and that, trying to make them fit.

The thing was, I didn't know what pieces she had that I didn't. And she wasn't about to offer them up.

"What'd you say about me and you talking?" she asked.

"Not much. They wondered why I'd gone to the game. Jack knew I didn't play anymore, so it's kind of suspicious that I went to a game where one of the men in the room ends up dead a few hours later."

She snorted, but not with humor. "Yeah, it's *really* starting to feel like déjà vu."

"I *really* need to start staying out of your games."

"Ya think? So, did you tell them why you went? Doesn't look good that you went specifically to see Johnny."

"Yeah, I told them everything." There was no reason not to. Nobody would be in trouble if the truth was out there. There was no crime I was trying to cover up. Not point shaving, anyway. The illegal loan sharking between Johnny (and Carla) and Niall wasn't my issue. No need to lie to cover for him anymore. Not that I would have anyway. Stupid Johnny.

"Yeah, me too," she said, surprising me. She rolled her eyes at me. "Well, not *everything*. But as it pertains to Johnny and that night. Morning. Whatever. I have nothing to hide."

She had a lot to hide. As did I. But I took her at her word that she wasn't holding back where the morning of Johnny's murder was concerned.

Johnny's murder.

Frank Botz and Peter Faxon had conducted my questioning. Jack, I was sure, had been behind the two-way mirror. They didn't tell me much, just that Johnny had been shot while in his car. It was in front of his apartment building, done at close range. So either the killer was lying in wait for Johnny or they'd followed him home from the Venetian.

It reminded me a little of poor Danny O'Hern's death. But his killer was no longer among the living.

"You taking off?" Carla asked.

"I thought I might stick around and talk to Raymond when he's done. If it doesn't take too much longer."

"He's here too?"

I nodded. And as if to prove my point, the elevator doors opened up and out stepped both Monty and Raymond. They came over and joined us. Monty and Carla nodded at each other. I wasn't sure if they'd ever met, but it seemed weird to do proper introductions in the lobby of Las Vegas Metro.

"Everything okay?" I asked both of them. They both responded with nods. The four of us stood there, warily staring at each other. "Raymond and I missed dinner. Anybody want to grab something to eat?"

"I could eat," Carla said with a shrug.

"Yeah, sure," Monty said. Raymond looked at his phone and then nodded.

Carla gave the name of a place, and we all agreed on it, splitting up as we left the building and went to our cars. It kind of felt like the beginning of a joke.

Four Persons of Interest walk into a bar.

I hoped the joke wouldn't be on me.

Fourteen

❖❖

WE MET AT A PLACE BETWEEN THE STATION AND
Summerlin. I didn't know where Carla lived (nor did I want to),
but she was the one who'd suggested the place, so I figured it was
on her way home.

We settled in and ordered drinks. Carla ordered a bunch of
appetizers for the table.

A regular Monday-evening happy hour. Except instead of
watching the game together, we were discussing which of us
were the most prime murder suspect. The primest?

"I'm sorry to have dragged you into this," I said to Monty.
"There was no reason for you to be at the Venetian that night
other than to look after me."

"Yeah, I still don't quite get that," Carla said. "He's like,
what? A sober companion or something?"

There wasn't a good way to explain who Monty was to me,
so I just shrugged. "Something like that."

She snorted. "Fat lot of good he did you that night. He'd be
better off getting a cut of your winnings."

"At least she didn't take those winnings and flush them
down the drain betting on football," Monty said. There was a
definite chip-on-the-shoulder tone to his words. The chip fell
when he looked at me and said quietly, "You didn't do that,
right?"

"Right," I said. Not a lot of conviction in my voice as I shared a glance with Raymond and we both remembered our meeting in the hallway to our bedrooms in the wee hours of Saturday morning.

"So, I have a question," Raymond said. "You two have a lot more experience at being murder suspects than I do." He motioned between Carla and me.

"Ha. Ha. Very fucking funny, kid," Carla said. "Murder, maybe. But suspected felonies of any kind? I'm guessing you're right up there."

Our drinks had arrived, and Raymond lifted his beer in a touché toast to Carla. After a healthy sip, he asked, "So, since they questioned us, and we were the last people to see Johnny before he got shot, how far are they going to start digging into our whereabouts and that kind of shit?"

"What do you mean? Johnny left. We all left after him. All went home. What's to dig into?" Monty said. I didn't call him on it, but Monty had gotten a phone call that made him leave the Venetian when he had. I wasn't so sure he'd gone *straight* home.

Carla didn't answer. Neither did Raymond. And I remembered the fact that Raymond didn't get home until well after I did, even though he'd left for the Venetian parking deck before me.

"Oh, they'll check to make sure we left when we told them," I told Monty, but it was for the whole table's education. They probably didn't need it. As both Carla and Raymond pointed out, it wasn't our first murder-adjacent rodeo.

Even Monty had been involved in the investigation into the death of one of our GREET support group members.

Hell, we were all old hands at this.

Still, I went on with what to expect. "They'll look at security footage in the parking deck—if there is any—and cross it against our statements. Stuff like that."

"What's that thing they do on the cop shows? Check the

pings on your phone or whatever?" Raymond said. "Think they'll do that?"

I took a drink of my beer, loving the coldness as it slid down my dry throat. Nothing like spending a few hours at a police station to make you crave a tall, frosty one.

"I don't know. I suppose if something in our statements doesn't ring true, or check out, they'll do stuff like that."

"They can see where we've been with that, right?" Raymond said. But it was all three of them that suddenly got quiet, put their heads down slightly in a movement that seemed a lot like guilt.

Or simply not wanting cops to know your business.

"Yeah, I guess," I said, not completely sure. Some PI I would make when I didn't even know basics like that. No wonder you needed to get years of hours in.

"And they can tell who you talked to?" he asked.

"Phone records, yeah. Different than the location pinging," I said, again not totally confident I knew what I was talking about. "But they might have to get a warrant to do that." But did they have to notify you about that? I didn't think so, but because of the look on Raymond's face, I kept that to myself.

"Kid, didn't Anna teach you anything? Burner phones," Carla said.

Monty shot Carla a look. Like her bringing up my colorful past was a blow below the belt.

It wasn't. It was fair game. Everything was in Vegas.

The appetizers arrived—nachos, mini tacos, spinach dip, and sliders—and we dove in, each of us eating like it was our last supper.

Or like we didn't want to talk to each other.

I thought about Raymond's look of agitation at his phone when I'd met him in our hallway. Could it have been a text conversation with his buddy at Ohio State that had him concerned? Was that what he'd been looking at when I met him?

But that would have been around eight a.m. on Saturday morning in Columbus, and I couldn't see a college basketball player being up that early after being at a party the night before. More likely he'd texted Raymond from the party itself hours earlier.

So if that was the case, what had bothered Raymond so much that morning?

Carla loaded up on the nachos, taking her fork to disengage a particularly stubborn strand of melted cheese that stretched to her plate.

She looked more hungry than nervous, but I had to figure that she wouldn't want the police tracking her movements and phone usage any more than Raymond would. I also wondered if she'd told the cops about being pissed at Johnny when she left me at the Coffee Bean. And why she was so pissed to know Niall was in the custody of his parents.

Monty popped a slider down in two bites, barely stopping to chew. He reached for another one. Somewhere in my office, Lorelei had a file on Monty's past. Something in it had made her cautious. At the time, I hadn't wanted to know. Maybe I should have asked.

"Um, I have to tell you something," Monty said after a swallow. "Something I did let the police know, so you two should know as well." He was looking between Carla and me. I glanced at her, and she shrugged. "If they do trace our phones, I got a call from Niall's mother that night."

So that was who had called him away. But wasn't she back in Topeka already? Trying to get Niall into some kind of treatment?

"Niall is no longer with them," Monty said.

"What?" Carla and I said at the same time.

"He gave them the slip at McCarran. They don't know if he's still here, got on a different flight, or, well, what happened."

I looked at Carla and could see the wheels turning. Could she get her money? Did Niall kill Johnny because of his debt?

Would he be coming for Carla next? Could she get her money?

"Has he been in touch with you?" I asked Monty.

He shook his head. "No, but he wouldn't. I was working with his parents, not so much him. And after the other night, there's no way he'd trust me now."

Nor me. But he hadn't seen Anna Dawson that night. He'd dealt with JoJo.

This new development sat with us, none of us knowing what it really meant.

Finally the aroma of the food did me in and I dug in myself, joining the other three. Were we all stress-eating or just hungry?

All of us seemed to be hiding something from the others. And I was faced with all I did not know about how any of this worked.

Yeah, I was sorely lacking in the ABCs of investigation techniques.

But I knew someone I could ask. Or, as Jimmy would say, "I know a guy." Only, in this case: I knew a lady.

Fifteen

❖

THE OFFICES OF CASSANDRA HALL, PRIVATE investigator, were not what I expected. Of course it wouldn't be like something out of a Sam Spade novel with frosted glass panes in the wooden doors, a transom overhead, and her name stenciled on the glass. It was not a tiny reception area with a bombshell receptionist who wore a tight pencil skirt and a smart, crisp blouse and sat behind a huge oak desk. Nor was it dark and filled with an atmosphere right out of film noir.

Her office was bright and sunny, with an impressive amount of greenery in the outer room and a receptionist who could have been a grandmother and who wore khakis and a knit top in a matronly print. And it wasn't a huge oak desk she sat behind, but a glass-top desk with sleek, brushed-nickel legs.

The kind I could never have because I had too much crap all over the place and needed to be able to hide it.

"You must be Anna Dawson," she said when I entered the reception area. "Cassie's running a few minutes behind. Can I offer you something? Coffee? Soda? Bottled water?"

"I'm fine, thank you," I said.

"I'm Brenda. Have a seat, dear, and don't hesitate to let me know if you change your mind about something. I even have some cookies I made and brought in, in the break room."

"Thanks, Brenda," I said, and took a seat on the plush love

seat that was part of a multi-piece set that was nicer than you saw in most living rooms.

The office building she was in was a newer one, lots of windows, three stories, and her offices took up a corner of the third floor.

I wondered if her office had always been this nice and located in such a luxury building, or if she'd upgraded after Vince's will had been read.

"Anna? Hi. Come on in," the woman herself said as she opened the door to her office. I hadn't even heard her.

I nodded at Brenda as I passed her desk and entered Cassandra's office, which was as tastefully—and expensively, if my inexpert eye was any judge—decorated as the outer area.

Understated. Minimalist. But very nice. And her windows had a spectacular view of the Strip. If she were putting in late hours, she'd have an amazing array of lights to keep her company.

I supposed her late hours were probably more likely to be in a car on a stakeout than here in her palatial office, but still not a bad place to come to each morning.

"I'm so glad you took me at my word and called," she said. "I really didn't think you would when I gave you my card."

I hadn't either. Then. But now?

"Thanks for seeing me so soon," I said.

I'd called that morning from breakfast with the boys, and her receptionist had worked me in for just a few hours later.

I'd brought Ben home, changed into something a little less degenerate gambler (though that was eighty percent of my wardrobe), and driven to her offices, which weren't terribly far from Summerlin, on the north side of town, near where the freeways merged—the Spaghetti Bowl.

"No problem. Kind of a slow morning, actually, so this worked out well." She sat in her chair behind her desk—another glass-topped one that was impeccably tidy on top—and waved me to one of the two upholstered chairs that faced her. "So, what can I do for you?" she asked once I sat. She pulled over a yellow legal pad from the side of the desk and took a thick, expensive-looking pen from a glass jar full of them at the front of the desk.

There was a desktop computer on the corner of the desk, but she ignored that and wrote on the legal pad as I explained the last five days to her.

I left nothing out. However, I didn't feel the need to flesh out everyone's backstory, either. No need for her to know Raymond's history. Or why Monty was fearful for me. Or why... Well, any of the stuff that happened Before.

I did tell her about Niall, and how that may or may not be connected. And how, honestly, any number of people could have killed Johnny because of his line of work and his less-than-friendly disposition. But the four of us who'd followed Johnny out of the Venetian were most likely whom the police would look at first.

And the hardest.

There wasn't any reason to go into Raymond's and my history. Cassandra had known about the feds looking into Raymond.

She never let on if she knew other things, though, as I gave her all the players and timelines of Friday night.

After I finished, she looked over her notes again while I sat in silence. Not wanting to just stare at her, I took in her office in more detail.

Besides the desk and facing chairs that we occupied, there was a long, sleek couch along one wall in a light gray leather that looked so soft I wanted to go over and dive into it. I kept my seat.

The artwork on the walls was breathtaking black-and-white photos of Vegas. Some bold and chaotic of the Strip and the iconic Welcome to Fabulous Las Vegas sign. But some were stark and bare shots of the desert and the canyons.

The whole office was like the photos—shades of black and

white—except for three bright yellow throw pillows on the couch.

It should have been cold, clinical, but it wasn't. The whole place exuded understated warmth.

Kind of like Cassandra herself.

"Okay. So, where would you like me to start?" she said when she looked up from her tablet.

"Um…"

She took my reticence for indecision. "Well, probably the first place to start is a little background on this Niall person. See if he really is back in Topeka or still in Vegas."

I nodded. "Right. I thought I'd ask Monty more about that. See if there's anything new there."

She blinked at me, then jotted something down. "Okay. And I'll do some digging too. Let's find out if he really has anything to do with this or is just a red herring."

Process of elimination. Yes, I liked that. It was how my brain worked too, coming into play in almost every poker hand I'd ever been dealt.

"And, of course, the other players in the game. And other associates of this Johnny Aces. And a deeper dive into him, of course."

"Right. But, um, I think the police will be doing all that."

She was studying me again, and I realized it was time to lay my cards on the table. Tell her why I was really there.

As if onto me, she said, "So, if you're working with this Monty on Niall, and the police are investigating the other players and Johnny's background, what exactly would you like me to do?"

"Well, I, I mean…"

She leaned forward, the sleeves of her silk blouse gliding across the glass-top desk. Clasping her hands together, she asked, "Anna, exactly why do you want to hire me?"

"That's just it," I said. "I don't want to hire you."

"You don't want to hire me?"

"No."

"Then why are you here?"

"I don't want to hire you. I want *you* to hire *me*."

Sixteen

❖❖

"AND SHE'S GOING TO DO IT? HIRE YOU?" LORELEI asked me later that night after dinner. I'd helped her clean up the kitchen, and then we went to our office to talk.

I had business to discuss with her. Apparently it was Anna Dawson Doing Business day.

I told her all about my meeting with Cassandra Hall and my offer to her.

"Yes. I think so. It kind of took her off guard," I said.

"Yeah, I'll bet," Lor said. She was clicking away on her laptop, but waving for me to go on.

"I explained to her about needing hours toward a PI license."

"Which she would have had to do herself, so I'm sure she's sympathetic to that," Lorelei said.

I wasn't as confident. "Maybe. I think she might have thought I was just some bored dilettante that was looking for some thrills."

Lor looked up from her screen. "Why would she think that?" As soon as I'd gotten home, I'd changed into my usual "in" outfit of jogging pants and tee. Nothing about my attire screamed bored dilettante. More like scary homeless.

"I said I didn't want any kind of payment, and that I'd even be willing to subsidize myself. For her time. For her taking me on."

Lor scrunched up her nose. Yeah, that sounded like boredom.

"I also explained that I'm unsure of this all myself, and I didn't want to waste her time—or anyone else's—until I was sure this was something I wanted to pursue. But the fact that I've, um, stumbled upon—"

"You're involved in a murder investigation. Again."

"Yes. Thank you," I said. She snorted and went back to her laptop. "That this was a perfect opportunity to start on hours, while getting to the bottom of Johnny Aces' murder."

"Oh God, what's going on now?" Jack said from the doorway.

"Nothing," I said while Lor said, "Everything."

He looked good. Standing in the doorway, wearing jeans and a Trail Blazers hoodie that I knew was a Father's Day gift from Casey. He'd missed dinner, but had apparently been home long enough from the station to change from work clothes.

He hadn't come to my room last night. I wasn't even sure when he'd gotten home from the station, or if he'd spent the night in his room or at his apartment.

I assumed he was trying to stay as involved as they'd let him. Which probably wasn't much due to both medical and Anna-involvement reasons.

He'd gotten his hair cut, but I wasn't sure if that had been while in Portland or since he'd gotten back yesterday. I hadn't noticed it before, but hadn't really focused on his hair as he had taken me into the station to be questioned about a murder.

I was focused on him now, though. He leaned one shoulder against the doorjamb and shoved a hand in his jeans pocket. Damn, he did it for me.

His head leaned to the side as he looked at me. "Do I want to know?" he asked.

"What we're doing, or what I'm thinking?" I asked.

I swear I didn't move a muscle. No facial tic. No raised

brow or batting eyelashes. No "how you doin'?" seduction in my voice. I gave nothing away.

And still, he barked out a laugh. "Oh, I *know* what you're thinking. And we'll get to that. Later. But what Lucy and Ethel are up to right now is the question."

Lor and I glanced at each other, looking for guidance from the other as to whether we should be offended or complimented by the Lucy and Ethel crack.

"Research. For possible employment opportunities for Jo," Lor said, with a bit of a sniff to her voice. No stuffing candies down our blouses here, no sir!

She turned her laptop around for me to see, pushing it across the shared writers' desk we had in our office.

It was the website for Cassandra Hall, private investigator. I leaned forward to take a look as Jack entered the room, came around to my side, stood behind me, and bent down to read over my shoulder.

I could smell his freshly laundered hoodie and feel the heat come from his freshly bathed body.

"Employment opportunity? With this outfit?"

"We're considering it," I said.

"Who's we?" Jack said. He looked at Lorelei, who held up her hands in surrender.

"I just do the research. All decisions made are on Jo."

"Cassandra Hall is considering taking me on in kind of an intern role," I said.

Jack reached over me and pulled the laptop closer to our side, scrolling down the webpage. I was quiet as we both read the fairly bare-bones website. It didn't say a lot, but then, discretion would be key in that type of business. No picture of Cassandra, which I assumed was a good idea so she could do more undercover-type things. Too bad, though, because there were a fair amount of men who would hire her just to be around a woman who looked like she did.

Probably another reason she went photo-less. Smart.

There wasn't a lot of information. Years in the business. Types of investigations handled. Utmost in discretion. The basic things you might have questions about. But it was a very professionally done website, looking like her office space: sparse, expensive, tasteful.

Jack finished before I did and leaned back, but moved his hand that had been on the trackpad to my shoulder. He gave a gentle squeeze.

"I thought the plan was to work on your list and then Frank would find the right PI for you to work with?"

"It was," I said. "But this kind of fell into my lap."

"How's that?"

I told him about running into Cassandra at the gun range. I almost derailed the story there at the look of surprise on Jack's face that I'd gone to the range at all. But I plowed ahead and told him about meeting her for the first time at Vince's will reading.

"And I really wouldn't have contacted her at all, except, you know, with Johnny and all."

His hand slid from my shoulder and he stepped back, leaning against the credenza that ran along the back wall. Crossing his legs at the ankle, he put both hands in his pockets.

"I'll leave you guys to it," Lor said.

"Thanks, Lorelei," I said. Jack waved to her, and she waved back to us both, closing the office door as she left. I rotated my swivel chair around to face Jack. "What do you think?"

He shrugged, but not in a petulant way. More like he was resolved.

"I think... Jesus, Anna, I don't know what to think. I can do some digging into her if you want. Before you commit to this. I'm too new to the town to know all the PIs personally, but Frank would know who is reputable and who isn't."

Probably a good idea. But I didn't want Jack to do it. He'd stretched the weight limit of the limbs he'd climbed out on for me. No need to throw an anvil at him and weigh him down even more. "That's okay. If she even says yes, we can just see how it goes with this one thing. There's no time frame for me, so if I don't like working with her—"

"*For* her," Jack corrected me.

"Right," I agreed. He quirked a brow at me. Yeah, I'd never really worked for anyone before. Part-time stuff in high school and college. But for better or worse—and there were lots of both—I'd been my own boss since moving to Vegas years ago. "I realize that to be my own boss in this, eventually, I have to pay my dues now."

"And you're okay with that?"

I didn't answer right away, only lifted a shoulder in a half shrug. Jack smiled. A full-on I-know-you-better-than-you-know-yourself smile. He had me there.

"Come on, Jack. I really want to know. What's your professional opinion of all this? Me? Taking on something like this? With Cassandra?"

He tilted his head back like I'd slapped him. Maybe in a way I had. Uncrossing his ankles, he took his hands from his pockets and laid them on the credenza behind him, as if bracing himself.

Oh, man. I probably shouldn't have asked.

"My opinions about you, Johanna Elizabeth Dawson, have never been, much to my partner's dismay—and everyone else's at Metro—professional. Not from moment one. Not from those steps in front of that building."

Oh, man, he was bringing *that* up. Not even meeting over Danny's death, but before that. I definitely didn't want to hear this.

"And the thought of you being mixed up in yet *another* murder has me wanting to head straight for that bottle of bourbon I hid in this house and sit in my room—*my* room, not yours—and drink until I can't even remember your name."

Oh, man, there was a hidden bottle somewhere? Should I be worried about that?

"But you have a talent for reading people, reading situations, and I'd never want to see you stifle those talents. I wouldn't stifle mine. They mean too much to me."

I started to say something, but didn't get the chance. I wasn't sure what I could say to that, anyway.

"Whether it's this Cassandra Hall, or some other PI, if you want to do it, do it. Pursue something that makes you happy. I love what I do. I know that sounds weird. The shit I've seen has probably cost me my marriage and my liver, but I couldn't imagine doing anything else."

My thoughts went to Hummers. Those brief moments when I was *truly* happy. But those moments were also tinged with fear of the unknown. Fear that it could all come crashing down. Adrenaline should not be construed as happiness.

I knew that.

"And I'll deal with it," Jack said. "You survived a lot before you ever met me. I'm not fool enough to think I'm going to keep you out of danger. Hell, I can't even keep you away from every damn murder investigation that comes Metro's way."

Oh, man. It wasn't every murder Metro had, was it? I mean, what would even be the odds on that? The over/under?

I could ask some retired bookmakers I happened to know.

"So do it. Let me know if you get in over your head. Otherwise I'll try to keep out of it and keep my mouth shut."

Oh, man, I knew what Herculean effort that might take. And I loved Jack for it.

He leaned forward, got right into my space, and said quietly, "And now, let's get to what you were thinking about when I was standing in the doorway." He brushed a hand down my arm and snagged my hand, pulling me out of my chair to leave the office.

Oh, man.

Seventeen

❖❖

TWO DAYS LATER, I SAT WITH CASSANDRA HALL IN FRONT of a seedy joint in North Las Vegas named the Moonlight Motel. It wasn't the place where I'd helped smuggle out Niall, but it was just as bad. This one, though, had all its room entrances on the outside of the building, so we were able to stay in the car.

We were in her 4Runner, having left my Porsche in the Aliante Casino parking lot, where she'd picked me up. She'd called early this morning saying she had a lead on Niall and asking if I wanted to join her. After making sure Lor could take Ben to breakfast, I said yes, anxious to start on the bank of hours needed if I was going to pursue becoming a PI. Even more anxious to see if Niall really was still in town, and if he knew anything about Johnny being shot Friday night.

And so we sat, sipping coffee that we'd picked up at a drive-thru on our way to the motel. "How did you find out Niall was staying here?" I asked, ready to begin my learning.

"*Might* be staying here," Cassandra answered. "It was just a tip. Could be a bum one."

"Right," I said. "I guess I'm asking how—"

"Listen, in order for this to work, you have to know that I'm not going to let you completely in on my network. I spent years building it up. It is, basically, my stock in trade."

"Yeah, of course," I said. I realized—again—how much I

didn't know about all of this.

"I'm not against sharing intel with you—you are, I guess, my employee. But there are certain things that I'm not going to give up. My sources being one of those things. You're just going to have to trust me on tips I may find out."

"Right. Yeah. I do. Trust you, that is."

She nodded and took another glance in the rearview mirror. We'd parked facing away from the motel and were watching the door through the side and rearview mirrors, and also the camera on Cassandra's phone, which she'd set on the dash, facing out the back window, and which was video-recording.

She'd explained when she parked that she faced away so that if the person you were tailing looked in your direction, they wouldn't be able to make out your face.

I guess that had been my first lesson.

My second lesson, apparently, was to protect your sources from wannabes.

"That's something you're already ahead of the curve with, and don't even realize it," Cassandra said. She took a drink of her coffee, her eyes moving from the mirror back to her phone, which was just a smaller, wider version of the same view.

"What do you mean?" I asked.

"As many years as you've been gambling in this town? Connections galore."

We sat in the parking lot for another hour. She gave me the ins and outs of doing a stakeout. Always have a bag in the car with a towel, change of clothes, bottles of water, and snacks in case you are stuck nowhere near food. Use a nondescript car, one people won't remember. Which is why she had me move from my Porsche to her older 4Runner. Probably why she still had the 4Runner after inheriting from Vince.

She advised me to get a couple of burner phones and keep straight their numbers and to whom I gave said numbers. I didn't tell her that I was already a champ with burner phones.

"Men have it a lot easier for this kind of thing," she said, lifting her empty coffee cup and then holding it down by her crotch, imitating something that women would not be able to do in a car without a lot of mess.

Not for the faint of heart, the PI business.

"When it comes to that, sometimes I just leave the camera on my phone recording and walk behind a building if there's no businesses around where I can use the restroom," she said.

"But what if you miss them leave?" I said. That seemed like a big no-no. Peeing-in-a-cup-so-you-didn't-miss-a-thing-level no-no.

She shrugged, setting her empty cup in a trash bag she had on the floor behind her seat. (Another good thing to have, I mentally noted.) "If I miss it, I miss it. If I leave my phone going, or a video camera, I've got them leaving, and if they left with anyone."

"But not where they might be going. No way to follow them," I said.

"Right. But, Anna, most of the cases you'll get are humdrum stuff. From the little you told me about why you want to become a PI, you've been neck-deep in murders lately, but this business is a lot more boring than that."

I didn't necessarily like the "neck-deep in murders" comment, but it wasn't like I could argue with it.

She continued, "Cheating spouses. Disability fraud. That type of stuff. Stuff where you already know where the person lives or where they might be going. Who they're with or what they're doing is more important. Yes, there's the occasional missing person. Then it's important for eyes to be on them at all times if you find them."

"And what do you do then?" I asked, motioning to her general crotch area.

"Depends," she said.

"Depends on what?"

"No. *Depends.*"

"Oh," I said. No good answer to that.

She smiled. "Welcome to the glamour life, Anna."

I laughed. Beyond the gross imagery, it was fascinating to me. "I can't thank you enough for doing this for me, Cassandra," I said.

"We're talking pissing our pants, I guess you should probably call me Cassie," she said.

Our chuckling was broken up by movement in the mirrors, and this time our vigil was rewarded with the sight of Niall walking out of room number fourteen, head down, phone in hand.

He looked much like he had the night I'd drugged him, over a week ago now. I had so many questions for him, not the least of which was how he'd gotten away from his parents, and if they were all right with his disappearance.

His poor mother was probably a wreck.

I reached for the door handle, but Cassie stopped me with a hand to my other arm. "Hang on. This would be a good time to follow your target, see where they're going. As soon as you talk to them, their behavior is altered. Especially if they know you know where they live. If you want to question them, it's best to do it in a neutral setting, looking like maybe you just ran into them, if you can manage it."

That made good sense to me, so I put my hand down and kept my eyes on the mirror.

Niall put his phone down and then looked around. Cassie's tip of parking with our backs to the motel paid off, as Niall's glance skimmed over the line of cars in the lot, not resting on any of them.

"He's waiting for a car, or for somebody," Cassie said, voicing the conclusion I'd also come to. Niall stood patiently waiting, calmer than he'd been the night I met him, when his leg had been constantly twitching. His glance was not a nervous one, but one of expectance. Was he no longer nervous because he knew the man who was coming to collect on his debt was dead?

And did he know Johnny was dead because he'd had something to do with it?

Down the side of the motel, another of the rooms opened and a young woman stepped out. She lit up a cigarette and took a deep drag, letting out a plume of smoke. I looked away from her and back to Niall, but something made me look back at her. A flash of red at her feet.

Red Chucks.

"Kaitlyn," I said.

"Who?" Cassie asked, turning to her side mirror so she could see the other door where Kaitlyn stood smoking.

Niall looked to his left at Kaitlyn. She was a couple doors down and was looking at him as she took another drag from her cigarette. She nodded at him, and he nodded back—a move that looked comfortable enough for me to surmise it had happened before.

A car pulled into the lot, and Niall checked his phone and then put a hand up, which had the car pulling toward his room. His Uber had arrived.

"Kaitlyn was the dealer the night Johnny was killed. She was one of the last ones out of the room."

Cassie looked at Kaitlyn, then over to Niall getting into the back seat of the car that had pulled up to his room.

"The woman who dealt at the game before Johnny was killed is staying a few rooms down from Niall?"

"Apparently," I said.

"Interesting," Cassie said.

"Do you think it could be a coincidence?" I asked, already knowing the answer.

"Do you?" she asked.

"Nope," I said.

"Right answer," she said.

Eightteen

❖❖

I KNEW WHAT I WANTED TO DO: FOLLOW NIALL AND talk to Kaitlyn. But we couldn't do both, so I stayed silent, hoping Cassie would have a plan. She was the pro, after all.

She eyed the Uber car holding Niall, stopped at the entrance of the motel, waiting for traffic. Then she turned to me. "Would Niall know you?"

I'd been in JoJo garb the night I'd drugged him, and he'd been pretty much out of it with anxiety before I'd even spiked his drink.

"Doubtful," I said.

She nodded. "What about Kaitlyn?"

I thought of the large tip I'd given her and the conversation we'd had about the different players at the table. Both were memorable, but I knew that in this town, people remembered those who tipped them well.

And those that stiffed them.

"Yeah, she'd remember me," I said.

A quick nod, and Cassie was in movement. "Give me the keys to your car."

It was a level of trust with me that she'd achieved quickly, obvious by the fact that I didn't question her, just handed over the keys to my beloved 911.

As she was exiting the car, she grabbed her phone and

looked back to me. "Move over. You take my car and follow Niall. If you get a chance to actually make contact in a way that he wouldn't know you followed him, do it."

"What about you?" I asked, already lifting a leg over the console to move to the driver's side.

"I'm going to talk to Kaitlyn," Cassie said.

A glance assured me that Niall's car was still in the lot waiting for traffic to clear. Thank God for a heavy flow of cars.

"What about not letting them know we know where they are?"

Cassie checked that her phone was done recording Niall's room, and put it in her back pocket. From the rearview, I could see Kaitlyn stub out her cigarette and return to her room.

"I'll come up with something," Cassie said. "We weren't after her anyway," she added.

I wasn't sure that we were exactly *after* Niall, but the logic still stood. We would have to divide and conquer at this point.

"I'll take an Uber to the Aliante and get your car. Text me with where you end up and I'll meet you there."

Before I could agree, she shut the driver's door and walked away. I started up her Toyota and eased from the parking lot just as Niall's car got into traffic.

There must have been a light a block back or so, because I easily got on Lamb and began to follow Niall.

Cassie and I hadn't gotten to best practices when tailing someone yet, but I basically just used common sense. It helped that the car Niall had called was a neon-green VW Beetle. Pretty easy to stay a few cars back and not lose it.

We all got on the 15 and headed south toward the Strip. I got my phone from my jacket pocket and turned it from silence back to sound in case Cassie called. I hadn't liked the idea of silent mode at all, in case Lor needed me, but I hadn't wanted to seem like a newbie in front of Cassie. (Even though that's exactly what I was.)

The Beetle took the Flamingo exit and headed for the Strip. That exit took them right to the center of the "L," where the Strip turned slightly. They could be going to any of the casinos. Taking a right at the light, the Beetle continued on, getting in the right-hand lane. So, could be Bellagio, but no, they kept on through the next light, and the next. The blinker of the Beetle came on and it became apparent that Niall was going to the Aria. I turned in behind the car and through the casino entrance until I saw Niall get out and walk to the front entrance.

I'm a self-parker in Vegas, always have been. The boys taught me that. Don't be at the mercy of valet when you might want to get off the property quickly.

Not because someone might be chasing you, but because, well, I guess it would be the demons chasing you.

But I liked having control of where I parked, when I could leave, and not having to wait.

Today, afraid of losing Niall if I took the time to self-park, I got out and waved to one of the valet guys, apologizing for being in the wrong lane. I pulled some money out of my pocket and handed it, and my keys, over to him.

"Sorry, I didn't realize I was staying," I said.

He took a look at the fifty I'd just given him (I thought it was a twenty—but oh well) and shrugged. "No problem," he said.

"I don't think I'll be long, if you can keep it close," I said, feeling like some kind of gangster or something. Or Sharon Stone in *Casino*, greasing the palms of the people who gave her tips on big spenders.

"Whatever," he said, and got into Cassie's 4Runner.

Some big shot—handing out fifties, but driving a ten-year-old Toyota.

I went through the doors and searched the tops of heads for Niall. Nothing. On instinct, I headed to the side of the casino that held the poker room and, beyond that, the book room.

I almost bumped into the back of Niall as he turned from the poker registration desk. "Sorry," he mumbled, and moved to the side, looking up at the board where the poker manager had just added his first name to the list of players waiting for a table.

"No worries," I said. Niall's head jerked. At first I thought it was because he recognized my voice, but his look showed no recognition. It did hold surprise, and I realized it was because I was a woman.

Yeah, there weren't many of us playing cash games daily, and a quick look throughout the room told me that I was the sole representation of my gender at ten in the morning on a random Wednesday.

I didn't know whether to be proud or ashamed of that fact.

Niall moved beyond me, to the far side of the poker room where the tables sat empty. He looked back at me, then took a chair at one of the empty tables.

Not to arouse suspicion, I moved to the registration desk that he'd just left.

"Hey, Anna, playing today? It's been a while," the man behind the desk said to me.

"Hey, Al, how've you been?"

"Good, good. You?"

"Yeah, good."

"Ben doing okay?"

I nodded. "He is, thanks for asking."

Al nodded. Al Rocklaw was in his fifties and had worked for Ben years ago in the book room at a different casino. Since I'd known him, he'd been one of the poker room supervisors, first at the Riviera before they'd closed and now at the Aria. I didn't play here a lot, but he knew Ben lived with me and so was always very sweet to me when I did.

"I think I will play for a while, yeah. Um, what table did the kid who was just here request?" I asked Al.

He didn't need to look around to know whom I was talking

about; that was the skill of a good poker room guy—they knew everything and everybody.

"He wanted on the $25/50 table."

Steep. More than I'd even play on a usual basis. Perhaps Niall was trying to win back what he owed. Even more curious— how'd he get the stake for his buy-in? Even if he was going to play tight, at the $25/50 table, he'd need to at least start out with a few thousand to just stay in the game for a while.

A few thousand I didn't have. I hadn't really expected that my day would take me to the poker tables at the Aria when I'd left the house to meet Cassie.

Another mental note to myself—be prepared for anything.

Cassie's talk of networks and sources came back to me, and I figured it was as good a time as any to test that out. Start building my own network. "Hey, Al, how long before you think a spot will open on that table?"

Al didn't look behind him to Niall, but instead at one of the poker tables in the front of the room. Even from this far, Al could probably guess to within five minutes when someone would leave the table, just by looking at the size of the stack in front of them. "I told him an hour, but it might end up being like a half-hour if Donny keeps playing like it looks like he is."

Not much time to talk to Niall before he got on the table, but I didn't have the cash to join a higher-stakes table. And it wasn't like I could question him about Johnny Aces while sitting with a bunch of poker players waiting for me to make my bet.

"Okay, thanks. I think I'll just wait for a bit before I sign up for a seat."

Al nodded and looked down at his list. "Not too many people ahead of you, but then, not a lot of people have left yet, either. It's pretty early for the after-breakfast player to be busted out. And the nooners haven't shown yet."

"I'm going to grab a coffee, want one?" I asked. Al looked over to the corner where a coffee machine stood for the players to help themselves. "Not from there. That coffee place by the shops, the one next to the chocolate place," I added.

"God, I'd love one," Al said. "One cream, two sugars."

I nodded and frowned at him when he tried to hand me money. "I got it," I said, and quickly made my way out of the poker area and down a hallway to the shops. As always, the line at the good coffee place was long, so after I was served, I hustled back with the coffee, hoping Niall hadn't gotten the call for an open seat yet. I didn't even take the time to go to the delectable chocolate shop next to the coffee place. Just like a professional PI would probably do.

Relieved to see Niall still sitting at the empty table, I took one of the coffees from the tray that held three and set it on Al's desk. He was busy with a player, but whispered, "Bless you, Anna," as I set it down.

I took my carrier over to the empty table where Niall sat. "Mind if I join you?" I asked, nodding at one of the empty chairs.

He'd been looking at his phone, and his head came up, then his eyes narrowed slightly as they fixed on me. "Help yourself," he said. He was returning to his phone when he looked closer at me. "Do I know you?" he asked, his expression one of curiosity, not suspicion. So far.

I nodded toward the tables behind me. "I don't know. From the tables, maybe?"

"You play a lot?"

"Some. I used to play more," I said.

He sighed at that. "Yeah, me too."

I gave him a small smile, like I got it. In a way, I did. "Funny how a run of bad luck can sideline ya for a while, hey?"

"Ain't that the truth," he said.

I took my coffee from the cardboard holder, which I slid, with the remaining cup, down the table toward Niall. "I got one thinking someone I know was playing, but they aren't here. Want it? It's black, but there's cream and sugar in the holder."

His eyes did narrow just the tiniest bit, but he reached out and took the coffee from the holder. He didn't bother with the creamers or sugar, then took a deep drag, wincing when the hot liquid hit his throat.

"Thanks. Are you sure we haven't met before?" he said. It was more decisive this time, not so much questioning. Probably because the last time he saw me I was also handing him a drink.

That one was a little stronger than the hot black coffee he now held.

Okay, a *lot* stronger.

"Like I said, I used to play a lot. Here, Bellagio, a lot of private games. You play in those much? Maybe that's where you know me from?"

"Maybe. I have played in a few, yeah. When I…"

"Didn't have the cash? Yeah, me too."

So now we were just two degenerate gamblers shooting the shit. He knew that I knew the lay of the land, recognized me, though he thought it was from poker and not the seedy hotel room I'd found him in a week ago.

"It can get you in some hot water, though, those games," I said. "Take it from me, you don't want to make a habit of those. Playing in casinos is much safer. You have to leave when your pockets are empty."

He let out a soft gurgle that I thought was supposed to be a laugh of bravado. I'd tried those when I wasn't feeling it—it didn't sound any better than Niall's attempt.

"Thanks for the tip," he said, like maybe I was bringing that info a little too late. I knew for a fact I was, but it still never hurt to hear it.

Ah. *That* was why Lor kept doing those damn interventions for me.

Which could be a good segue for the kid.

I did give a laugh, better than Niall's, but still halfhearted. "I know, I know. Easy for me to say. You can just ignore me."

I took another sip of coffee and swiveled in the chair, ostensibly to look at the board where the players waiting for a table were listed.

"Sorry. Didn't mean to be an ass," Niall said behind me.

I spun back to face him. "Dude. I get it. Nobody wants to hear it. I sure didn't."

"Didn't or don't?"

I lifted one shoulder in a half shrug. "Both, I guess. I've had interventions done on my behalf, so, past tense. But..." I let that drift off, hoping he'd take the bait.

"No shit? I just had one myself."

I rolled the chair tighter to the table, close to him. "Yeah? Were you the guest star or the one who bitches about the guest star?"

He smiled. God, he was young. His overall unkemptness made him look a little older, but when he smiled, it was all kid.

A small pang of regret wafted through me for young Anna, who came to Vegas to play poker.

A *lot* had happened in thirteen years.

Shit, a lot had happened in the past seven months.

"Guest of honor," he said, a little bit of pride in his voice. He was right: it was no fun to be the one bitching. Better to be bitched at.

I swung a hand out to encompass the poker room, including us. "I can see it really worked for you."

The smile grew broader, and I couldn't help but return it with one of my own. A genuine one.

"Neither did yours, apparently."

We both laughed softly, then took drinks of our coffee. When his smile had dimmed, and I knew he was thinking of his intervention, I quietly said, "Was it family or friends?"

I didn't have to explain my question further. "My parents," he said.

"Oof. That's a rough one," I said.

"Yeah. Yeah, it was."

I wanted to tell Al to cancel Niall's seat. To make Niall come home with me. Call his parents (were they back in Topeka or here in Vegas looking for Niall once again?) and have them get Niall solidly booked into a facility. Because whatever they'd said to him, it hadn't been enough if he was here playing at a table with the largest blinds.

"Listen, why—"

"And I guess they meant well. I mean, of course they meant well. They're my parents, and I love them." He took another quick drink of coffee, then put his cup down a little too forcefully. He wasn't looking at me as he continued. "And yeah, there was some reason—well, they had cause for concern, I guess."

Um, yeah, owing Carla Rossetti 100K and having Johnny Aces looking to collect would be cause for concern.

"But I dealt with that. That's all taken care of, so it's not like they need to worry anymore, you know?" He glanced at me, but didn't wait for a response. "And I'm a good player. Most times I win. I've had some great hands. It's just...*fuck* those bad beats, you know?"

Oh, I knew a bad beat. Had them against me, and in my favor. They were part of the game. You could be the best player in the world, but if that river card gave your opponent a flush, not a whole lot you could do.

But wait, what had he said?

"Right. But you had it dealt with, you said?"

He glanced at me again, his thoughts catching up, or going back, to what I was saying. "Yes. What my parents were concerned with. That's all settled now, so I don't see why I can't just keep playing. I'm good."

Every poker player sitting in this room secretly—or not so secretly—thought they were a good player. That was why they were here.

Most would go home with empty pockets.

"Sure, but they're your parents. They probably think whatever it was could crop up again."

"No. It won't. It's been dealt with in a very *final* way. It won't come up again."

Holy shit, did Niall really kill Johnny? Could it be that easy? Day one and case closed?

Probably not going to confess to murder over coffee at a poker table, though. Nobody could have that much good luck on their first day of PI training.

"Well, that's good. But, you know, they're parents, so they worry."

"Sure, sure, but I have this all under control. The poker. Vegas. The money. All of it." His voice was becoming manic, and it was clear that Niall very much did *not* have it all under control. No gambler ever did.

"I'm glad you do, kid. Really. Sounds like you know what you're doing."

"I do," he said.

He absolutely did not.

"I'm glad the heavy threat is gone. Must have been hard to shake."

My words were innocuous enough that he could read them any way he wanted to. Staring down at the table, he ran his thumb along the green felt, the grain springing up in his wake.

"Easier than I thought it would be," he said. He looked at me. "But I thought it was going to be a bitch."

I nodded. "Kid, it's all a bitch."

His expression went blank, his shoulders slumped, and his gaze returned to his thumb on the table, making waves in the grain of the felt. "Yeah," he said.

Now was when I should take him out of here. He was pliable at this moment. I could probably take him home, call Monty, and try for intervention number two.

That one didn't work for me, either. But you never knew

which one would take with Niall.

But then what? Hand him over to his parents, or Jack? Call for Monty? Or Metro? If Niall did kill Johnny, and the cops were looking at me and my friends, would I serve the kid up to them?

Yes, in a heartbeat. But I still didn't know that all the cryptic shit Niall was going on about—the threat no longer there—had anything to do with Johnny being killed.

Taking the decision out of my hands, Niall's name came up on the board with a ping and an announcement from Al over the poker room PA. His spot at the high-roller table was available.

"That's me," he said. "Thanks for the coffee."

"No problem," I said. I watched as he got up from the table, chucked his cup in the trash can, and started walking away from me, toward the full tables.

About ten feet away, he froze in his tracks and spun around. I looked at his spot at the table to see if he'd left his phone or anything, but his area was empty.

Striding back, his eyes were on me, recognition on his face.

Holy shit, he recognized me.

"Holy shit, I recognize you," he said when he got right in front of me. I had to lean back in my chair to look up at him.

"Look, I—"

"You're the Black Widow. I've watched you so many times. I can't believe I didn't recognize you right away." He was in fanboy mode now. It'd been a while, but I still got it from time to time.

I guess if he was going to recognize me, it was better that it be from televised poker and not me putting a mickey in his drink.

"I look a lot different in my day clothes," I said to him.

"Totally," he said. Thinking that was a knock—which it was—he back-pedaled. "I mean, you look fine. Good. Today. It's just—"

I held a hand up to stop him, a smile on my face. My this-happens-all-the-time smile. "It's fine. Really. I do it up when I'm on a final table. But most days, this is me."

He stuck his hand out. "Niall. It was really great to meet you."

I shook his hand. It was steady and warm, and I thought that maybe—*maybe*—Niall was right and whatever threat faced him was gone. "Good to meet you, Niall. Anna Dawson."

"I know. It was so great talking with you."

"Feel free anytime you see me at a table," I said.

That made him smile, making him look about seventeen, and I thought again about hustling him out of here and driving far from the Strip.

"Today is going to be lit, I can feel it," he said. He turned and walked back to the table and the players who were waiting to take all his money.

I was about to call out "good luck" to him, but knew he wouldn't hear me.

And that it wouldn't matter.

The cards fell how they fell.

Nineteen

❖

TO EXCHANGE CARS, CASSIE AND I MET AT THE twenty-four hour café at the Red Rock Casino. While we waited for our lunch (salad for her, BLT and fries for me), I filled her in on my conversation with Niall.

Our food arrived just as I finished my recap, and I started dipping fries into ketchup and shoveling them in as I nervously waited for Cassie's assessment. I was pretty sure it would match mine: that Niall had killed Johnny.

"Okay, so that's something to think about," she said as she sparingly poured her dressing onto her salad.

I could learn a lot from Cassie, not the least of which being how to eat better.

"Think about? Seems pretty obvious to me," I said. I kept on with the fries, not wanting a mouthful of triple-decker BLT while conversing.

As she placed her napkin in her lap, Cassie gave a small shrug. "I've learned not to get too excited about things over the years," she said. "Lots of leads turn into nothing."

"Lead? Or confession?" I said.

She smiled, her fork stopping halfway to her mouth, a grape tomato skewered by the tines. "Confession? That's grasping a little, isn't it? Think about what he actually said." She ate the tomato and gathered some greens for her next bite as I thought about my conversation with Niall.

"That he'd gotten rid of the threat—Johnny, of course."

She chewed and swallowed, patting her mouth with her napkin. "Not really. You made that leap—that Johnny was the threat he was talking about. He could have meant any number of things. His debt. His parents. Things we have no idea about how he was living his life. Everybody has secrets, Anna, and gamblers have more than the average."

Couldn't argue with that, so I didn't try. And she was right about Niall, of course. He could have been talking about a host of threats that had been taken out of his path. He may even have been talking about Johnny, but had nothing to do with his death.

"One thing to remember is not to let your hunches guide you. They may be strong, and they may be right, but you can't dismiss other avenues just because you want to follow a one-way street."

"Confirmation bias," I said.

"Exactly," she said. "The cops are big at that, because it's expedient. And they've been proven right most of the time. So they tailor their investigation to the outcome they would have predicted. It's smart, but it can be dangerous."

"Like the thing about eighty percent of the time it's the husband or boyfriend, so they look at him first," I said, not really asking.

She nodded. "Right. And they should. But what I try to do—what any *good* investigator should do—is not forget about that other twenty percent out there. Look in that direction too."

"Right. Yeah, I get it," I said. Out of fries, I tackled a bite of my sandwich, making as much of a mess of it as I assumed I would. Tomato squirted out and mayo sloshed onto my thumb.

Worth it. Awesome sandwich.

"So, if we're to do that on this case, I'd say the other twenty percent—to stick with our analogy—could be split in half between who we know and the unknown."

At my confused look, she continued, which was just as well, as I was still chewing.

"So ten percent would be the group that was in the room earlier, the poker game. More specifically, those who followed him to the parking deck. You. Monty. Raymond. Carla. All have motive, all had opportunity and means."

I didn't agree with all that, but I kept chewing.

"After the whole thing about not jumping to conclusions and confirmation bias, I probably shouldn't say this…"

"But?" I took another giant bite, riveted to Cassie's words, hoping they soaked in. If I was going to learn, I was going to *learn*.

"If I was betting, I'd put my money on Carla."

"Really?" I said.

She lifted her hands and dropped them to the table. "Just a feeling. Niall had to gain, yes. But that's a big leap. A gambler in debt to killing a muscle man? A kid, no less? Doesn't feel right."

As she said it, I realized she was right. It wasn't inconceivable that Niall had killed Johnny, and I knew from experience that age didn't determine a killer. A kid in my former support group— another degenerate gambler—was proof of that.

But yeah, Carla had more motive with Johnny working for her. If he was skimming, or holding out on her. Or had told her Niall had been taken care of when he very much had not.

But I didn't think it was her. My vote leaned toward Niall. Cassie was right, though: all roads, not just the one-ways.

"Raymond and Monty, I think, are safe to rule out," I said.

"If you think so. We won't spend a lot of time on them, but we should cross our T's on them at least."

"No motive," I said.

She leaned forward, and I put down my sandwich before taking another bite. "They could have been protecting you. Or Niall. Or themselves. What would Raymond do to protect you?"

He *shouldn't* do anything. I was the one who had turned his life upside down. He had every right to laugh at my funeral.

But he wouldn't. We'd reached a truce of sorts. Not quite that. An understanding. We'd both fucked up (me first), but we came through it and his family was safe. His life, if not how he'd imagined it, was on track.

If I was in danger from Johnny, would Raymond kill to protect me? Once again, I remembered him coming home later than me that night.

And Monty. If not to protect me, what would he do to protect Niall? Did any of Monty's other clients owe money to Carla or Johnny?

"Jesus," I whispered.

"Exactly," Cassie said. "And don't forget the remaining ten percent."

"Who would that include?"

"That's just it. That's all the other people that wanted harm to come to Johnny, and also the chance that it was a random shooting with Johnny just being in the wrong place at the wrong time."

"Do you believe that?" I asked.

"No. Not when there are so many strong suspects."

"Me neither," I said.

"Which doesn't mean that we should discount that ten percent. I'll do some digging into Johnny's other hustles. You said he hadn't been working for Carla all that long?"

"Right," I said.

She nodded as she tapped something into the Notes app on her phone. "And we don't know who he was working with before, or if he was sharking on his own, too, not just muscle for others. If his name was spoken in circles."

"What do you mean? What circles?"

She looked up from her phone at me. "You know...his name was *spoken*."

I shook my head, not getting it.

"I thought you'd been in Vegas a while," she said.

"I have. Thirteen years and change."

"Gambling, right. I mean, obviously you knew Vince and Carla."

"Yes. But I don't know what you mean by *spoken*." I tried to put the same emphasis on the word as she had.

"If your name has been *spoken*, someone wants you dead, and is willing to pay for it."

"Oh. Like a contract out on you?"

"Right," she said.

"You think that's a possibility? That Johnny's name was... spoken?"

"Could be. Seems like the circle he was running with. I'll check into it."

"You can do that?" I asked.

She seemed amused. "Yes, Anna, I can do that. See why I didn't want to share my sources?"

If your sources included people who knew when a contract was put out on someone, then yeah, absolutely I understood keeping that shit quiet. I nodded. "Okay. What should I work on?"

"You think Monty, Raymond, or Carla would open up to you? More than they already have?"

I thought back to the night the four of us went out after being questioned. It seemed like each had something they hadn't said. I hadn't pushed it at the time, but maybe if I was one on one with each of them?

"I can try," I said. "I'm not sure how to go about it."

"That's why it's good to practice on them. You know them; you'll be able to tell if they're off in any way."

"I'm supposed to be able to do that with anyone. I made my living doing that."

She smiled, sat back, and pushed her mostly uneaten salad

to the middle of the table. "Then you're already ahead of the curve. I got a few things very wrong when I first started."

"Oh, I'm not saying I won't get it wrong, just that I'm *supposed* to be good at reading people."

Putting my keys on the table, she said, "I parked your Porsche next to my car where you parked in the east garage. Stay and finish your sandwich. I have a prospective client I need to meet back at my office."

I thought about asking if I could join her, see how she went about that part of the business, but I didn't. I had enough to work on.

"Keep track of the hours you work on this; I'll vouch for them if you're doing the work on your own," she said.

"Thanks," I said. I wiped off my hands and handed her the keys to the 4Runner, hoping I hadn't gotten stray mayo on them. I took my key ring and put it in the pocket of my cargo pants.

She started to slide out of her side of the booth when I remembered something. "Oh, man, I completely forgot. What did Kaitlyn say? Were you able to talk to her?"

Cassie smiled and sat back into the booth. "I wondered when you'd ask about that."

All the good mojo I'd felt about my chances of becoming a PI after getting Niall to open up came crashing back to reality. I had no idea what I was doing.

Thankfully, Cassie did.

"So, what did she say? Could you get anything out of her without her being suspicious?"

Cassie waited for our server, who had just dropped off a fresh Diet Coke for me, to leave. "There was nothing in her room that seemed odd. Just the regular things. Looks like she's been there a while, though. Nothing in there to connect her—at least outwardly—to Niall or Johnny. No men's clothing or anything like that."

"You got in her room? She just let you?" I'd thought Kaitlyn seemed like a sharper cookie than to do something like that, no matter how unthreatening Cassie appeared.

Cassie smiled—it was warm and genuine and it changed her face from striking to breathtaking. Again, I wondered about her and Vince's relationship. How could he have been interested in me with Cassie around?

I'd never know.

"Okay, here's a freebie for you," she said. She dug into the pocket of her jeans and pulled out a lone earring. A tasteful silver drop with a ruby on the end, almost like an exclamation point. Long enough to be noticed, but not so long as to be a focal point, or stab Cassie in a sensitive area from her jeans pocket.

"Always carry around one earring. Make it distinctive. Then, in places where you want to get in, like a motel room, or an office, or someplace that has public access, you can just say you lost an earring there and wanted to look for it."

"That works?" I said, dumbfounded. And then I wondered what I would do if a woman who looked like Cassie knocked on my door and said she had lost an earring. Yeah, I'd probably let her in.

Idiots. All of us.

"It works for a couple of reasons. One, you describe the earring specifically, and that it means a lot to you. Husband gave it to you. Mother. Whatever. Then, when you're in the room, or wherever, you discreetly pull this from your pocket and 'find' it." I stared at her, my admiration obvious. She shrugged. "If they were suspicious, finding this specific item lessens that. It doesn't always work. I've gotten shut down. Said I was there last week, but they'd been there a month. But it works enough of the time."

"Wow, that's, that's…"

"All part of the job," Cassie said.

"Thanks again for taking me on," I said.

She put up a hand, not in a full stop motion, but a yield at least. "We're still trying this out, right?" she asked. I nodded.

"Right. Well, it's what Vince would have wanted."

I wasn't sure that Vince Santini would have wanted me to become a private investigator, but I didn't argue the point.

She put the earring back in her pocket and again moved to leave the booth. This time I didn't stop her. When she left, I thought about all I'd learned from just one day in the "employ" of Cassandra Hall.

Sure, I'd learned plenty on my own the last seven months since murder had invaded my quiet life. (Okay, my life hadn't been quiet since I left Wisconsin for Vegas years ago, but whatever.) And I'd certainly learned a lot from watching Jack and Botz work a case. But this was different. These were good, usable trade secrets.

I tucked into the rest of my BLT, not knowing if it was the tasty sandwich that made me so happy, or the day I'd had.

Yeah, I knew which it was.

It was still a damn good BLT.

Twenty

❖❖

"GREAT TRICK," JACK SAID LATER AFTER I'D RECAPPED my day. "The earring thing."

"I know, right?" I left the chair in my bedroom where I'd been sitting and went to my dresser, opening my jewelry box that I'd had since my tenth birthday. I pawed around its meager contents. Mostly key cards from various Strip hotels. Way more cards than jewelry.

Behind me, Jack was sprawled out on my bed, still wearing what he'd worn to the station that day. He'd kicked his shoes off and made himself at home, and I had to admit it was a lovely sight to come in on. Seldom in our relationship had we had such a relatively normal day—both out at our "office" and home with time to relax a little before dinner.

Jack was only home this early because he was still on restricted/limited duty. And I was here because I wasn't sure what avenue to follow next. Or what avenues were actually worth following.

"That's the kind of stuff PIs can do that we cops can't. Bullshit our way into a suspect's hotel room."

In the mirror above my dresser, I gave Jack a skeptical look. He seemed to shrug, but his shoulders were so enmeshed with my upholstered headboard that it was too hard to tell. "Well, we can't *legally* do that, anyway," he added. I nodded and returned to my search.

I had filled him in on my stakeout and following Niall to the Aria. I'd also let him know about Niall feeling that there was no more pressure on him. And, of course, the cool earring trick that Cassie had told me about.

"Any luck?" he said.

I put down the lid on my jewelry box and turned to him as I shook my head. "Nope. All I have are a few pairs of basic hoops. I wanted them to be something memorable."

He did a chin nod toward my walk-in closet. "Anything in there?"

He meant the suitcase I kept in the way back, full of JoJo's things. Granted, there were some god-awful, gaudy baubles that went along with her getup.

"Too memorable," I said. We both smiled. Jack's smile faded first and he got a look in his eye that—even though I found Jack incredibly hard to read—I knew in an instant.

I slid a few steps to the right and shut and locked my bedroom door.

"How long before dinner?" he asked.

"Long enough," I said, and walked toward him.

"I don't think that's a compliment," he said.

When I reached the bed, I started undoing the button on my pants. "Do you care?" I asked.

He sprang from his lounging position, sitting up and opening his legs. Pulling me between his legs, he brushed my hands aside and finished the task himself.

"Not in the slightest."

HE'D SHOWN ME A TRICK that topped Cassie's earring one and we'd taken a quick shower after. (I was really starting to like multiple-shower days.) We were re-dressed and about to head to the kitchen to help Lor when he said, "So, you never mentioned the motel where Niall was staying."

About to unlock my door, I stalled. Jack was lacing up his shoe on one of the chairs in the seating nook, and I walked back and joined him, sitting on the ottoman that was placed between the two chairs.

"That's right, I didn't," I said.

He looked up as he finished tying his shoe. He studied my face and nodded once. "Guess it's time to have the talk, yeah?"

"Yeah, I guess it is," I said.

"You wanna start?" He sat back in his chair, resting his hands on his lap.

"You can," I said.

One of his hands flopped a little in his lap, like he didn't know where to begin. I wasn't buying that for a second.

"You have, what, like, five years of hours to get in?" he asked. I nodded. "So, it's not unlikely that we'll come across this kind of thing from time to time."

"Right. Although Cassie said that working on a murder case is pretty rare. That most of the work is for cheating spouses and insurance fraud. That type of stuff."

"Makes sense," he said.

"In fact, the only reason she's working this one is because of me being involved. I'm, I guess, both the client and the investigator."

"And a suspect," Jack added, but there was a bite to his voice. Just a taste of sarcasm. I guess it meant we'd come to a place in our relationship where Jack automatically discounted me as a murderess every time I was a likely suspect.

Some women got roses. I got innocent until proven guilty.

Roses died. Presumption of innocence lasted longer. Hopefully.

Rolling my eyes, I sat back, propping myself with my arms behind me. "And a suspect. The trifecta, if you will."

"Always an overachiever," he said, causing me to laugh. He leaned back in his chair, as if this conversation were no big deal. We both knew better.

It wasn't the gushy love stuff—which was hard enough—but it was important to set boundaries. If only so we knew when we breached them.

"Are we, what? Looking at a don't ask/don't tell situation here?" Jack asked.

"Like, just live our lives and if we happen to have a case, or person, or whatever, that overlaps, we don't talk about it?" I asked. That didn't seem like it would work very well.

"Or how about this: you tell me if you have information you think will help a police investigation. Like any good citizen would do."

"And you'll do things like run license plates for me, and prior records and aliases, known associates, and that kind of stuff?"

He leaned forward, a smile on his face. "Known associates? Already have the vernacular down? Oh, this is going to be fun, Johanna."

He could have been patronizing me, but he wasn't; that wasn't Jack's style. "Nah, I can't do any of that for you. No matter what you've seen on TV," he said.

I knew that, too. Sure, there were cops out there that would do that sort of thing. Cassie probably had a few she considered part of her network. But Jack had a strong, albeit skewed, ethical code. He wouldn't break that for me.

I respected that. Didn't like it. But respected it.

"So I'm supposed to show my hand, but you hold your cards close to the vest?" I said.

He placed a hand on my knee. "Oh, come on, you know there's power in showing your cards. Mind games of another kind."

"And you say you're a bad poker player." I knew firsthand

he wasn't. I'd found that out at a poker game in Pittsburgh that felt like several lifetimes ago.

A squeeze from his hand on my knee had me thinking about the other places he'd squeezed just a half-hour ago. Which was no doubt his intention.

"Come on, Jack. What's in it for me to give you—the cops—any intel I come across?"

"Besides your civic duty?"

I scoffed, and he smirked. "Yeah, besides that," I said.

"The cops have resources that you don't. Or that even someone as seasoned and connected as Cassandra Hall doesn't have."

"Of course. But like you said earlier, we can do things that bend the law a little. We're not so worried about things holding up in court like you have to be."

"And that's the biggest advantage we have over PIs."

"What?"

"Fear," he said.

"Like intimidation? Because you're a man? I mean, there—"

"No. Not that. Fear of being caught by the cops. Because that means arrest. If a PI catches you, or catches on to you, they can tell your wife you're cheating, or the insurance company that you're faking. But only the cops can snap those cuffs on you."

He was making sense, and he knew he had me on the ropes. "If you tell me where he is, we can bring Niall in and get his official statement on where he was the night of Johnny's murder."

"I think we're going to need, like, a signal or something," I said.

"What kind of signal?"

"You know, like those couples that have signals at dinner parties and stuff? When they want to leave?"

"You think we're the kind of couple that's going to be invited to dinner parties?"

I did not. "No. Not for that."

"What would our signal be for?"

"When we are entering into territory that we won't discuss with each other. Just so there's no misunderstanding or, I don't know, coercion of any kind."

"You think I'm going to coerce you?"

"No. I don't know. It would work both ways," I said.

"Anna, you're talking about a safe word."

Was I? Yeah, I guess I was. Huh.

"Do you agree?"

"Like if I ask where Niall is staying and you say…"

My mind rushed to come up with something. "Iceberg," I blurted. He smiled, thinking about the same thing I was—the night we first met in front of a municipal building when we'd decided to let our particular icebergs float a while longer instead of going into AA or NA meetings.

"And you say Iceberg and then I have to let it drop?"

"Right. Exactly," I said.

He took a long breath and then slapped his knees and rose from the chair. "Deal. Let's get some dinner."

I walked to the door with him, loving that he respected me enough to let it drop. But I still thought that it was a good idea for the cops to talk to Niall. If he had done it, it would get a killer off the streets. If he hadn't, then it was another suspect eliminated.

"He's at the Moonlight Motel on Lamb in North Las Vegas."

Jack put a hand on my shoulder and kissed the back of my neck. "Got it," he whispered. I kind of liked that he didn't say thank you.

Twenty-One
❖

"How's Lorelei taking all this? You working with Cassandra Hall?" Jack asked me as we left my room and walked the long hallway toward the main living area and dining room.

"Fine. Why wouldn't she?"

He shrugged one shoulder that brushed against mine. "I don't know. She's just been the one around here that you looked to for—"

"Everything," I said.

"Exactly. And to have somebody new that takes up your time, your attention, is a mentor of sorts, might ruffle her feathers." He looked down at me, stopping in the hallway when he saw my expression. "What?"

"I'm trying to figure out if that was incredibly sexist or incredibly astute."

He snorted and kept walking. About four steps ahead of me, he said, "Probably a little of both."

"Yeah," I said, catching up to him as we neared the corner to the main living area. I heard Raymond's door open and close behind us.

"Man, that smells good," he said.

"Sure does," I said over my shoulder. To Jack, I said, "You really think Lor is feeling left out? I mean, when I was gambling heavily, I'd be gone for long periods of time. Days, even."

"But you weren't with anyone else. Didn't *need* anyone else."

I thought on that as we rounded the corner to the dining room, where Ben and Jimmy already sat. Ben smiled when he saw us, his eyes staying on his son with warmth that at one time had made me feel a little excluded. I'd pretty much come to terms with those feelings. I think.

"Yeah, okay. I'll think about that. Lor's feelings," I said.

Another shrug from Jack as he took a chair. "Could be nothing. But maybe throw her a bone or something if you find the chance."

"Hannah, dear, you look lovely tonight," Ben said as I sat down next to him.

My hair, still wet from our shower, was hanging limply down my back, and I'd thrown on old jeans and a UNLV tee shirt. Not lovely in the slightest.

Seemed like Ben was throwing some bones of his own. I'd take it.

"Thank you," I said, squeezing his hand. Raymond rounded the corner and joined us as we waited for the true head of the household.

AFTER WE DEMOLISHED LOR'S tuna noodle casserole, and the kitchen was cleaned up (thanks to Jack and myself at our insistence), we all gathered back around the dining room table to have coffee, warm brownies, and conversation as the playing cards came out.

Jimmy had joined us, but not Gus. He hadn't been to dinner lately, but had been at breakfast with the boys each morning, so I knew he was fine. Probably had his sights on the next Mrs. Gus Morgan. Yeesh.

As we played gin rummy, I asked the boys about the networks they'd built up while they'd been oddsmakers. Jimmy regaled us with stories of "I got a guy" who had given him tips throughout the years. The hiding in hedges in South Bend during practices in the eighties. The woman who worked in the cafeteria where the team ate in Tuscaloosa. The moles he'd had report back from the different college towns.

Ben had joined in with stories of his own, and I glanced at Jack's face as he watched his father tell stories of his younger days.

Days they missed together.

"What brought all this up, Hannah, dear?" Ben asked after we'd stopped laughing over Jimmy's last tale.

"I'm trying to cultivate my own network," I said. "Around here. In case I do become a PI."

Jimmy pointed at Jack. "You know all about that too, right? Or in your case, it's snitches."

"We use the term CIs—confidential informants," Jack said.

Jimmy snorted. "Snitches."

I'd noticed Raymond had been on his phone most of the night, playing when it was his turn and laughing in the right spots, but head down most of the time, looking at his phone.

I supposed that was normal for a kid in his early twenties stuck playing gin rummy with a bunch of oldies. Some oldies. Some a very respectable early thirties.

Okay. Mid-thirties.

"Speaking of starting my own, I saw Al Rocklaw at the Aria today, Ben," I said. "He said to say hello to you."

"Ah, Al. You'd be wise to keep him as a friend. Al knows everybody in town. And he's still in the game, not like us old farts."

Jimmy frowned at that, but didn't say anything.

Ben looked toward Jack. "Al used to love your mother's rugelach. When she'd make a big batch, she'd have Saul bring some to me at the casino. I'd share them with Al because I knew he loved them so much."

Jack's face got soft, then his mouth tightened. Knowing what he was thinking, Ben said, "She was a lovely woman, your mother, Jack. And she made wonderful rugelach. I'm so sorry you never got to meet her."

"Me too," Jack said quietly. I wished he wasn't so far down the table from me, as I would have liked to touch him just then. Just so he would know he was no longer alone. He was with family.

The room got silent and emotion bubbled in the air.

"Yeah, she did good rugelach. But her lasagna sucked," Jimmy said, making us all laugh and breaking the tension.

We continued playing, Raymond ultimately winning even though he'd barely paid attention.

Lor and I sent the boys into the TV room when we were done, and she and I took the brownie plates and coffee cups to the kitchen.

"Hey, do you have any plans for tomorrow?" I asked her.

"No, nothing that's important. What do you need done?" she said.

"I was thinking about updating my wardrobe a little. You know, now that I might be doing some more professional-type things."

She put the dishes she was holding into the sink and then slowly turned around, studying me. "Yes?" she said, expectation—and excitement?—in her voice.

"And I thought maybe you'd go with and help me out—"

Jack ran into the kitchen at the sound of Lorelei's squeal. "Everything okay in here?" he said, a little out of breath. Good thing he was still on desk duty.

"Perfect!" Lor said. "Absolutely perfect!"

Jack winked at me and left the kitchen.

And Lor started making a list.

Twenty-Two

❖

I SHOULD HAVE KNOWN WHAT I'D BE IN FOR WHEN
Lorelei insisted we take the Lexus shopping instead of my
Porsche or her BMW.

"Trunk space," she said.

"Just a few things is all I need, Lor," I said. She nodded, but
I caught a smile before she could turn away from me and look
out the window.

And if that wasn't bad enough—needing an empty trunk
and back seat—she directed me to The Shops at Crystals, the
mall next to the Aria on the Strip.

The very expensive, designer-only mall.

"Oh, and besides clothes, I need to get a pair of earrings.
Something small, but really distinctive."

"Ooh, Tiffany," Lor said.

"I was thinking like Claire's," I said, only to get an eye roll
from Lor and a wave out the windshield for me to continue on
to her chosen destination.

The only consolation she gave me was allowing me to park
in the Aria deck instead of the valet at Crystals so that I could
walk past the poker room on our way to the mall.

No Niall. But a wave from Al, who was working the poker
room desk. I motioned drinking, asking if he'd like anything,
but he held up his Starbucks cup, so I just waved and then Lor

and I moved on to the shops.

"Really, Lor, I think this is my limit," I said three hours later after coming out of the dressing room wearing yet another one of the outfits Lor or I had picked out. I'd told her I wanted casual professional. She was an aged-out showgirl and I was a reforming gambler. Neither of us knew shit about what professional women wore on a daily basis. But Lor had a better idea than I did, and her selections of tailored slacks, soft sweaters, and understated blouses were spot-on.

"Oh, that one's a keeper, for sure," she said when I made my exit. The black slacks felt like butter against my legs. I typically wouldn't pick out red for a top, but the crisp cotton button-down with a little flare at the hem went perfectly with the pants. Sharp. Not too flashy, but noticeable.

Probably not something to wear sitting in a 4Runner while peeing into a Depend, but there would be times for an outfit like this.

"Okay. Done," I said, to which Lorelei squealed and clapped her hands like a three-year-old. "And seriously, we're done, I think."

"There should be one more outfit for you to try on in there," she said. Even sitting in this lovely area of the fitting rooms, where champagne was served and trays of cookies were on ottomans in front of the plush seats, Lor knew exactly what was piled back in my dressing room.

"The one you picked out on your own. The jeans, top, and boots," she said.

"Okay. Then we're done," I said.

"Fine," she agreed, and took a sip from her glass and a bite of the cookie. When I started to grab for a cookie, she pointed back to the dressing room. "One more, then you can have all the cookies you want."

"Sheesh," I said, walking back to my room.

"Most women would *kill* to be able to do this, and you

want to end it as soon as possible. You're a buzzkill, Jo," she said loudly. There was no one else in the large fitting room area, with our salesperson—Darlene, she'd introduced herself as—coming in now and then to replenish both treats for Lor and clothes/sizes for me.

Poor Darlene had gotten the short end of the stick between the three members of the Dolce & Gabbana staff when we walked in. You could just read their minds as they'd eyed us up.

Oh God, more tourists.

They'll probably take pictures to tell their friends they shopped here.

Wait until they look at their first price tag.

Poor Darlene was shuttled to the front of the group, given the task of taking us on. She took it like a champ, though, hiding any exasperation she may have felt at being saddled with us as prospective buyers.

Somewhere I think it might have clicked with her that we might in actuality be big shoppers, as we kept adding more and more clothes to my dressing room and never once looked at a price tag.

I put on the last outfit, one I'd taken to the changing room on a lark. Fancy jeans, a crisp white blouse, and over-the-knee suede boots.

The boots were so soft that I couldn't stop touching them. When I zipped them up, then stood in front of the mirror, I wasn't even sure it was me at first.

"Is that what she looks like?" Lor said once I'd stepped out into the sitting area.

"Who?" I said. Maybe she knew who I was supposed to be, because I wasn't really sure myself.

"Cassandra Hall."

I looked at the three-way reflection of myself. If I had a blond bob instead of my chestnut mop of hair, currently up in a ponytail, I could probably pass as Cassie's, if not sister, at least her good friend that tends to dress like her. Like those women you see where they're all wearing variations on the same basic outfit.

"Yeah, I guess," I said. "Not intentionally. Probably more so the other outfits."

Lor nodded. "What's that they say? 'Dress for the job you want, not the job you have'?"

"I guess."

She studied me some more. "The other ones, yes, I can see it. But this one. This is you, Jo."

I looked again in the mirror. The jeans hugged my curves, showing them off much more than my baggy cargo pants ever could, even giving me the illusion of curves where I was less than plentiful.

And the boots. Oh God, I really couldn't stop touching them.

"Really? You think this is me?"

"This is the Anna Dawson that was meant to be."

I heard a sound from a changing room about halfway down the sitting area from us. A noise that sounded like a gasp. I guessed someone had just looked at a price tag.

There was only around eight inches of space between the long doors of the fitting rooms and floor, but you could see the inhabitant's feet and ankles.

And the feet were wearing red Chucks.

No. Couldn't be. Here?

And what if it was Kaitlyn? Should I confront her? Talk to her? I mean, we did have that conversation after the poker game, so it wouldn't seem too strange to strike up a conversation, right? And she'd have to know I wasn't following her, since I'd been in the fitting room area first.

She was still wearing her jeans and shoes, so it seemed like she was just getting started.

"Okay. Good. Let me get changed and we'll assess the

damage," I said to Lorelei.

"Take your time," she said as I nearly sprinted back to the dressing room. I was gentle taking the boots off, but quick, too. I got my own clothes back on in record time and made it back out to the main sitting area just as I saw Kaitlyn's back leaving.

"Kaitlyn," I said.

She didn't stop, but there was enough flinch of her back to assume that she'd heard me. The heavy curtains closed behind her.

"I need to talk to that woman," I said to Lor and Darlene, who had come back to join us as we wrapped up.

"Okay, we'll wait," Lorelei said, and Darlene nodded. Darlene was now smelling a big sale. Yeah, she'd wait as long as it took.

I opened up the curtain to see that Kaitlyn was walking quickly—very quickly, near a run—to the front of the store.

"I might need to leave the store," I said back to Lor. "Just pick out what you think looked best. Maybe the best six or seven outfits?"

Lor nodded. "You got it." It was going to be Lor that paid the tab anyway. My money, but Lor's purse strings.

"If I'm not back in the store by the time you're done, I'll meet you in front of the poker room at the Aria," I said.

"Got it."

"It was a pleasure working—" Darlene started, but I was in a hurry and had one more important thing to say to Lor.

"The boots and jeans. That one for sure. The boots."

"On it!" she said, her smile bright.

That sorted, I dashed through the curtain and started a half jog to the front of the store.

Twenty-Three
❖

THE SHOPS AT CRYSTALS WAS A BEAUTIFUL MALL, FILLED with gorgeous stores offering extravagant wares.

But it was big. Really big. And it had lots of corners and angles. Really architecturally cool. Not so cool if you were trying to find someone.

And especially if that someone did not want to be found, as I was beginning to believe was the case.

Had Kaitlyn put together Cassie's visit yesterday with me somehow? Had she and Niall spoken about me?

Would he have mentioned meeting the Black Widow at the Aria and then Kaitlyn had told the story of me playing in a game she dealt last week?

And why was Kaitlyn dealing a game for a man to whom Niall owed money? Were they working some kind of angle together?

Or could it all be simply explained away if I could only catch up to Kaitlyn?

After forty minutes of weaving through stores, dressing room areas, and the main mall itself, I was slowly heading back to the entrance to the Aria when my phone rang. Jack.

"Hey," I said. "I'm just finishing up shopping with Lor. That was a good idea you—"

"They got nothing from Niall," he said, making me realize

this wasn't a "hey, honey, how's your day going?" call. Not that we ever had those.

"You pulled him in for questioning?" I asked. I sat down on a bench that was formed to look like it was made of glass. Deceivingly comfortable, though.

"Yeah. Well, Botz and Faxon did. He was in the motel room that you told me about."

I had mixed feelings about that, giving Niall over to the cops. It felt like a snitch move, and we all knew that snitches got stitches. But if Niall—or Niall and Kaitlyn—were involved in killing Johnny, that would at least absolve Monty, Carla, and Raymond.

Oh yeah, and me too.

And yeah, if Niall killed Johnny—no matter how much I saw a young me in Niall and how much I despised Johnny Aces—he should have to pay for that.

"And did it lead to anything?" I asked Jack.

There was a pause on his end, and I knew what was coming. "You know I can't tell you everything, Anna."

"And we're back to that," I said. "Already using the safe word?"

He chuckled, a sound that normally made my insides warm. But not today. Not when I'd lost Kaitlyn and the info I'd given the cops would not be reciprocated.

"Jack?" I said when he didn't go on.

A heavy sigh. "Botz doesn't know. He thinks this Niall kid is hiding something, but that would be true of a gambler with debts. Not necessarily a murderer. Right?"

I didn't know if he was asking my opinion as an aspiring investigator or my confirmation as a gambler with debts.

Previous debts.

"Right," I said, covering all my bases.

"Faxon thinks Niall's good for it. Johnny Aces' murder."

"Yeah, but Faxon's a tool," I said.

Another chuckle from Jack. "You're not wrong. But he has some good instincts."

"His instincts got you shot," I said.

"That's true, too. But they didn't have enough to hold Niall. And the search of his room while he was being questioned didn't turn up anything to tie him to Johnny Aces' murder. God, I hate that nickname."

"Me too," I said. "So you didn't hold him?"

"Nope. Didn't have enough. But he didn't have a solid alibi for the time frame, either."

"He wasn't still with his parents?"

"Nope. He ditched his parents at McCarran airport earlier. Never left Vegas."

"Oh, his poor parents."

"He told an interesting story about a woman coming to his hotel room and drugging him before his parents tried to take him back to Kansas. You wouldn't know anything about that, would you?"

"Iceberg," I said.

Jack laughed. "Yeah, I figured as much. Okay, I gotta go. Just wanted you to know we talked to him."

"Okay, thanks for letting me know."

"Oh! We also tried that Kaitlyn's room. No one there. Room's been cleared out. Looks like we just missed her if she was there yesterday when Cassandra Hall spoke to her."

"I just saw her! She's here at The Shops at Crystals."

"That ritzy mall at the Aria?"

"Right."

"What are *you* doing there?"

I rolled my eyes even though Jack couldn't see me. "Don't ask. Spending way too much money with Lorelei."

"Some bone you threw her," he said.

I thought about the boots I'd bought and a possible fashion show for Jack. Just the boots. "You might like some of it."

He spoke to someone who must have been nearby. "Okay, I have to go. Talk soon. If you see Kaitlyn again, follow her and text me the location where she ends up."

"I don't think there's much chance of that."

We said our goodbyes, and I took one more loop around the mall, but I knew she'd left. As surely as I knew when a guard was going to miss a free throw to put me over on the point spread.

Bone-deep intuition.

Lor only had one bag with her when I met her by the poker room entrance of the Aria. I wondered if she'd been just blowing smoke about liking all of the clothes on me, or if perhaps her/my credit card had been declined or something.

"That's it?" I said, pointing to the one large shopping bag she held. A large box was the only item in it.

"The rest is being couriered to the house later today."

"Wow. They do that?" I asked. Stupidly. Money made certain things possible. This I knew only too well. I'd just never needed that knowledge for something like a shopping spree.

"Yes. I guess we didn't need to bring the Lexus after all. But these had to come home with you. They're just too delicious to wait for." She handed the bag for me to carry. I didn't even look, knowing they were the suede boots.

"That was fun," Lor said as we made our way off the Strip and back toward Summerlin.

"Fun for you," I said.

"Oh, come on. You didn't like playing dress-up? Even a little bit?"

For so long, the thought of playing dress-up was to become JoJo and don her attire. That had not been even a little bit fun. But today? Becoming a version of myself that I hadn't really explored? One that was within my grasp?

"Yeah, I guess," I admitted.

"Well, I had a great time. Thank you for taking me."

I had told her several times throughout the day to try on some things, to buy a few outfits for herself, but she'd declined, saying today was all about me.

"You're the best, Lor," I said. "Truly. I couldn't do any of this without you being my safety net."

"I'll always be that, Jo." We rode in silence, and then she said, "This was just what I needed. I was feeling, I don't know, a little left out, I guess."

Jack had been right. I wondered if I'd tell him that. I certainly wasn't going to tell Lor that this had all been his idea.

"Well, we're all kind of carving out new phases. Things are shifting," I said.

"I know. And I love that for you. And Ben having Jack and Casey in his life. And Raymond joining our little family and going to school."

"But?"

"I don't know. I think I'm like an empty-nester mom or something, getting used to people not needing me as much."

"Are you kidding? We all need you. You're helping with Monty's business. You got Raymond set up. My research on private investigation."

She sighed. "Yeah, I guess."

I wanted to reassure her that she was needed, but I also didn't want to hold her back. "Lor, if there's something you'd like to be doing, do it. We'll figure out how to make it work. Hire a cook or whatever."

"Oh no, I love doing that."

Phew. I did not want a kitchen that didn't have Lor at the helm. And there was no way we'd ever see Jimmy again if she gave up the meal making.

"Okay, well, think about it," I said.

"I will. Thanks. Today was great," she said.

As we pulled into our driveway, I realized I'd never looked for a pair of earrings.

Just as well. Earrings to be used as a prop should probably come from somewhere besides Tiffany.

Twenty-Four
❖❖

TWO DAYS LATER, I MET CASSIE BACK AT THE KOFFEE Klatch, where we'd gone after meeting the first time.

Well, not the first time, that would have been at Vince's will reading.

She was already there when I arrived and had only a coffee in front of her. Despite having gone to breakfast with the boys a few hours earlier, I was disappointed there wasn't one of those amazing cinnamon rolls in front of her. I ordered coffee only too.

Maybe it would be a short meeting.

"Thanks for coming over here. I have business on this side of town, so my office wouldn't have worked as well."

"No problem," I said. "I might even go over to the shooting range when we're done and get a little practice in."

She nodded as she took a sip of her coffee. "Good idea. Tell Buddy I sent you—you'll get a little discount."

"Thanks. Unless you'd like some help on whatever you've got going on this side of town. I really don't have anything else going on today. I'd love to—"

She held up a hand, stopping me. "That's what I want to talk to you about."

Was I already being used on cases other than my own? Had she been impressed enough with the way I'd followed and questioned Niall the other day that she thought I was ready to work on something different?

"You're fired," she said.

Oh. Not a promotion.

"I'm sorry, what?"

Her hand floated gracefully, flicking like my future was lint on her sweater, then settled back on her mug. "Unhired. Un-interned. Un-whatever it is you're playing at."

"I don't understand," I said.

"Clearly." She sat back in her seat, the back of the booth coming up nearly a foot above her head. My coffee arrived, but I couldn't take a sip.

"Cassie, what happened? Or didn't happen?"

"Oh, a lot has happened. And all because of you."

Confused, but then it became clear. "Niall's gone again," I said.

"Yep. Should have used those smarts a little sooner."

"He left because he was questioned by the police."

"Right again."

"And the police knew where he was because I told Jack." I filled the last piece of the puzzle she had already solved.

"Might have been nice if you'd mentioned you live with a cop," she said. I didn't ask her how she found out about Jack and me. It wasn't like I was keeping him a secret or anything. And her network was good.

"I didn't think it was relevant," I said.

She didn't do an actual eye roll, but the effect was the same.

"Besides, it's up and down with Jack. It's not just that he lives with me. His father lives there too."

"And Raymond Joseph," she said. I nodded. "And does Jack Schiller know that Raymond Joseph was being investigated in a point-shaving scheme?"

"Yes, he knows. And Raymond was never charged with anything." She raised a brow. "Thanks in part to you," I conceded.

"So, you what? Went home all excited about your first stakeout and told your boyfriend all about it?" That was exactly what happened, but it sounded much more juvenile the way she put it. "And you handed Niall over to the police on a silver platter."

"He is wanted for questioning in a murder case," I pointed out.

"By the police, sure. But he's much more useful to us if we know where he is. Now he's in the wind again. Digging deeper underground, no doubt. I mean, how did you even think being a PI would work with you living with a cop?"

That confused me. Beyond the Iceberg parameters. "What do you mean? In the end, we're on the same side. We have different ways, legally and otherwise, to get the information, but at the end of the day, we both want to find the truth."

She scoffed at that. "Jesus, how could you have survived in this town, in the gambling circles you must have been in, and still be so naïve? PIs aren't always the good guys, you know. We find out information. Sometimes that information is used in not-so-great ways."

Sure. Right. Of course. I guess I was naïve. "I just—"

"And asked to do not-so-great things, too. I mean, you could make a lot more money than just your hourly fee if you're willing to work with some of these people."

I could claim that I wouldn't do that, that I wouldn't be hired by those kinds of people. But I knew from experience that sometimes you didn't know who those kind of people were at first. Or that you had to do business with that sort sometimes.

Or shit, that you may even have briefly dated one.

I played it safe: "It's not about the money for me. It's about…the puzzle, I guess."

If she'd known about my foray as JoJo for Vince, she'd have thrown it in my face. Nothing but a half snort and a "Must be nice."

I didn't mention that she was now in a position not to worry about money either, with Vince leaving her the bulk of his estate.

"So you think you'd just ignore the fact that you live with a cop? And it would never be a conflict of interest?"

"We talked about it," I said.

"When?"

"Last night," I said.

"And then the cops hauled in Niall this morning, and now he's MIA. I have to start all over again."

I kept it to myself that if she had indeed fired me, there was no reason for her to keep working on my case. Maybe I could salvage this whole thing yet.

I eased forward on my bench seat, putting my hands on the table, clasping them together like some recalcitrant child begging for forgiveness. Not far off the mark.

"But this is different, Cassie. It's *my* case. I was a suspect. Still am a suspect, I imagine. Yes, I want to learn how to be a PI, but I also need this case solved, so I took a calculated risk in telling Jack. We can do so much, but police questioning is something else entirely."

"Obviously. Enough to make us lose Niall."

I was scrambling for ammunition, but I found I really wanted to convince Cassie to keep me on. That I *really* wanted this whole thing.

Even if it took three to five years to get there.

"Nobody can stay hidden forever. Not in this town. Your sources found him once, and—"

"Exactly. And you basically shit all over that source for me," she said.

"Why? They don't need to know that I…"

"Fucked up?" she said.

I took a deep breath, let it out. I could *mea culpa* and beg for the gig back, but that would set the tone for our future interactions. A tone I did not want to carry for years.

"Yeah, see, I don't think I did fuck up," I said. She raised a brow at me, reminiscent of Jack's move. Cassie got the same reaction out of me. Almost. But I forged on. "It was the right call to have the cops question Niall. And the fact that he ran afterward is going to just make him look guiltier. This is probably a good thing. The cops, or you and I, will find him."

"It's a good thing that he looks guiltier to the cops, because that takes the heat off you and your pals," she said.

It was true. Raymond, Monty, Carla, and I, all having motive and opportunity (shaky as motive was in some of our cases), could breathe a little easier today if the cops thought Niall was guilt-running.

"Yeah, maybe," I said. "What's wrong with that if it catches the killer in the end?"

"*If* being the operative word," she said.

I waved a hand like finding Niall was already a done deal. "He'll be found. Somebody will see him. Word will get back to us somehow."

I was already thinking about the network the boys had and if I'd be able to call any of them in. I already had Al in my web. Which made me realize…

"Niall's a gambler. He can't stay away from the table. He'll show up eventually at either a legit game in a casino or a backroom game."

"You know all the backroom games that go on in this town?"

A lot, I was sure. "No. Not all. I played in Vince's and a couple of others from time to time."

"Those are the ones in beautiful hotel suites with professional dealers and a lovely buffet and bar, right?"

I nodded. Yeah, I knew I played at the high end in Vegas. But that wasn't always the case.

"I've done some seedy games too," I said, remembering my first few years in Vegas. Pre-Vince. Pre-Ben.

"Lately? Would you know the people running them?"

I shuddered at the thought of some of those guys, and said a silent prayer that my misspent youth ended with only a foot that ached when it rained. "No. Not lately. But I'll keep an eye out for some of the guys I used to play with."

She seemed to be softening to the idea that I was still working on this whole thing. "You think any of them are still alive?" she said, but there was no bite.

I chuckled, relaxing a little. "Actually, that is kind of doubtful. But I'll check it out just in case. I can talk to the poker room managers too, ask them to keep an eye out."

She nodded, and I took that to mean I was back on the Hall Investigations team. "Be careful when asking for favors. In this town, people bank those like hard currency. You never know what you'll be asked to do in return."

"I know. I know. I take full responsibility. It's all on me." She seemed satisfied with that, so I pushed on. "As was telling Jack where Niall and Kaitlyn were staying. But I stand by that."

Studying me, she slowly nodded once, as if it was all settled. "Well, did it at least work two ways? Did your boyfriend tell you what the cops found out?"

"As much as he could, being that it isn't his case and I'm involved."

"And?"

I relayed what little intel Jack had given me to Cassie. "So, it seems that Johnny was into a whole bunch of pies. You were probably right about his name being spoken. It opens up the field of suspects a bit more," I said when I'd finished.

"So why would Niall run?" Cassie asked.

I shrugged. "Because he's a suspect in a murder case, his parents are desperate to get him into some kind of rehab back in Topeka, and all he wants to do is play cards all day and night."

"And Kaitlyn? Where does she fit in?"

Another shrug from me. I supposed there was a lot of

shrugging in the PI biz. "I don't know. But it fits that she'd be shopping at high-end stores if Niall felt all threat was gone, as he alluded to the other day at the Aria. I mean, she had some money from what I'd tipped her, but…"

"They scored big."

"He won, and wouldn't have to use it to pay Carla back."

"Because Johnny was dead? That doesn't erase the debt to Carla."

She was right, and I was at a dead end. For now. But it seemed I was back on the case with Cassie.

Crisis averted.

"Okay, so what now?" I said, hoping I was right about assuming we would continue to work together.

"You work on trying to find Niall through your poker buddies. I'll try to track down Kaitlyn. Hopefully they're still together. If they ever even were, in whatever capacity. But them both leaving the Moonlight at the same time makes it even more likely."

Anticipation zinged through me. Yes, I wanted to do this. Maybe I truly had found my calling.

She laid down a ten-dollar bill and got out of the booth.

"Okay. Stay in touch," she said. I nodded and stayed sitting. Cassie leaned down, one hand on the edge of the table. "And Anna? Next time keep the pillow talk with Detective Schiller to sex, okay?"

I smiled and nodded, not sure who would enjoy me keeping that promise more: Cassie or Jack.

After she left, I ordered the cinnamon roll and ate the whole thing as I made a list in my journal of people I could recruit for my network.

CARLA MET ME FOR DINNER at the noodle place in the

Bellagio. She had a game there later in the evening and told me she had a few hours prior that were available when I had asked her to meet me.

"So, what's all this about?" she said after we'd both ordered the pad Thai. A working night for her, she only had a Diet Coke, so I joined her with that. Good to keep my head about me, anyway.

"I was putting together a list of people that used to play in backroom games a while ago. And guys who hosted them."

"You mean like my competition? Why are you making a list of them? Am I on this list?"

"No, it's not like that. I mean, yeah, you're on the list. But it's just for me. I'm trying to connect with some people. People who might be able to watch out if Niall shows up at a game."

She snorted. "Well, he sure as shit isn't dumb enough to show up at one of mine, is he?"

God, I hoped we were dealing with someone smart enough to avoid Carla's games. With a degenerate gambler needing a fix, who knew? But if Niall had been playing at the Aria the other day, maybe he had enough cash to play in casinos and not go to games that gave credit.

Credit with a very steep vig.

"Do you use Kaitlyn as a dealer often?" I asked, taking the subject away from how smart Niall was or wasn't. Hummers outweighed smarts in most cases.

"No. I never used her myself. Johnny did a couple of times before that night. I don't know where he found her originally. And I don't have her contact info, so I haven't used her since the night…"

She didn't need to finish the sentence. Our food arrived, and we dug into the deliciousness.

"So, turns out Johnny was dealing all over the place," I said when I came up for a breath.

Carla nodded as she finished a bite. After wiping her mouth, she said, "I'm finding that out too. What an asshole. I'm sure he was skimming from me, too, but I can't figure out where."

"Oh, man, sorry." I didn't point out that that knowledge would have given Carla more motive to take Johnny out than, say, Monty, Raymond, or myself.

And maybe as much as Niall, who owed a ton of money to Johnny, and ultimately Carla.

"No honor among thieves anymore," I said, making Carla laugh.

She motioned to my journal, which I'd brought with me and sat on the corner of our large table. "Speaking of thieves, let's see this list of yours. I'll tell you what I know. If this stays just between us."

"It will," I said. I knew protecting your sources was just as important as finding them, so I would not be sharing this info with Jack.

No matter how much I might like his bad-cop persona.

He had his CIs, and I would have mine.

I grabbed the list that I'd tucked into my journal, and we spent the next hour going over it, telling stories of players of days gone by, finding out from each other which people were dead or done gambling, or had left Vegas willingly.

It was like a night out with a girlfriend, reminiscing about old boyfriends.

Except Carla was not my girlfriend but had worked for my longtime loan shark. And those we remembered weren't past loves, but poker players who had—and had not—weathered the sometimes-hostile world of Vegas backroom games.

After she left to get to her game, I took my list, now with new notes in the margins thanks to Carla, over to the book room, where I could sit in one of the horse-betting carrels and go over it again.

After I was done, I drove home and realized I'd never once looked up at the odds board while I had been in the sports book.

A smile on my face, I drove my Porsche out to Summerlin with a plan to start building my network the next day.

Twenty-Five

❖

I SPENT THE NEXT THREE DAYS REVISITING MY OLD haunts. The places where I'd played when I first arrived in Vegas and had no money. The places I played after I lost all the money I'd won. The places I played at all points of money in pocket in the past thirteen years.

The Ghost of Anna Past was a bitch of a travel guide.

I saw men I thought had died, who looked as surprised to see me as I did them. Men I assumed had left the Vegas scene. And a few women who probably should have left the Vegas scene years ago.

Playing almost exclusively in Vince's private games and in the casinos with mostly tourists had taken me out of the circles I now revisited. I should have marveled at how far I'd come. Been proud at all I had achieved.

But it all felt like a monumental *there but for the grace of God go I* moment.

I did feel good about the reception I received, though. Apparently I'd been a player's player back then and still had the respect of my former competitors, which was comforting in a weird way.

I reminisced with some about bad beats and monster bluffs. Of those who didn't assume I'd been whacked for debt along the way, about half had followed my career and congratulated me on "making it."

I didn't tell them about JoJo, harboring a point-shaving college basketball player, or currently being under investigation in yet another murder case.

I let them all know I was looking for Niall. Monty had texted me a photo of Niall, and I showed that around to a bunch of players and poker room managers and workers.

If I saw a dealer I knew on break, I'd talk to them too, but knew enough to not talk to them at the table while they dealt.

After describing my first day of doing this, Lorelei quickly printed up some business cards for me to give out with my phone number on them, which was way more helpful than me writing it on a square of bet sheets from the casinos.

I thought for a moment about getting a burner phone for all the PI-related stuff and then decided not to. I still had the one Monty gave me the night we "rescued" Niall for his parents, but that should be kept separate.

Besides, this PI stuff was all legit. I was looking for Niall for perfectly legal reasons. And I'd want the network I was building to be permanent, not one that might have to get tossed out the window while driving over a bridge.

Not that I'd ever needed to do that with a burner phone. I just gave them to homeless guys at street corners.

I was leaving the backroom game in the basement of a family-owned restaurant when I crossed the last name off my list of people I wanted to connect with.

None had seen Niall recently, though a few had said they'd played with him in the past. And nobody had heard of a dealer named Kaitlyn. At least, none would say they had.

Realizing I was now in wait mode, and not far from Buddy's shooting range, I decided to go and practice.

"Do you think I should try a different gun this time?" I asked Buddy when I approached his counter.

"What was your score with the Colt?"

"Score?"

"You do know the targets have numbers on them, right, so you can score?"

I looked at him blankly. "Yes?" I said.

He snorted and shook his head, but pulled out one of the targets. Oh yeah, it did have numbers on it.

"Use the Colt today. Get a base score with eight shots. Do that a few times today. Write down your scores. Come back and do it more. When you double your score, we'll try a different gun until you get proficient with that one."

"Would it be better to be an expert with one gun, or pretty good with a few different kinds?"

"It would be *better* if you never needed to be good with any gun," he said.

"Amen," I said, then remembered whom I was talking to. "That would be bad for business, wouldn't it?"

"I'd survive," he said. Then he gave me what was supposed to be a wink, but on his weathered, wrinkled face, it might have been a small spasm.

"Aw, Buddy, thanks for caring."

He snorted again, and got me set up.

After I finished, I wrote down my scores in my journal, on the sheet of paper that had my PI prerequisites on it. I even kept the best target, thinking I'd bring it home to show Jack. Like a good grade on a report card or something.

As I was walking out of the shop, I passed the bulletin board by the door. It was filled with flyers for various things like you see in the lobby areas of grocery stores.

These were a little different than those offering house-cleaning services and looking for lost dogs. This bulletin board had a few of those, but also many that clearly applied to the clientele of the gun range.

Guns for sale. Shooting lessons. Excursions where you could shoot at various things, including animals.

A bright pink piece of paper stood out to me, and I stopped to look at it. A flyer for a women's self-protection course. It was newer, and none of the little half-torn strips at the bottom with the phone number had been removed.

I read the flyer. It was an ongoing class and held on Monday nights, not too far from Summerlin.

Perfect to avoid *Monday Night Football.* I tore off one of the slips at the bottom and took it, my target, and my journal out to my Porsche.

I put my loot on the passenger seat, and was wondering if maybe I could get Lor to do the self-defense classes with me, when my phone rang.

Hopeful it was one of my recent contacts already paying off with a Niall sighting, I pulled it out of my pocket to see it was Cassandra calling.

"Hey," I said. "I'm just leaving Buddy's."

"Do you have plans? Are you on your way somewhere?"

"No. Not really. Just going home, I guess."

I didn't want to say I was waiting to hear from people I'd met with the past few days. That seemed like a passive thing, and I didn't want Cassie to think I wasn't a go-getter.

Even if I wasn't sure what I should be going and getting.

"Do you want to go with me while I work on another case? It's not going to be very exciting, probably just—"

"Yes," I said. "Tell me where to meet you."

I was already firing up the Porsche while she texted me the address.

Time to get going.

THANK GOODNESS I HAD thought to use the restroom after I'd finished at the range. Because it was another boring stakeout in front of another fleabag motel in North Las Vegas.

Cassie was following a philandering husband for his curious wife. He was currently in room five. We assumed not alone, but Cassie had followed him here from his office and hadn't seen anyone else enter the room.

Kurt Gunnell's lover had gotten to the room before him.

That had been three hours ago.

I looked at my watch. "He can take a lunch hour this long? I mean, it's impressive and all, but doesn't he have to get back to the office?"

"He's a sales guy. Out on a call. No one wonders where he is as long as he makes his numbers," Cassie said.

"Seems like he's making his numbers, all right," I said. "Looking like possible bonus territory."

A sigh from Cassie, which was all that joke deserved, I supposed. Maybe not even that much.

I'd told Cassie about how I'd spent the last few days reaching out to old cronies, reconnecting with players, dealers, and others in the poker world that the Black Widow had passed by.

When I'd finished, she gave me a look that said she was impressed. She didn't come right out and say it, but I could tell.

The feeling was embarrassingly satisfying.

"And so far nothing on Niall? No sightings of him?"

"Not yet," I said, my feeling of accomplishment slipping a bit. I *thought* those I'd reached out to would contact me if they saw Niall. It wasn't like I was a cop or anything. I was one of them—degenerate gambler.

I had the scars to prove it.

But who knew? Maybe narcing was narcing no matter to whom you gave it up, and the mere idea was anathema to those living on the edge.

Snitches get stitches and all that.

"Well, it's early yet," she said, making me feel better. "And the cops will be looking too. They're probably pissed they didn't put a shadow on him when they let him go after questioning."

"Yeah, probably," I said. Jack hadn't mentioned that, but then, we hadn't really talked about it at all after they'd picked up Niall at the Moonlight Motel from the info I'd given them.

"Except…"

"Except what?" Cassie said.

"Oh, they'll still want to find Niall. But I think they're finding out a lot more about the stuff Johnny was into, and so the playing field is expanding."

"In what way?"

I told her about my conversation with Carla and the feeling she and I both had that she, Monty, Raymond, or myself weren't considered true suspects anymore. There just seemed to be a lot more people out there with more powerful grudges against Johnny.

Yes, the four of us had the best opportunity—literally following him out of the Venetian parking deck. And we all had motive, though more of it was to protect others than ourselves. But as more was known about Johnny, and those he was dealing with, it seemed like we were falling further down the list.

Niall was rising higher, and all of those Johnny colleagues unknown to me were climbing as well.

"Well, that's good and bad, right?" Cassie said.

"In what way?"

"Well, good in that you and your buddies aren't being looked at more seriously."

"Yes, that's very good."

"But bad in that even more suspects are in play. Ones you don't know, can't check on."

"Right," I said. That didn't seem like a real negative. But maybe that was because I was one of the ones being looked at less.

"And if his name was spoken, and this was a professional job, then you're looking at layers between the actual killer and the one paying for it."

"How many layers?"

"I have no idea. At least two. Maybe more middlemen. The means they connected."

"Right. About that. So, if your name is 'spoken,' how does that even happen?" I asked.

"In the old days, word of mouth. Street connections. Now it can be done online."

"Like…like a hit portal or something?"

"I guess? Something untraceable, obviously," she said.

I had this vision of an Excel spreadsheet floating around a public Dropbox folder. Or like the portal that college athletes used when they wanted to transfer to a different school.

"That's messed up," I said.

"It's always been messed up. Now it's just more streamlined," she said, shaking her head and taking a deep breath.

We sat in silence for a bit, waiting for Kurt Gunnell to exit his room. Until Cassie broke the silence, apparently still thinking about the growing list of suspects in Johnny's murder.

"So you're basically turning it over to the cops. Which is fine. But I thought you'd want to…"

"What?" I said.

She shrugged, her eyes still on her phone on the dash, recording the motel room. "I thought this was more about you solving the case than making sure one of your friends wasn't arrested."

I thought about that. It was a relief that Carla, Monty, Raymond, and I were, if not off the hook, at least being left to swim in the pond a little longer. But yes, Cassie was right.

"I do. I do want to solve it. But I don't have access to Johnny's dealings like the cops do. Carla learned about a few, and I'm sure she'd share them with me. But I'm guessing there are a lot she doesn't know about. Not to mention this dark net where names are spoken."

We were both quiet, then Cassie sighed again. "Okay, we'll

switch it up a bit. You concentrate on Niall, since you've already spread the word on him. And I'll tap into my sources on who would most want Johnny out of the way. Besides all of you."

"Thank you. Really," I said.

She nodded like it was no big deal. But after having spent the last few days trying to cultivate a network of intelligence gathering, I knew it was no small thing to call in favors, or promise to make good on a future one for a bit of information.

Yes, this was what she did for a living, but this case was one that was more of a favor to me. We'd never even discussed who would pay whom. Me for the case, or her for my "assistance." I was guessing it was a wash, though if she handed me a bill, I'd gladly pay it.

I was about to thank her again when she motioned to her phone. "Looks like Kurt got the sale."

The curtains on the room were opening. Cassie kept her phone in place, still recording video, but also pulled a digital camera with zoom lens from the floor of the back seat.

She scooched low in her seat so her head was below the headrest, as did I. Contorting her body, she curved around her seat to get a clear view out of the back window. Her shoulder showed up on the corner of her phone, but the rest of the frame was still on the room of Kurt's motel room.

Poetry. Clearly a move she'd done before, balancing taking zoom photos while not being seen, with still recording on her phone.

Kurt came first, putting the finishing touches on his necktie, his sport coat hanging loose over one arm. He was in his early fifties, in good shape, hair graying at the temples.

A woman came behind him. Blond, tall, and slim. Almost taller than Kurt. I had expected her to be young, or at least younger, but she seemed to be around Kurt's age. She was not dressed to go back to work, wearing only a black slip/nightie that ended barely below her crotch.

Kurt turned and wrapped an arm around the woman's waist, pulling her close for a last embrace. Their kiss was passionate, desperate almost. Like maybe this was the last time they'd meet?

Or was that what they told themselves every time?

Cassie's camera continued to click through the kiss and the swat Kurt gave the woman's ass before he turned and walked to his car. The woman watched him from just inside the doorway, the look of bliss slowly turning to one of pain. Click. Click. Click.

I thought about someone capturing such raw emotion on my face.

"Okay, that wraps that up. We can leave now," Cassie said.

Good. Because I couldn't wait to take a shower.

Twenty-Six

❖❖

TWO DAYS LATER, JUST BEFORE DINNERTIME, I GOT A
call from a number I didn't have programmed into my phone.
In the old JoJo days, that would have scared the crap out of me.
But now, I was thinking (hoping?) I'd be getting those calls a lot.

"Hello?"

"Anna? Anna Dawson?"

"Yes?"

"Hey, Anna, it's me, Al Rocklaw from the—"

"Hi, Al. What's up?" Al had never called me before. My
pulse picked up a couple of beats; this had to be about Niall.

"It's about that kid. The one you were talking to in the
poker room last week."

"Niall," I said.

"Yeah, I guess. Yeah, Niall, that's right."

"Is he there now? At the Aria?" I was already moving
around my room, grabbing my sneakers, looking for my keys.
It was almost six, nearly dinnertime. Jack wasn't home yet, but
probably would be soon. We'd all told Lor that we'd be home for
dinner, and she said she'd be trying a new recipe.

Looked like I'd be eating leftovers later. If it got me to Niall,
I'd be okay with that.

"No, not here. But I was just talking to a couple of guys and
it sounds like your guy, this Niall kid, is playing in a game right

now. Private game."

"Do you know where?"

"Basement of the Shangri-La. It's a strip joint over by—"

"I know where it is," I said. I'd paid a visit there a few days ago to put the word out about Niall. The guy who was running the game when I'd stopped by hadn't known me, and looked at my card with disdain when I handed it to him. No big surprise that he hadn't called me when Niall had shown up.

"Thanks, Al. If I show up there now, looking to play, that won't blow back on you in any way, would it?"

"Nah, I don't think so. And if it does, so what? What the hell do I care about some assholes running a private game?"

Exactly. They were eating into Al's business by playing in a private game and not at a casino. Would serve them right if I brought Jack and the vice squad in with me.

"Okay. Thanks again, Al. I appreciate it."

"Well, here's the thing, Anna. The reason I dug around and found your number. I think your kid is on tilt. Sounds like he's not doing so great. Throwing more money after bad, edgy."

I looked at the time on my phone again, in case I'd been wrong. Vegas could do that to you—both days and time all seemed to be one nebulous cloud.

Nope, it was only nearly six at night.

"So, early in the night and he's already off the rails?" I said, my concern for Niall rising. He may have killed Johnny (though I was rooting for it to be some unknown person with an axe to grind with Johnny), but I felt invested in Niall. Mainly because I had helped his poor parents try to get him back to Topeka. And also because I was the one who told the cops where to find him for questioning. That had led him to going underground.

A degenerate gambler needing a game was one thing. A degenerate gambler needing a game when he feared he was wanted for murder was something a little bit steeper.

"When you get there, if you want to play, you're going to

have to tell them, 'Shorty says I'm cool.' Got that?"

"Shorty says I'm cool. Got it. Thanks, Al," I said, and we hung up.

The kitchen smelled amazing when I popped my head in to tell Lorelei I was going out.

"Should we hold dinner for you?" she asked with her back to me as she did something at the marble island.

"No, you guys go ahead. I might be late. Really late."

She turned around at that. "Are you going alone, or will Cassandra be with you?"

"Alone," I said.

"Do you want me to go with you? Backup?"

I smiled at her. "Won't need it, but thanks. Just going to see if I can help a friend out of a poker game."

She nodded and turned back to the vegetables she was cutting. "Be careful, Jo," she said.

I picked up some cash from my cigar box in my office as I passed by, then said a goodbye to Raymond and Ben, who were watching a movie in the TV room.

The Shangri-La was a low-end strip joint. When you read the stories of pro athletes getting into trouble at strip clubs in Vegas? Those places are about five notches above the Shangri-La.

After paying the cover charge just to get into the place, and walking by the array of bored, sad dancers, I told the bouncer at the door to the basement the password and was allowed down the stairs.

The bass from the club seemed to reverberate off the walls, which were barely visible due to the cloud of smoke that filled the large room.

There was a man at the door playing cashier with chips, and a bar set up along the wall, but those were the only similarities between this and one of Vince's games.

Seedy. Depressing. A blast from my past.

And I felt a Hummer rushing through me the size of the

Hoover Dam.

Until I saw Niall's foot tapping furiously as he raised his bet at the table.

"There a chair free?" I asked the man at the table near the door.

"Yeah, but I don't think this game has much life left in it. It's been a long one. I'm guessing when one of them packs it in, they all will. Nobody wants to be the first guy to cash out."

I nodded. I knew those games. Everybody just limped along, hoping the tide turned at the right time, and then the game would break up. Men, more than the women I played with, were hesitant to be the first player to leave with money in hand.

I even knew players who subconsciously tanked so that they'd lose their money and then could just go home. It was one pitfall I'd never fallen into.

Not too deeply, anyway.

"I think I'll still hop on, if that's okay," I said to the door guy.

He was white and around thirty, with a greasy mullet and dressed in jeans and a torn hoodie. Couldn't hold a candle to Raymond in his dapper suits from Lorenzo's.

"How much?" he asked, nodding his chin to the racks of chips.

"What's the average right now?" I asked.

"Twenty grand. That's what most of them bought in originally. Some have come back for more. Not all."

"I'll do twenty," I said, and handed over the cash—it came from my winnings when I played the night Johnny was killed.

The last time I played poker.

Let's hope this game didn't end with murder.

Twenty-Seven

❖

NIALL RECOGNIZED ME FROM THE ARIA THE WEEK before. And, of course, from being the Black Widow once he'd recalled that. I could tell as soon as I neared the table, but I purposely didn't look at him, or react to his recognition.

One of the other players was a man I'd seen playing in casinos from time to time. His name was Todd and he was around the same age as Kurt Gunnell—the cheating husband—with the same graying-at-the-temple hair. He wore a dress shirt with the top two buttons undone. I suspected I'd find a tie and sport coat somewhere in the room behind the table.

A good player, Todd. I wondered why he needed to play in this place that was straight out of a movie where the reformed-gambler hero has to play in *one last game* to get a kidney for his mother or some other bullshit.

"Hey, Todd, how've ya been?" I said as I took my seat at the table.

"Pretty good, Anna, you?"

"Ups and downs. You know how it goes," I said. I put my chips on the table and pulled the chair up closer, getting comfortable. I kept my jean jacket on. Never knew when you'd need to quickly get out of a hellhole like this.

"I do know how that goes, yes," Todd said. The current hand ended and the dealer started shuffling while the other players all looked at me.

"Hi. Anna," I said. There were nods and a few hellos. All six of them looked like hell, bleary-eyed and with shadows well beyond five o'clock.

"Hi," Niall said, expectation in his voice. He wanted me to remember him.

I focused on his face for a second and then said, "Oh, hey. Hi. The Aria, right?"

Niall nodded, pleased. The Black Widow remembered him, which was very cool in his book. Little did he know that JoJo remembered him too.

Not so cool.

"All set?" the dealer asked the table as a whole, but particularly me. Nodding, I put my chips out for the small blind position, which was where I'd ended up on the table.

"Shuffle up and deal," I said, causing a few smiles at the table full of weary men.

THE SADDEST PART of it all was that Niall was actually a pretty good poker player. It reinforced to me that when he said he'd taken care of his problem, he'd probably meant that he'd won enough money, not that he'd killed Johnny.

With Niall beginning to be eliminated as a suspect in my mind, and my hopeful belief that Carla, Raymond, and Monty weren't involved—no matter that each of them had some sort of motive and/or opportunity—I relaxed into the game a little.

It must have been one of the many randos that Johnny likely pissed off or stole from. Or it was big enough that his name had been *spoken*.

Yes, Niall was a good player, and probably did win some big money from the time he'd ditched his parents, but he was also a compulsive gambler.

And it showed.

There were times he blew a hand because he rushed it. His leg jittered beneath the table constantly. Eyes were so bloodshot that it looked like he'd been smoking weed nonstop for a week.

I was guessing his leg wouldn't be quite so jittery if he actually had.

He should have left the table hours ago. But the compulsion wouldn't let him. Even when I started winning some of the pots, mostly off him, he wouldn't take his winnings and go home.

So, even if he'd gotten rid of a debt once, he would forever be in the win/lose/loan/lose/win cycle.

A cycle I knew well.

A cycle that created JoJo.

"That's it for me," Todd said after another two hours. He held his hand up to the dealer to skip him and started picking up the meager stack of chips he had left.

It was a "lose some" night for Todd in the world of win some/lose some.

"Good to see you, Anna," he said as he slid his chair back and moved to get up.

"You too, Todd," I said. In other instances of seeing people you knew but didn't see often, there would typically be more in the goodbyes, a "tell the wife I said hi" or a "don't work too hard at the office." But gambling was such that you didn't often share those things with people.

Either you felt they wouldn't care (they probably wouldn't), or you didn't want anyone to know too much about you (that could be used against you).

"Yeah, I think that's it for me too," one of the other guys said. He had fewer chips left than Todd did.

I could sense Niall's impending panic. The darting of his eyes to his chip stack, the mental addition of what he had left. What he'd lost. How much he could still win. Glances at the others' chip stacks, falling primarily on mine as the big stack.

Two of the other players made moves to start counting their chips, ready to go home. Or at least move on.

"Oh, come on, it's not that late," Niall said, the desperation seeping from his voice. "A few more hands, is all."

"Kid, we've been at this for a lot of hours," the oldest man at the table said. I'd put him in his early sixties, certainly not Ben's or Gus' ages, but older than Todd. Impressive he'd played for what had to be almost twenty-four hours.

I shivered thinking about doing this for so long in my sixties.

"Okay, just one more hand. An agreed-upon last hand," Niall said. Everyone looked to Todd for guidance.

Leave. Get this over with.

"Okay. One last hand. What the hell," Todd said, sitting back down.

The dealer looked to the other players, who all nodded, as did I, then dealt the cards.

The other thing about playing when you were so tired was your tells showed up more easily. And Niall's was a tiny movement with his tongue touching the tip of his upper lip when he had cards.

The tongue stayed longer this time—a movement he surely wasn't even aware of, but one I picked up on immediately. He had a good hand.

I had a queen and jack suited. A hand worth playing. A hand I might have thrown away, though, and taken my winnings and gone home. Which was probably what I should have done: tossed them in, then waited for Niall to leave and pull him aside as he left the Shangri-La. Or follow him to wherever he was now crashing. And keep that info to myself this time.

But I stayed in, calling Niall's bet. His stack was low; mine was high.

Would it count as enabling if I let him win? If I only kept out my original stake and lost all my winnings to him, could it help or hurt?

Long term it would hurt. It would just perpetuate the cycle. Put off rock bottom another day, which couldn't be good.

If his parents were worried enough to beg for help from Monty, and Niall was a suspect in a murder case, plus owing 100K to Carla wasn't rock bottom, then losing this card game probably wasn't going to move the needle much.

The flop contained a ten and an eight of hearts. My suit. A shot at an inside straight flush. But a long shot. The other card on the flop was a two of clubs. The two didn't help me, probably didn't help Niall.

Niall's tongue tapped his lip. I put him on holding a pair of tens. Now three of them.

He bet, but not too big, not enough to scare me off.

I called. A couple of other guys did too.

The turn card was an eight of spades. Now he had a full house and I had even less of a chance for anything. A measly pair of eights from the board wasn't going to do it.

Help him out.

JoJo's voice played in my ear.

Niall bet, a bit bigger than last time. I called. The other players folded.

It was just Niall and me.

Most of the other players, now done for the night, started gathering up their remaining chips and personal stuff. I noticed Todd stayed to watch, as did the older guy.

"What's your chip count?" I asked Niall. Meaning, how much did he have so I could cover him when I bet, forcing him to bet everything he had.

Without looking, he said, "Ten thousand." So, if he had started with the same amount that I had, he was ten thousand down. At least. He could have pulled out more money at any time in the past twenty-some hours.

I nodded and started to count out ten thousand from my

chips, but stopped when he added, "But if you take an IOU, you can go higher."

The old guy at the table scoffed as he was picking up his stack of chips.

IOUs were not something that were taken in drop-in poker games. That was something you did with friends and family. I couldn't even remember anyone ever bringing it up at a game I'd played.

Niall needed money and thought his full boat was good. It was. No way was I going to hit a nine of hearts to get my straight flush. Not with just one card remaining.

The river card. A card that had made me millions and cost me probably just as much.

"An IOU? Are you serious?" I said. There wasn't disdain in my voice. I tried not to sound like "are you some kind of idiot?" and more like "and how would we go about doing that?"

"I mean, yeah, we could. If you're good with that?" His voice got softer as he finished, as if realizing himself how daft he sounded.

Then a thought struck.

"You easy to find, Niall? Because I don't want to have to hunt down my winnings if I accept your chit."

"Yeah. Of course. I'm staying at the Queen of Hearts out by the airport. Where that group of cheap motels are? Room 154. There, I let everyone here know. So for sure you can find me."

Everybody chuckled at that, like it didn't occur to me that Niall could be giving me fake info, or be gone in the night if he lost.

Niall looked confused, and that made me think maybe there was still hope for him. It hadn't occurred to him to give me a false motel, or that he'd duck out on me.

That was when I decided to let him win. Big.

He had the winning hand, but now he could win more than the ten thousand he could only currently bet.

"Okay, Niall, sure. Shit, why not," I said.

Todd looked at me with an eyebrow raised. The old man stared at me like I'd lost my mind. The others who had left the table already started drifting back toward us after having cashed out with the hoodie-wearing doorman.

"Seriously? You'll do it?" Niall said.

I nodded. "Anybody got some paper and a pen?" Todd pulled out a pen from the inside pocket of his sport coat, which he'd just put on. After he handed it to me, I realized it was the same style of Montblanc pen I'd given to Raymond. The same as had been in a jar of pens in Cassie's office.

Were those pens following me? Or were they always around and I was just now noticing them after shopping for Raymond's?

Head in the game, Anna.

Which wasn't really necessary, as I was about to lose all my winnings, but still.

One of the other guys had an envelope in his pocket that he emptied out and then handed to me.

I did a count of my chips for everyone, even though I knew them to the dollar. Ninety thousand. I wanted to walk away with my starting twenty, which would give Niall seventy thousand. Plus what was already in the pot.

"Write the IOU for sixty K to check," I said, handing the envelope and pen to Niall. "Otherwise you're folding. My raise is seventy thousand."

"Kid, I don't think—" Todd stopped himself when he saw Niall was already furiously scribbling on the envelope.

"Put that hotel info on there too," I said. "And your cell number." He only nodded and kept writing.

The guys watching were of two minds: half thought I was crazy to be taking an IOU, and the other half thought I was a dick to be putting this kid in that kind of debt. It didn't occur to them that I'd lose.

I guess I should have been flattered.

"Okay, I'm all in, with this," Niall said, shoving his remaining chips and the IOU to the middle of the table. He started to turn over his cards, but my upraised hand stopped him.

"Hang on," I said. Taking out my phone, I reached for the IOU in the pot. "Turn your phone on."

Niall got what I was going to do and quickly pulled his phone out of his back pocket and took it off silent. I dialed the number he'd written on the envelope, and seconds later, his phone started to ring. I memorized the name Queen of Hearts and the room number, then threw the IOU into the pot at the center of the table.

Niall would win the pot in another minute and take the envelope back, but at least I had his phone number in my phone and his most current whereabouts memorized.

"I'm good if you are," I said to Niall, motioning to the pot.

"Whoa, Anna. Do you think that's wise?" Todd said.

"He's good for it, aren't you, kid?" I said.

Niall nodded a bit too quickly. "Yeah. Yes. But that's only if you beat me."

By now all the players were standing around the table and someone had explained to the doorman what was happening. He leaned over the table, arms locked, hands gripping the edge. "Hey, this is between you two. This doesn't involve the game, or the room, right? It doesn't blow back on us. Shorty has no liability in this, yeah?"

"Got it. No liability if he takes a runner," I said.

"I'm not going to take a runner," Niall said, seemingly hurt. He might have meant it. The truth was he had been in Vegas when he owed money before. It was JoJo and his parents who'd tried to get him out of town.

"Okay, let 'er rip," the doorman said to dealer.

"All in, you can show your cards," the dealer said.

We both flipped over our hole cards. I'd been right; Niall had a pair of tens, and now a full house.

I had a queen, jack, ten, and eight of hearts. Which was nothing on its own. A pair of eights on the table, beaten by his full house. Only a nine of hearts, giving me a straight flush, could beat him.

It was a terrible call and all the other players knew it. I sent up a silent wish that none of these players would talk about the stupid-ass move I made, taking an IOU for the chance to draw to an inside straight flush.

My reputation would survive, but seeing the confused, stunned, and almost pitying looks of the guys I'd just taken money from was a bit hard to swallow.

Niall sat back in his seat. It was a good thing the betting was over and our cards revealed, because the kid had totally lost any semblance of a poker face.

"Holy shit," he said. The shock on his face morphed into laser focus on the pot, and I could tell he was already thinking about where the money would go.

Pay off debts? Money for him and Kaitlyn to get the hell out of this town?

Or put it right back into the next poker game?

The dealer rapped once with his fist on the table, discarded the burn card, and turned over the river card. I had already started to pick up my remaining chips when I heard a collective gasp.

A nine of hearts.

I'd won.

And Niall owed me sixty thousand dollars.

I thought for a second he was going to make a dive for the envelope, and perhaps the dealer did too, because he pushed the pot in my direction quickly.

I took the envelope and put it in my jacket pocket, and quickly stacked my chips in a rack and handed it to the doorman to cash in.

The others looked like they'd all been kicked in the balls.

Bad beats were like that. Even if it wasn't you, you felt it to the core.

"Unbelievable," Todd said.

Guess my reputation would survive the night after all. It was a crazy-ass move with a huge payoff. Even if it wasn't the one I'd been after.

The other players shuffled away from the table. Most patted Niall on the shoulder and spoke a variation on "tough one, kid."

They'd been ready to leave before, but now it was like they wanted to replay that last hand over, because only two of them left; the others, along with Todd and the old guy, went to the bar and got a drink.

Niall and I were the only two at the table besides the dealer, who was stacking up the chips that had been cashed in already.

"It was a bad beat," I said softly. Niall only nodded, still staring at the table where the pot had been. His finger was moving back and forth on the felt of the poker table. It was the same nervous habit he had done the day we'd been talking at the Aria. There must have been some dampness on his fingers, because they left a trail against the grain.

"Let me get you a drink and then we can talk," I said.

He swallowed hard and nodded again. He thought I meant payment plans. And I guessed that was what it would have to be, so that I could keep his whereabouts on my radar until we found Johnny's killer and Niall was cleared.

Or charged.

Then I'd give him back the envelope and cancel the debt. And turn him over to Monty once again, to try to get him some help.

Because this? Right here? Getting beat like that to go deeply, deeply in debt?

If not rock bottom, it was pretty damn close.

I walked over to the bar and poured two whiskeys. The other men parted for me like the Red Sea. They weren't sure if I was an idiot, a genius, or just lucky as hell.

The answer was all three, but unfortunately, never the right one at the right time.

Bringing the drink back to the table, I was stopped by the doorman with my winnings.

"Give the dealer two thousand," I said. He took some from my envelope and then put it down on the table in front of me. He handed the money to the dealer, who thanked me.

I nodded back and then handed Niall his drink.

"Drink this and let's talk for a bit, yeah?" I said.

I realized what I'd said the second I saw the confusion on Niall's face. Or, actually, *remembered* that I'd said the same thing to him when JoJo handed him his laced drink a couple of weeks ago.

No semblance of trying for a poker face, he scanned me, then clearly went back in time, trying to make the pieces fit.

They didn't. He couldn't wrap his mind around the fact that the woman who'd drugged him was a famous poker player.

Neither could I, for that matter.

"Who… I mean, why…"

I kept my voice low, happy the dealer was leaving the table, allowing us to do our "business."

"Niall? It's okay. It's not what you think," I said.

It was probably exactly what he thought.

"How did you… So, what, was this all a setup?"

"No. No setup. Tonight's game was totally on the up and up."

He looked at me skeptically. I didn't blame him. I didn't know off the top of my head what the odds were that I would hit the nine of hearts on the river, but they'd be pretty astronomical.

"So, what the hell was that the night my parents showed up? Who the hell are you, anyway?"

"I'm Anna Dawson. You know that. You said you—"

He abruptly stood from his chair, causing it to fall behind

him, instantly ceasing the conversation of the players at the bar and creating complete silence.

"You fucked me over that night. Do you even know what you did?"

"I was helping out a friend," I said softly, trying to get him to take it down a notch. But that was not to be. The sleep deprivation—undoubtedly longer than just this marathon game—and the gambling desperation, mixed with some paranoia probably brought on by owing loan sharks money, sparked a wrath in Niall that I hadn't seen in the other times we'd interacted.

"You bitch! What, am I some kind of mark to you? Who are you working with? Carla? Johnny? Escada? Torrini? Are they out there? Waiting for me?"

I put my hands out in a "hold up" manner. "Niall, no one is waiting for you. This isn't a setup. I'm not working for anyone. I just—"

Suddenly he lunged at me and pulled the envelope out of my pocket. "Fuck you! This isn't legit at all." He crumpled up the envelope and started to throw it to the ground, but thought better of it and shoved it in the pocket of his jeans. "This is all fucking bullshit!"

He turned to see all the other players staring at him. Staring at us. Panic flashed across his face, and he took one more glance at me before darting for the door that led up the stairs from the basement.

He was fast. Very fast.

I should have just let him go. But I thought as soon as I did, he'd bolt from the motel room he'd given me and block my number on his phone.

And I still thought maybe I could explain it all to him. Help him out somehow.

I took off after him, shoving my winnings in my pocket and not bothering to say any goodbyes, thankful I'd kept my jacket on the entire time.

The beat of music and glare of the lights from the stage threw me off for a couple of seconds, but when I got my bearings, I headed straight for the front door.

As I reached the parking lot, I heard a car peeling out from the other side. Running to get to a position to see, I only managed to catch a quick glimpse of a dark-colored Tesla driving off.

No Uber this time. Some of those winnings, or whatever Niall had "taken care of," went toward a new car. I was too far away to get a plate number.

My car was on the other side of the lot, and I knew that no matter how quickly I got to it, I wouldn't be able to catch up to Niall. The entranceway to the 15 was a block away and the Strip just further than that. I'd lose him on either of those routes.

I slowly walked to my Porsche, tossing the envelope the doorman gave me onto the passenger seat.

It was full of money, but this one wasn't the envelope I'd wanted in my possession at the end of this night.

Twenty-Eight

❖

I DIDN'T WANT TO GO HOME. IT WAS ELEVEN AT NIGHT, not late by gambler standards. Ben would be in bed. I checked my phone to see if Jack had texted or called. Nothing. Either he was working late or Lor had filled him in on me working and he'd left me to it.

If you could call what I'd just done working.

I'd driven from the Shangri-La, but instead of heading to Summerlin, I did a GPS on the Queen of Hearts motel. It was a start, anyway.

There was a Sonic about a block before getting on the freeway to the motel, and I got myself a shake and a chili dog, having skipped Lor's new-recipe dinner. The Queen of Hearts was a motel like Niall had been in before, and Kurt Gunnell, with the entrances to the rooms on the outside of the long, one-story building.

Did guys like Niall and Kurt pick these types of places so they could see the parking lot? Those in debt and those cheating on their spouses? Always on the lookout, ready to go on the lam at any minute?

I shook my head at my thoughts. *On the lam?* I sounded like some schlocky Sam Spade rip-off.

These types of motels were probably just the cheapest kind. It was dark enough that I didn't do the reverse park thing once I'd reached Niall's motel. I pulled in so I faced his door, albeit at an angle of a few doors down. There was a light that shone through a small crack in his curtains. Could be home, or could be he left a light on. Or could be that Kaitlyn was in the room. There was no black Tesla in the parking lot, but that didn't mean Niall wasn't there. It might not even have been him peeling out of the Shangri-La parking lot.

Ostensibly, he could still be at the Shangri-La in a private room at the club, getting a lap dance while I sat staring at his motel room door.

At least I had food.

Before I dug in, I got out of my car, walked to his room, and knocked loudly on the door three times. I waited a minute and tried again, putting my ear close to the door.

No movement detected, either by sound or fluttering of the drapes. I rapped one more time and, after no answer, went back to the Porsche to wait for him. Or Kaitlyn. Though if Kaitlyn was making money as a dealer, she'd most likely be working right now.

It wasn't Lor's cooking, but it was an amazing chili dog. The frosty shake soothed my throat, which was scratchy from the smoke in the basement poker game. I cracked the window to get some breeze through just to take a bit of the smoke stink from my jacket and clothes. I pulled my ponytail down to my face. Damn, even my hair smelled.

It had been a long time since I'd played in a smoke-filled room. The poker rooms in the casinos were now nonsmoking, as had been Vince's games. The odor reminded me of my early days, when playing somewhere like the basement of the Shangri-La felt like I was making great strides as a player.

Tonight, it felt like a giant step backward.

But I had found Niall once again, and was going to explain things to him as soon as he came home.

If he came home.

Would he assume I'd memorized his motel and room because he said them out loud and I'd had the IOU in my possession before he yanked it out of my jacket pocket? Good assumption, because that was exactly what had happened.

So did that mean he'd *never* come back here? That didn't seem likely. Maybe Kaitlyn had a room here too, like they'd had at the Moonlight Motel? I looked at the other rooms, which were all dark except one.

I thought about knocking on that one, but by now it was nearly one in the morning and it didn't seem like the safe thing to do, knocking on a stranger's door so late.

I almost choked on my last piece of chili dog thinking about how many hotel rooms JoJo had walked into.

But JoJo was in control in those instances. And you don't really have any idea what you're doing in this new venture of yours.

Another hour passed with still no sign of Niall, a Tesla, or Kaitlyn peeking out a window.

It became clear how much of a rookie I was at this when I realized I would have to find a bathroom relatively soon.

And as the chili dog began to bark back, I raised a white flag and surrendered, starting up my car and heading home.

There may come a time when Depends would enter the picture, but I was not to that point. Yet.

JACK WAS ASLEEP WHEN I got home. I didn't bother to wake him, but took a long shower, washing my hair several times. After I put on some pajama pants and a clean tee, I brought my smoky clothes right to the laundry room, threw them in the washer, and turned it on.

I'd be asleep when they should go in the dryer, but at least that smell was not in my nostrils any longer.

When I crawled into bed with Jack, he moved to let me

cuddle close to him.

"What time is it?" he asked, still mostly asleep.

"Late. Early, actually. Go back to sleep," I said.

"Mm, you smell good," he murmured. It seemed to register what I'd said about it being early in the morning, because he tried to sit up a bit. "Everything okay?" he asked.

Pushing gently on his shoulder to get him to lie back down, I said, "Everything's fine. I'll tell you about it in the morning. Nothing monumental. Go back to sleep."

"Okay," he said, the word long and slurred because he was already back in slumber land. At least, I hoped that was why his words were slurred. I leaned into him, sniffing his exhales for signs of bourbon. I hated that I did it, and it wasn't even in a "gotcha!" way. No, it was more of an "I played poker tonight and at times I felt so alive I wanted to burst, and though I don't want you to start drinking again, it doesn't seem fair that I got to enjoy my Hummer and you didn't" kind of way.

As I drifted off, I thought about what all I'd tell Jack the next morning. And what I would leave out. Definitely leave out the part about sniffing his breath.

Iceberg.

WHEN I WOKE UP to my alarm for breakfast, Jack was already gone from my bed and my room. When I went over to the other side of the house to make sure Ben was up and getting ready (and of course he was) I saw Jack's room was empty, so he'd already gotten ready and left the house. Eager to resume that desk duty he loathed so much.

It was probably just as well I didn't have to recap for him. After breakfast and dropping Ben off back here, I'd hit up the Queen of Hearts again and try to find Niall and/or Kaitlyn and explain that they weren't in trouble. At least not from me.

Twenty-Nine
❖❖

THIS TIME, WHEN THE BOYS PULLED OUT THE ODDS sheets when breakfast was over, I happily pulled out my journal to get my thoughts down on paper.

No wistful glances at their papers, or pretending not to listen to them as they discussed games, injuries, and idiot coaches. Instead, I was immersed in jotting down the latest info on Johnny Aces' murder.

Kaitlyn's name with a big question mark took up the upper corner of the page. I still wasn't clear how she and Niall were working together, and what their relationship was. If it was romantic, why did she have a separate room at the Moonlight? Was she purposely working the game the night Johnny was killed? Had she signaled Niall when the game had broken up?

So, I was back to Niall being the top suspect for killing Johnny. Even though I'd said to Cassie and Carla recently that it was probably one of the many other people that Johnny had done business with.

Cassie had suggested that was what I wanted to believe so it wouldn't blow back on Raymond, Monty, Carla, and myself. Which was true.

But I didn't want it to be Niall either, for no other reason than that I had a soft spot for the kid. His running from me last night when he'd recognized me from drugging him had me putting him firmly in the "yeah, probably" column.

After we finished up, I dropped Ben off at home, but didn't even go in, anxious to get back to the Queen of Hearts.

I helped him out of the Lexus and brought his walker around for him, then he shooed me away.

"Go. Go do your things, Hannah, dear. I can make it the rest of the way myself."

"Are you sure, Ben? I can take you inside, make sure Lor is home." Her BMW was in the circular drive, out of the way, so it was a safe assumption that she was, but still.

"And what if she's not? I can make it to my room, or the living room, you know."

Of course he could. I had to remember not to baby him too much, even if I wanted to. He was a man in his eighties who had seen a shit-ton of stuff in his day.

"Right. Sorry. Okay, see you later, Ben," I said.

He put his hand out on mine. "Hannah, dear, you seem to be enjoying yourself with this new adventure."

I nodded. "Yeah, I am, I think. It's still a lot to learn, but…"

"Ah, when we stop learning, we stop living."

"I guess," I said.

He patted me on the hand, then wrapped his bony fingers around the handle of his walker and shuffled to the front door. "It's good. To be excited about things," he said, his voice growing softer.

I made my way slowly from the Lexus to my Porsche, taking my time to make sure Ben made it in okay. Once he was in, I sped off to the Queen of Hearts.

Ben was right. It was nice to be excited about something other than gambling. I caught my reflection in the rearview at a stoplight. I almost didn't recognize myself—a lightness, an almost-smile on my resting face.

That quickly changed when I turned the corner on Warm Springs Road and saw the police cars at the Queen of Hearts.

♠ ♥ ♦ ♣

I PULLED INTO THE parking lot, even though a uniformed policeman was waving me away. "Is there a detective on the scene?" I asked him when I rolled down my window.

He was taken aback by the question, but quickly regrouped and gave me a curt nod.

"Who is it?" I asked.

"Ma'am, I can't dis—"

"Is it Frank Botz?" I asked, gaining not only another look of surprise, but then a narrowing of his eyes while he determined that maybe I was someone who needed to be dealt with.

"I'm not press," I said. "I'm not sure what's going on here, but could you tell Detective Botz that Anna Dawson is here and would like to speak with him?"

"Spencer! Let her through," Botz yelled from across the parking lot, startling both me and officer Spencer.

Officer Spencer waved me through, and I parked just a couple of spots down from where I'd staked out Niall's room only hours earlier.

There were cops milling around and the door to Niall's room was open. An ambulance was parked in front of the room three down from Niall's, with no apparent urgency emanating from its crew, who were having a smoke while leaning on the vehicle.

A crime-scene van was also parked nearby. Several reasons why Botz and crew would be here floated through my brain. But the tingle in my spine knew the truth.

Niall was dead.

I got out of my car and started walking toward Botz, but he held up a hand, stopping me. He called behind him, into the room, then walked over to me.

"Anna, what are you doing here?"

"Is Niall dead?" I asked, not wanting to play any kind of

cop games.

"How did you know Niall was here?"

"Cut the shit, Frank. Is he dead or not?"

"Why would you ask that?" Peter Faxon, who had come out of Niall's room and joined us, asked.

"Because two of Metro's homicide detectives are directing what appears to be a crime scene around his room," I said. Faxon bugged me, and my tone made that clear.

But I bugged Faxon too, and that was evident when he said, "And how did you know this was his room?"

Oh, what the hell, if Niall was dead, everything was going to come out eventually. "Listen, I've got nothing to hide, and am willing to tell you what I know, but just tell me if he's dead."

"He's dead," Faxon said. Botz nodded in confirmation.

"Drugs?" I asked. I hadn't really noticed anything that would definitely indicate Niall was doing drugs, but it wasn't uncommon in players who went on playing binges. Uppers to keep going. Downers after the game was over. Circular destruction. He was always crazy fidgety, barely covering it when he played.

"OD?" I asked in a different way when neither detective answered me.

They glanced at each other, and Faxon said, with a little more satisfaction than the moment dictated, "Not OD. Murdered. Looks like the same MO as Johnny Aces. Up close. One shot to the head."

Shit.

An officer came out of Niall's room with a baggie that he brought to Faxon, who made a show of accepting it, turning it so I'd get a look at it.

The envelope IOU from Niall to me. I could even see the wording from the angle Faxon held it.

Niall Hendricks owes Anna Dawson sixty thousand US dollars. Followed by his contact info and his signature. What caught my attention this time was that I had been so intent on memorizing the motel and room number that I hadn't even paid attention to his full name.

Niall Hendricks.

I realized it was the first time I'd even registered Niall's last name. I'd drugged him and smuggled him to his parents. Tracked him down once and turned him over to the cops. Found him again and got his whereabouts out of him. And all that time, I'd never even known his last name.

Or maybe I had heard it somewhere in there and it'd never registered?

How fucked up was that?

I pointed to the IOU Faxon obviously wanted me to see. "If you had that, you know how I knew where Niall was."

"Yes and no," he said. "It has his contact info on it, yes. But it was in his possession, not yours, so I'm still asking how you knew to come here."

"And when else you've been here," Botz added.

"Hey, guys, if I'd killed Niall, why would I be showing up now?" I asked. "And why wouldn't I have taken the IOU? It would have been stupid to leave it behind."

"Murderers aren't the sharpest tools in the shed," Faxon said. Botz suppressed an eye roll at his partner. He probably missed Jack more than Jack missed being back in the action.

Well, not that much. But a lot.

"I think it's time to take this to the station. Ask some questions," Botz said.

"Okay," I said. "Like I said, I'll tell you what I know, but it's not a lot." Faxon held out a hand toward his car, but I shook my head. "I'll drive my own car there."

"No, that won't—"

"That's fine," Botz said, cutting off Faxon. "But you'll go straight to the station, yeah?"

"Yes. Sure," I said. I wasn't sure if Niall's body was still in the room or in the back of the ambulance already. Or if some other kind of vehicle was coming for somebody who definitely didn't need medical attention.

I wanted to ask so many questions, but I wanted to get out of there before Niall's body could be brought out (if it was indeed still in the room), so I turned and made my way back to my car.

Botz jogged a couple of steps to catch up with me. He was wearing a Road Runner tie today. Usually the sight of his ties made me smile, but not now. Not while Niall's body was probably only a few feet away.

"Hey, Anna," Botz said when he'd reached me. "Might be a good idea to call a lawyer to meet you there."

For Botz to suggest that made my spine tingle even more. I only nodded and got in my car. Botz returned to his car to wait for Faxon, who was speaking with one of the officers, then walked to their car and got in. Faxon waved like I should follow them.

I did, but not in any rush, not to give him any satisfaction.

I called Lor from the car and asked her to get in touch with Marvin Harrison and ask if he was available to meet me right away at Metro headquarters.

"Oh, Jo, what happened?" she asked. I guess I should've been pleased that it was surprise and concern in her voice and not resignation, like she'd been expecting this call for years.

She probably had, but my recent good behavior had knocked it down a few notches.

"Somebody was killed last night. No one you know. But I saw him last night, so they're going to want to question me to get the time frame."

It sounded like the words I'd said when Johnny Aces had been killed. I was just needed to give them the tick-tock.

But it was different this time. I knew it. And not just because Johnny being dead fed no emotion in me while Niall's death stung. Deep.

"Just a precaution to have a lawyer sitting next to me," I said to Lor, trying to convince myself, as well as her, that it was true.

"Okay, yeah. I'll call Marvin right away. If he can't meet you there, I'll get somebody else."

"Thanks, Lor, you're the best. And maybe don't say anything to Ben just yet. No need to make him worry. I should be home by dinner, I would think."

"That's a good idea. I won't say anything to Ben. I'm assuming you'll see Jack there anyway, so no need to keep him in the dark."

"Yeah, probably. Thanks again, Lor."

"Be careful, Jo," she said, then we both hung up.

I followed a few cars behind Botz and Faxon, thinking about how long it would take until word got to Jack's desk that his girlfriend was being brought to the station in conjunction with a murder case.

Again.

Thirty

❖❖

IT DIDN'T TAKE LONG. JACK REACHED ME BEFORE my lawyer did.

"What the hell?" he said when he walked into the interrogation room, where I sat drinking a coffee that Botz had brought me before disappearing and leaving me alone.

"I don't think you're supposed to be in here until my lawyer arrives," I said.

"Quit the crap, Johanna," he said. Johanna. He only used my full name when we were in bed or shit was getting real. And I guessed it was, with him standing over me like I was some murder suspect he was about to question.

Oh.

"You're not allowed to question me, are you?"

"No, why?"

I shrugged. "You've got your cop face on."

"This is just my face," he said.

I couldn't help but let out a little snort. "And you say *I* have a tell. Maybe. But you have *faces*, Jack Schiller, and this is most definitely your cop face."

"What's my concerned boyfriend face look like?" he asked as he pulled out the chair opposite me and sat down, placing his forearms on the table between us.

I studied him for a second. Every line on his face had been earned, either through the job or through the bottle. Both. I hated that being with me was going to cause a few more.

But damn, he wore them well.

"It's very similar to your cop face, and I'm sorry for that," I answered.

He scrubbed a hand across his face, making a clump of hair skew out of place. It only made him better looking.

"I'm not," he said quietly, more to himself than to me. He breathed deeply, then sat back in the chair. "Lor got in touch with Marvin Harrison. He'll be here in a half-hour. Need anything until then?"

I lifted the cup of coffee Botz had brought me. Bless him, it was the good stuff from a coffee shop, not the stuff that they made here. "I'm good, thanks."

Jack nodded. "I don't think Frank will let Faxon back in here until Marvin is here, but if he does, you know not to say anything, right?"

I nodded, then leaned forward, my hands sliding on the table. Not reaching for him, but open. "You do know I didn't kill Niall, right?"

"Of course," he said quickly. Quickly enough that he wouldn't be sleeping back at his apartment tonight. "But that doesn't mean that your words couldn't get twisted, or used against you."

"Got it," I said, leaning back in my chair, my hands dropping down off the table to hang at my sides.

Neither of us moved, just stared at each other, until I finally looked away and took another drink of my coffee.

The silence broken, Jack stood up, nodded once more, and left the room.

I'D FIRST MET MARVIN HARRISON when he helped me out after golfer Lion LaGasse was killed. He then asked me to attend the will reading for Vince Santini. Then I called him when I woke up next to a dead body. If he was surprised to be called yet again for me being mixed up in a murder case, he had the good grace to hide it as he made his way into the room.

Making sure that we were not being monitored, he gave me the go-ahead to tell him why I was here, which I did.

When he was up to speed, he let Faxon and Botz know I was ready to be questioned.

Botz asked if I wanted more coffee or anything else, but I declined, ready to get this over with.

I wanted to ask some questions too.

"Okay, let's start at the top," Botz said. "From the point you gave Jack the Moonlight Motel as Niall's whereabouts, where and when have you seen Niall Hendricks?"

I told them everything as it pertained to Niall. About seeing him at the Aria after staking out the Moonlight. Then losing him after he'd been questioned by them. I made a point of clearing my throat there, because they should have been keeping an eye on Niall if they really liked him for Johnny Aces' murder. Faxon slid his eyes to Botz, and I guessed that it was Faxon that had dropped the ball there.

I told them about the previous night, getting a tip about where Niall was playing and going there.

And then I replayed the night for them, giving them times as best as I could remember.

"And this IOU he wrote. Is that a normal thing? Taking an IOU from somebody you don't know well? Barely know at all?" Botz asked.

"No," I said. "Not usual to suggest it like he did, and definitely not usual to accept it like I did."

"Why do you suppose he suggested it?" Botz asked.

"Ms. Dawson has no knowledge as to Mr. Hendricks' thought process. To suggest that—"

Botz held up a hand to alleviate Marvin's fears that they

were trying to trap me into something I couldn't possibly know. "I know she didn't know. But she's a professional poker player. Someone who reads other people for a living. I'm just asking if she had any idea why Hendricks would do something so unorthodox."

I gave a chin nod to Marvin, an "I got this," and then answered Botz. "I'm just guessing, but I think it was twofold. One, he was desperate. That was obvious. Either he was actually, really desperate, or he was gambler desperate."

"What's *gambler desperate*?" Faxon asked. He was wearing one of his expensive suits, the tie an understated navy. I wondered how much he hated Botz's ties, and it made me the tiniest bit happy.

"Gambler desperate is the belief that you only have this *one* chance left. That this will be the last time—because maybe you've told yourself you'll quit, or you just don't have your next game lined up—your last chance to win. It's a mindset. Actual desperation is most likely debt. Either debt you're trying to get out of, or debt you're trying not to get into."

"And which type of desperation do you think Niall had?" Botz asked.

Marvin didn't balk this time at me being asked about Niall's state of mind. He seemed just as interested in my answer as the two detectives.

"Both," I said.

"So, he probably owed several people money," Marvin said. "People with much more motivation to see him dead than my client, who had just granted him an IOU. All the more reason to see that Niall lives, so he can pay back the debt he owed her."

Good point, Marvin. Although I didn't think Botz and Faxon actually thought I killed Niall.

Well, Botz, at least.

"I still don't get why you then went to his motel right after the game," Faxon said. "Surely you didn't think he'd be able to pay you back so soon? Or did he say he had the money, just not with him?"

"No. He didn't say that. I had no reason to believe he would pay me last night. That's not why I went to the Queen of Hearts."

"So, why then?"

A bit sticky, this territory. I'd gone to tell Niall that he had nothing to fear from me. That the JoJo incident, which he'd remembered, was not some part of a larger nefarious plot against him.

"I wanted to tell him that he could forget the IOU. And mostly to make sure that he'd given me a legit address."

"Why would you let him off the hook? You won the game, right? Or was it not on the up and up?" Faxon asked.

Botz had the decency to look as affronted at Faxon as I did. Even Marvin let out a little snort of disgust.

"I don't play in games that aren't on the up and up," I said, mustering as much indignation as I could. Indignation that took an internal beating as I remembered a card game in Chicago not too long ago that had Raymond as the pot.

To be fair, I didn't know the game was fixed until after I had my prize and was bringing him back to Vegas.

"So, then, why not keep your winnings?" Faxon said, smug that he'd gotten the rise out of me that he'd been looking for.

Poker face, Anna. Don't let this SOB get more emotion out of you than Phil Hellmuth and Daniel Negreanu ever could.

"The money was irrelevant. I didn't lose anything. I made sure my stake was covered. And I didn't want a debt to make him do anything stupid," I said.

"Like killing the person he owed money to?" Faxon said.

"So, you're still thinking Niall killed Johnny Aces? I would think him being murdered in the exact same way would at least take the suspicion off him," I said.

"Could be a copycat thing, to throw us off," Faxon said.

Botz looked down, not wanting anyone to see what he

thought of Faxon's theory.

"That's idiotic," I said. "Besides, very few details were given out about Johnny's murder. Who could copy it?"

It was true. Other than the location of Johnny's shooting, and that it had been a shooting, very few details had emerged. Make of gun, that type of stuff.

Jack hadn't offered up anything either. Because he wasn't aware, not being on the case or because of Iceberg, that I didn't know.

"Wait, you said twofold earlier. That one of the reasons Niall would offer up an IOU was because of desperation. What was the other reason?" Botz asked.

I thought it was obvious, but apparently not, given the looks of curiosity from the three men in the little room with me.

"He thought he would win," I said.

It wasn't quite eye rolls, but it could have been.

"No, you don't get it," I explained. "That *certainty* that a gambler has. You absolutely *know* you can't lose."

"But you do. All the time," Botz said softly. I wasn't sure if we were still talking about Niall or myself.

Brushing past those thoughts, I said, "Gamblers have very short memories. While also remembering everything."

Faxon looked puzzled, but Marvin and Botz both nodded a little bit.

"So you staked out his place just to talk to him?"

"Yes," I said.

"And you say you gave up around"—Botz looked down at his tablet of notes—"two in the morning?"

"Yes," I said.

"Why?"

"Why what?"

"Why did you pack it in at two? Why not wait until morning? If it was that important to you?"

I hesitated, which put Marvin's antenna up. He sensed his

lawyerly skills would be coming into play.

Not quite yet, Marvin.

"I had to go to the bathroom," I said.

Botz and Faxon looked at each other, then back at me. "Excuse me?" Faxon said.

"I'd recently eaten and had a shake and I…needed to go home."

"Where did you eat? Would you have paid by card?"

They could get a timestamp on a credit or debit card payment. To make sure my times matched up with what I'd told them.

"Cash," I said. "But it was at the Sonic on Sahara. They might have had cameras. I didn't notice."

Botz wrote that down on his tablet.

"In fact, the Queen of Hearts probably has cameras, right? Wouldn't they catch when I arrived and left?"

"We're checking on that," Botz said, earning a look from Faxon.

"What I don't get is, why did Niall have the IOU in his possession, and not you?" Faxon asked.

Well, that one was a little tricky to answer honestly. The truth was that Niall had assumed something was hinky with the game when he realized I was also JoJo, the woman who'd drugged him and turned him over to his parents.

But I didn't *know* that. Not for certain. And so I could honestly say, "I'm not sure. It surprised me, for sure. He grabbed it out of my pocket, and I was shocked enough that I couldn't stop him. Then he was gone."

All true. And none of it bringing up JoJo and her illegal drugging of a young man. Even if it was for a good cause this time and not part of a point-shaving scheme.

They seemed satisfied with that. Or not. Hard to tell. But that was all they were going to get from me about that aspect of it all.

I didn't want Monty to get into any trouble. And I definitely didn't want anyone sniffing around JoJo's past activities.

Botz sighed, and I assumed we were wrapping up. There were no clocks in the room, and I didn't have a watch on, but I was guessing it had been a couple of hours since Marvin had arrived and the official questioning had begun.

Botz looked me over and said, "I'm assuming you've showered this morning?"

"Yes," I said. "Well, no. Not since I got up. I showered last night when I got home."

"And is there someone in the household who can verify what time that was?"

I shook my head. "I woke up Jack, but I don't think he was aware of what time it was. I wasn't even really sure myself."

Botz wrote something down and underlined it. Probably Jack's name. That would be an interesting conversation.

"Okay. No need for powder residue testing, then. We'll at least need the clothes you wore last night," Faxon said.

"Okay, but they're in the washer. Probably still there. I forgot about them. If Lor sees them, she'll just switch them to the dryer, but I can maybe text her to stop—"

"You get home at the early hours of the morning and still take a shower and do a load of laundry? Is that normal?" Faxon asked.

"Nothing's normal in a gambler's life," I said. "But no, I don't usually do that, but the Shangri-La allowed smoking, and I reeked. I knew I'd never sleep with the smell of smoke in my hair. My clothes stunk too, so I took them right to the washer. Not usual, no. But necessary."

"So, you showered and washed the clothes you were wearing," he said, like he'd cracked the case.

"Do you want me to have Lorelei pull the clothes from the washer for you or not?" I said.

"Not necessary," Botz said before Faxon could speak. "I

think we have enough for now. Thank you for coming in, Ms. Dawson."

Marvin started to put the few papers in front of him back into his briefcase. They might have been done with me, but I had a few questions for them. Or one, at least.

"What about Kaitlyn? Was she in the room with Niall? Did she find him?"

Faxon let out a snort. "Again with this Kaitlyn? This mysterious Kaitlyn. The dealer, right?"

"Right," I said. "From the game when Johnny was killed. And with Niall at the Moonlight Motel."

"We saw no signs of that," Faxon said.

"Because you scared her off. Both Kaitlyn and Niall."

I knew if I did go forward with this PI thing, there would be a lot more Icebergs between Jack and me.

Him, and his police work, I trusted. Even Botz. But Faxon was a well-dressed clown. To not even take Kaitlyn seriously as a witness, accomplice, or suspect was incomprehensible. She might have had nothing to do with any of it, but to not follow up on her was doing what Cassandra had accused cops of doing: one-way streets.

"There was no sign of her, or any other woman, in his room this morning," Botz said. "The cleaning woman found him."

"So, they're not together anymore? Or she…" I looked at both cops, willing them to fill in the blanks in my supposition, but neither one did. "I'm not sure where she fits in, but I'm sure she does."

"Why?"

I told them about her running away from me at the shops at the Aria. "It doesn't make sense. There was no reason to avoid me."

Faxon chuckled at that, and I guess it was supposed to be an insult, but I let it pass. "Maybe she just didn't see you?" Botz suggested.

Maybe. But I could have sworn we locked eyes. Did we?

Crap, this was all playing head games with me.

"Well, I think she's someone to look at, anyway," I said. "So, we're done, then?"

"For now," Faxon said, emphasizing the words like it would be just a matter of time before they'd have me in cuffs.

What a dick.

"I can walk you out," Botz said, rising from his seat.

"No need. I know the way," I said, throwing that line at Faxon. *Yeah, dickwad, I've been this way before. No cuffs on me yet.*

Marvin and I left the interrogation room. I said my thanks to him, and he said he'd keep me posted of anything I needed to know, and for me to do the same for him.

Jack met me in the lobby of the main floor after Marvin and I had parted. "How'd it go?" he asked.

"You know how it went," I said. He shrugged, confirming that he'd been watching the whole time. "How do *you* think it went?"

"Good. You told them important info to establish a timeline. Anything you left out?"

Jack always said I had a tell that only he could see. If that was true, there was no reason to lie. And probably not worth invoking Iceberg.

"Yeah, but nothing that would help them. Or hurt them. Just hurt others."

He scrubbed a hand over his face, not liking my answer. When his hand dropped, he nodded. "Fair enough."

"I'm heading home. See you later?"

"Yeah. I shouldn't be late. A little after six?"

"It's a date," I said. I knew better than to kiss him goodbye in the middle of the police station lobby. Notorious suspected murderess that I was and all.

But Jack surprised me by sliding a finger inside my jeans pocket and pulling me toward him. He leaned forward and kissed me soundly, as if it was a declaration.

I guess it was.

And if I hadn't been in love with Jack Schiller before, I would have tumbled deeply in right then.

"See ya at six," I whispered as he pulled away and released my pocket.

He smiled. I turned toward the door but stopped when I saw Monty entering.

With Niall's parents.

"What are you doing here?" Monty asked when they entered the large vestibule.

"I was…um…just talking with the detectives about…" I didn't know for sure if the Hendrickses had been notified about Niall until I looked at his mother.

It was the face of a shattered woman. They'd been told. Hopefully by Monty and not some asshat like Faxon.

"They said they were questioning someone right now," Mrs. Hendricks said. "Isn't that what they said?" she asked Monty.

"Yes, but that doesn't mean—"

"You. You're…*her*. Right?"

I shouldn't have been surprised that Mrs. Hendricks made me as JoJo right away. Women were much better at that than men. It was hard for them to reconcile the flamboyance of JoJo with the ho-hum Anna.

That was why I had never been cuffed.

Yet.

"Mr. and Mrs. Hendricks, I'm so sorry for your loss. I was with Niall last night, and—"

"So it *was* you they were questioning. I thought you were helping us. That night at the hotel. You did help us. Why would you hurt Niall now?"

"I didn't," I said. But was that really true? Yes, I didn't kill Niall, but had I hurt him? Was my involvement with all of this what got Niall killed?

"Anna has been helping, Lois," Monty said. "She's been trying to find Niall since he left you."

Mr. Hendricks flinched at that, and I only guessed at the shitshow that had ensued when Niall had ditched his parents.

"You saw him last night?" Mrs. Hendricks asked, obviously both confused and hopeful. Like there was something I could say that would make this all go away.

God, I wished there was.

"I did. Yes, I was with him last night."

"But you weren't involved?" she asked.

"I don't know who hurt him," I said, not willing to cop to total noninvolvement.

"You were with him, but couldn't protect him?"

No. No, I couldn't. The truth was that nobody could protect a gambler on the trajectory Niall was on.

"I'm so, so sorry," I said.

"But—"

"Let's get upstairs," Monty said, putting an arm at the back of Mrs. Hendricks and nodding over her head to Mr. Hendricks, who picked up on his cue.

"Lois, let's just go speak with the detectives. Find out what's really going on."

They walked toward the elevators. At the door, Monty pushed the button. He and Mr. Hendricks stared at the elevator door, but Mrs. Hendricks turned to stare at me.

The pain on her face.

I felt Jack's warm, reassuring hand on my shoulder. As if he knew that Mrs. Hendricks blamed me.

And she might not have, but I took her pain and twisted it in my gut, trying to block it out.

"She's a mother grieving," Jack said after they'd entered the elevator and its doors closed.

"Yeah, I know," I said. We said goodbye again, and I walked to my Porsche to drive home.

The whole way, I thought about poor Niall. I hadn't really let myself think about him being dead, having been hauled into the police station so quickly. But now it hit me.

When I got out to Summerlin, instead of turning into our gated community, I went to a nearby park and just sat in my car for a while.

I thought about Niall and the demons that chased him. The ones that finally caught up with him.

And then I thought about my mother, back in Wisconsin. And how, ten years ago, it could have easily been her being brought into a police station because her degenerate gambler child had been killed.

I pulled out my phone and texted Monty.

I know you're dealing with the Hendrickses for a while. And I don't want to intrude on that. But when you're free, I could really use someone to talk to.

Before I'd even put the phone back in the car holder, I got a response.

Of course. As soon as I'm able to, I'll call.

I started up the Porsche and heard another chime from my phone. Monty again.

I'm so proud of you for reaching out.

I put the car in gear and drove out of the park toward home. Proud of myself, too.

Thirty-One

❖

THE NEXT MORNING, I GOT A TEXT FROM CASSIE asking if I was available. I quickly texted back that I was.

It's not about Johnny Aces. Different case.

Oh. Well, I could definitely use a distraction of some sort.

Besides, I didn't think Cassie was aware of Niall being killed. Or maybe she was, given her contacts.

I was growing my list thanks to Al Rocklaw and Shorty and others, but she had a lot of years of this PI stuff on me.

Of course, my greatest asset had always been the Corporation. Nobody knew old-school Vegas like they did.

But Johnny Aces wasn't old school. Neither was Niall.

Cassie told me to meet her at the Koffee Klatch in an hour. Ben and I had been home from breakfast for a couple of hours already, so there was no conflict with timing.

Cassie was already at the Koffee Klatch when I arrived. Instead of one of the booths, she was seated at a larger table in the middle of the restaurant. It would seat six, and I wondered if there would be more than just me joining her.

Which must be the case, because she directed me to sit on her side of the table, next to her.

"Order something to drink, but no food," she said as I sat.

The waitress was already at my side and I went with a Diet Coke, having already had my coffee fix with Ben and the boys.

"A client is meeting us shortly," Cassie said by way of hello. "I don't have time to brief you now. Just follow my lead. When I get up to leave, come with me. We'll go to your car and drive for a bit, then circle back to get my car. Okay?"

"Yeah, I guess. Who is the client?" I asked, eyeing the couple coming in the doorway. They were young, Hispanic, and with a baby in a stroller.

Probably not here to meet a PI.

Probably not a good idea to assume.

The couple waved at an older woman who was sitting at the table behind ours and walked to join her. The baby had a little Raiders onesie on and a wide smile, gurgling as they were pushed through to the waiting grandma.

"Remember the Kurt Gunnell stakeout?" Cassie said. I nodded. "This is the other end. Meeting with the one who hired me."

"Mrs. Gunnell?"

"Yes?" answered a woman who was approaching our table.

I didn't know what I'd thought she'd look like. But this wasn't it.

Mrs. Gunnell was a beauty. Older, in her early fifties, probably. About the age of her husband. She could have passed for younger, especially given the youthful, very cool leather jacket, deep-vee white tee with silver necklaces hanging down, jeans, and ankle boots she was wearing. She looked like an aging rock star's longtime girlfriend.

Kurt Gunnell was an idiot.

"Greta, this is my associate, Anna Dawson. Anna, this is Greta Gunnell. Please sit."

The waitress brought my Diet Coke as Greta sat down. She started to take off her jacket but looked from me to Cassie—both of us still wearing ours—and kept hers on.

"What can I get you to drink?" the waitress asked Greta, who looked to Cassie's and my beverages.

"Coffee. Black, please," she said.

"Thanks for meeting us here," Cassie said. "We have a meeting nearby shortly, and it helps us out."

I wasn't aware of any meeting afterward, but perhaps I wasn't invited to join Cassie for that one.

Or perhaps there wasn't even another meeting.

Now was the time to just shut up and learn. Because if I wasn't mistaken, we were about to rip Greta Gunnell's world apart.

Given the way she was wadding up the paper napkin that was at her place setting, I wasn't the only one who thought so.

"Okay. Please go ahead," she said as soon as the waitress had delivered her coffee. She didn't touch it, and I didn't drink from my Diet Coke either.

It would have felt rude, somehow.

"You were correct, Greta. Your husband is having an affair. With a woman named—"

"Maris Fleming," Greta said, finishing Cassie's sentence for her.

Or maybe she hadn't.

"Perhaps," Cassie said. "But the woman we have proof that he's seeing is Sarah Ellison."

The color drained from Greta's face, her eyes following Cassie's hand as she reached to the empty seat beside her and picked up a nondescript brown envelope, the size that held 8 1/2 x 11 paper.

Or photos.

The Hummer rushed through me as I thought about how like a movie this all was. Cassie placed the envelope on the table and slid it across to Greta. She flattened her hand on the envelope, which Cassie then released. Her nails were short, but trimmed and shaped nicely, a soft seashell coral polish on them. Two rings, and both looked expensive to my untrained jewelry eye.

"Sarah?" Greta whispered. "You're sure?"

"I believe so. That's the information I gathered. If you take a look in the envelope, you can confirm it."

One tiny tap of Greta's fingertip on the envelope. "You can see her? Her face? In these?"

Cassie nodded. "Yes. There are three photos where her face is clear. Two from the same occasion, and one at one other location. There's a list of the meetings that I was able to document. If there were other times, or with the other woman you mentioned…"

"Maris."

"Yes, Maris. If your husband met with her, I did not witness it."

I couldn't tell if that bit of information made it better or worse for Greta. She bit the bullet, slid her finger under the top of the envelope, and opened it. I couldn't see her take a deep breath, and I hid my own, but it was there for the both of us.

Cassie, presumably having done this hundreds of times, showed no movement at all. She didn't touch her glass, so I—as much as I wanted to take a big drink of Diet Coke—left mine untouched as well.

Greta pulled out a few black-and-white photos, 8 1/2 x 11, and laid them on top of the envelope on the table. She didn't try to hide them from our view, which made sense, since we were the ones delivering them to her.

The top one was of Kurt and the woman we'd seen at the motel we'd staked out. They were in a passionate embrace as he left her. The second one, which Greta looked at more closely, was of Kurt walking toward his car and the woman watching him go. The woman's face was unobstructed, and Cassie had been able to get a good shot of her.

"Yes, that's Sarah," Greta said, defeat in her voice.

"And she is known to you?" Cassie said, even though it was obvious.

"She's my sister," Greta said softly.

Twist! All my years of poker face training came into play as I sat unaffected while Greta's world—marriage, family, sisterhood—fell apart.

I fought the urge to reach out and touch her hand. If Cassie didn't do it, it was probably the professional move. I made a mental note to ask Cassie about it later.

I had a whole lot to ask her about later.

Just as I was about to look at Cassie and see if we should do something, Greta lifted her head, her long, expertly highlighted hair falling behind her.

"That fucking asshole," she said.

I only nodded, though I wanted to offer her a high five.

Or a gun. Whichever she needed more.

No, not really. I would never condone violence of that sort.

A horrible accident, though, wouldn't be too much to ask for.

"The flash drive in the envelope includes all photos taken, as well as a spreadsheet of the times they met. And the times you mentioned that Kurt was gone for long periods of time. Many of the times, he was where he said he was. The other times he was…"

Greta lifted the top photo. "With her." It wasn't a question.

"Yes," Cassie said, her voice devoid of emotion. I noticed she didn't placate Greta with anything along the lines of "I feel your pain."

Business. It was a business.

"My statement is also in there. I'm very sorry, Greta, but Anna and I have to be at an appointment soon and will have to leave you now. Will you be all right here?"

She didn't wait for Greta to answer, just started to rise from the table, covertly jabbing me in the arm to do the same. Which I did.

"I…I…" Greta's resolve started to waver as she looked up

at Cassie and me.

"You're okay here," Cassie said again, more of a statement to let Greta know she was indeed okay.

"Yes. Yes. I'll be..." Greta looked from us back to the photos, then nodded. "I'll be fine. Thank you, Cassandra." She looked at me. "Anna, thank you."

I didn't tell her that all I'd done was sit in a car with Cassie as Greta's husband and sister did the nasty a few hundred yards away. Best she not think about that anyway.

Like that wasn't *all* she'd be thinking about.

"Of course. It was nice to meet you, Greta," I said. She let out a half sigh/half snort. Yeah, real nice to meet me—the messenger from hell.

Cassie put down two twenties—way more than would cover three drinks—and we left the Koffee Klatch. She scanned the parking lot and saw my Porsche, which she walked toward.

Following her, I unlocked the doors, and we got in.

"Why did—"

"Just drive. Get us out of the parking lot. There's a park two blocks over—why don't you head there." She pointed in the direction, and I drove, both of us quiet until I reached our destination.

Being the middle of a school day, the park was mostly deserted. Only a young mother and her toddler were playing on a nearby swing set.

After I parked, we got out and went to sit on one of the picnic tables. It reminded me of sitting with my GREET co-member Seb not too long ago.

"Okay, so you probably have a bunch of questions," Cassie said, to which I nodded. "Yeah, okay. Well, let me just explain why I do it this way, and then you can ask what you want."

I put my hands on the table, clasping them together, like a student ready for the teacher. She smiled at that.

"So, I learned this the hard way. It's better to do the bad-news reveal in a public place rather than your office, for a few reasons."

"Like when you're dumping someone. You do it in public to control the reaction," I said.

"Exactly. It doesn't always work. But people are less likely to fall apart—or get into a homicidal rage—if there's a waitress checking in to see if you need a refill."

"Makes sense," I said.

"Their pride has just been torn to shreds. Sometimes they have nothing left to lose on that front and just freak out. Sometimes they conjure up any decorum they have left to save face for those around them."

I was nodding as she continued, "The other reason to do it somewhere public, and not my office, is for what we just did. You can get up and leave. At the office, they have to leave."

"And they don't?" I asked.

She shrugged. "Sometimes. If you drop enough clues. But not even then sometimes. I learned that the hard way, too. And it's actually the men who won't leave the most."

I pondered that, but had no insight on gender discrepancies when handling gut-wrenching news.

Women were just more programmed to suck it up and get on with it? Who knew?

"So, do it somewhere public. Get there first to get a table that has easy out access. Don't order food that you'd have to wait for, or finish. When they sit down, mention you have a meeting in the area so you lay the foundation for having to leave once you've delivered the information."

"Yeah, about that," I said.

"Why the big envelope and the photos?"

"Exactly. Black-and-white, too. I mean, it was all on the flash drive, right? Couldn't it all have just been emailed to her? Of you just give her the flash drive and leave?"

Cassie watched the mother push her toddler on the swing

nearby, a look on her face I couldn't quite discern. Wistfulness? An appreciation for innocence when we'd just witnessed the antithesis?

She turned back to me. "Let me ask you this. When I pulled that out and handed it to her, did you think something along the lines of 'oh, just like on a TV show'?"

"Yes. That's exactly what I thought."

"So does everyone over the age of thirty. They grew up on that shit. That *is* what a PI is to them. Envelopes with black-and-white photos. That's what they're paying for. To just email them a zip file full of everything robs them of the payoff they thought they'd be getting."

"Even if the payoff is devastating?"

She waved a hand off the table, then let it fall back to the scarred wood. "They knew they'd be getting devastating news the minute they Googled PIs. Nobody hires a PI to prove a negative. They know. They always knew. Now they want confirmation that they aren't crazy."

"Even if that confirmation signals the end of their marriage?"

"Maybe. Maybe not. Couples stay together all the time after an infidelity is uncovered. Sometimes, the one who hires me never even brings it up. It's for them. To just know, you know?"

I nodded. "Yeah, I get it."

"So, public place. Then old-school proof, but new technology backup. Thus, the flash drive. She can do whatever she wants with it all. Then get the hell out of there."

"I noticed no comforting. Is that standard?"

Another shrug. "I don't know how other PIs handle it. Lots of times you're working directly for a divorce attorney, so you never have to deliver the news yourself. But I found out—again, the hard way—that people really don't want your comfort. Not then, anyway. Maybe later, but by then you're out of the picture. At first, they just want to lick their wounds."

"Okay, but—"

"Listen. You're not their priest, or their therapist. You're their employee. They hired you. They'll remember that later, and then they'll resent you if you patted their back and handed them tissues while they cried. A lot of this business is referrals and, sadly, repeat customers. You don't want them to remember you as someone who saw them totally lose it."

I thought about that while Cassie continued to watch the mother push her baby girl. We could hear the occasional shriek of laughter come from the child and cooing from the mother, though I couldn't make out her words. But the tone was all encouraging mother.

"Hey, I told you early on that the majority of cases for a PI are cheating spouses and insurance cheats. Either way, you're dealing with cheaters. It's not all glamorous murders, you know."

I almost laughed until I remembered poor Niall.

And Niall's mother.

"It's dirty laundry day every day in the life of a PI."

"Does that get to you?" I asked.

"Sure. Of course. More in the early years. You start to block it out. Much like you probably block out the fact that the people you play poker with are…"

"Degenerate gamblers?" I finished for her when it seemed she would not.

"Something like that."

"So, what drew you to it, then? Or why do you keep on doing it?"

Especially now that she had Vince's inheritance. I'd never asked her about it, but it must have been sizeable. For all I knew, she gave it all to charity.

"I like solving puzzles," she said. "I don't want to know that they're cheating on their wife. But I want to know *how* they think they're getting away with it. *When* and *where* they think they won't get caught. The puzzle part of it."

"Not the 'why'?"

"You'll never know the why of why someone cheats. There are the obvious reasons, but all marriages go through that. Just like you'll never know the real 'why' people kill other people."

"Revenge or money," I said.

"What?"

I shifted on the bench, the wood hard on my butt. "A conversation I had with Jack when we were first getting to know each other. That there are really only two reasons people kill. Revenge or money. Other than just random violence."

"Not love?" she asked, the same question I'd asked Jack all those months ago. We'd been at Danny's funeral. I'd said crime of passion, but Cassie meant the same thing I had. The same emotion.

That conversation with Jack seemed like a thousand years ago.

"Love is just revenge with a twist," I said, the same answer Jack had given me. All these months later, I saw that Jack had been right all along.

About that and so many other things.

Dammit.

"Hmmm. Not a bad theory," she said. Checking her watch, she started to rise from the picnic table. "It's probably safe to bring me back to my car."

As we drove past Buddy's shooting range on our way back to the Koffee Klatch, she asked if I'd been keeping up with my shooting practice.

"I haven't been in a week or so. The last time I went, Buddy had me actually, you know, target practice."

"What did you score?"

"A fifty-six on the human outline target."

"Not bad for a beginner, but you should be better than that."

"I know," I said as I pulled into the Koffee Klatch parking lot and in front of her 4Runner.

"You'll get there," she said. "It took me a long time to get really comfortable shooting."

"Have you had to use your gun a lot?"

"No. Thank God. But I'm always prepared. You just never know."

"Right." I didn't want to think about all the unknowns out there. The knowns were scary enough.

She laid a hand on my forearm that rested on the gearshift. "Anna, I was pretty skeptical when you came to see me. Thinking you were just someone who was bored. Or lost."

That was probably true, but I hadn't put it that way to myself. And bored was just the feeling I had when there wasn't a game to bet on.

So yeah, true, but weird to figure out.

"But I think you really have what it takes to do this. You just need to decide that it's what you want to do. Because as you've seen today, it's not all puzzle solving. It's dealing with the completed puzzle."

She squeezed my arm, then got out of my car and into her 4Runner.

I pulled out of her way and drove home, anxious to spend time with my family and my non-cheating (I assumed) boyfriend.

Thirty-Two

❖❖

A FEW NIGHTS LATER, WE STILL DIDN'T KNOW MUCH about Niall's murder.

At least not Monty and me. If Jack knew more, he wasn't saying. I didn't ask, thinking I'd just get, at the least, the cold shoulder, at most, the whole Iceberg.

Cassie said she was working on a case up at Mount Charleston for a few days. She asked if I wanted to go with her. It was another cheating spouse, this time a wife. (Should I be a proud feminist that women were out there cheating too?) I didn't really want to be away from Vegas while Niall's case was so hot, so I declined her offer and spent the time doing more research on things I felt I should know.

The night Monty, Carla, Raymond, and I went for food after we'd been interviewed, we'd wondered about the legalities of phone ping tracing and tapping. I wasn't sure then, so I did a bunch of research on that. Usually I'd ask Lor to do that for me, but I found I liked it.

Internet rabbit holes of legal procedures kept me busy for a couple of days.

When I emerged from my office for more than meals and sleep, it was Thursday night, and I found the gang watching an NFL game and a couple of college ones in the TV room.

When I walked in, they had four of the screens on pause.

Each had a close-up of a different player on it. All of the players were Black and all had their helmets off. Each screen was frozen on close-ups of the players' heads.

Confused, I tuned into the ongoing conversation.

"Okay. One more time. Upper left, braids. Lower left, dreads. Upper right, twists. Lower right, natural," Raymond said, pointing at the screens with the remote in his hand.

"Okay. I got it now," Jimmy said. "It's complicated, no?"

"Not if you're Black," Raymond said.

"Touché," Jimmy said.

"Don't be hating just 'cause y'all only have a couple choices."

"Thank God for that," Gus said, having stuck around after dinner to watch games. "I could *not* navigate today's hair situation."

"Boring is what you got," Raymond said. Everyone chuckled, and more than one old man's hand ran through their graying, boring hair.

"At least we have hair," Jimmy said, his pitch-black hair completely intact.

Raymond rubbed a hand over his head. "It's growing back. No time at all before I'm hunting down someone in this town that can do Black hair."

"Probably not as many choices here as in Chicago," Lorelei said, almost apologetically. I wouldn't be surprised if she didn't figure out how to do twists, braids, or dreads herself.

"But probably a lot more than Dubuque," Jack added.

"That's for sure," Raymond said. He noticed me in the doorway first. "Hey. What's up? You wanna watch, or do you need one of us?"

A rush of love for the family I'd created bubbled up my spine, and I had to take a deep breath.

I needed them all.

Lone wolf that I'd been throughout my gambling career, I needed them all.

Desperately.

"I don't want to watch, thanks." I handed a sheet of paper to Raymond. He took a look. It was the outcome of my research about how his phone *could* legally be pinged by police without anyone having to notify him or get a warrant. He let out a breath, nodded more to himself than to me, then folded the paper back up and put it in the pocket of his joggers. He touched his phone, which was on the arm of the recliner he sat in, probably thinking of whomever he'd been talking or texting with the night Johnny had been killed.

Or beyond.

His finger running along his phone reminded me of Niall playing with the grain of the poker table.

Niall, whose parents had made arrangements to have his body shipped back to Topeka after the autopsy.

"Hannah, dear, we can watch something else if you—"

"No, that's okay, Ben. I just wanted to give that to Raymond and…"

"What, dear?"

The emotional torrent continued to pour through me. I needed to let it out somehow or I'd burst. Rather than shock everyone by professing my love for them all, or my sorrow over Niall, I looked at Jack, who was carefully watching me.

"I need you for a minute," I said.

He nodded once, got out of his chair, and walked to the door. I stepped aside to let him past.

Calls of "that's all it takes, Jack? A minute?" and "get a room" from Jimmy and Raymond followed us, as did Ben's cries of shushing.

"Enjoy the boots, Jack," Lor called from the room, reaching us in the hall.

"You got me some boots?" Jack asked me, confused.

"Sort of," I said, following him down the hall and toward my bedroom.

THE NEXT MORNING, as I walked slowly with Ben through the Arizona Charlie's casino on the way to our breakfast place at the back, I stopped in my tracks as I saw a door open to an office area and Kaitlyn walked out.

She was shaking hands with an employee of Charlie's and thanking him. He was an older gentleman and was holding a piece of paper that I couldn't get a look at but was guessing, from the professional way Kaitlyn was dressed and his demeanor, was her résumé. It seemed like she was just finishing up with a job interview.

"Hi, Ben," the man with Kaitlyn said when he saw us approaching.

"Hello, Ernie, how's Evie?"

"Good, good, thanks. I'll tell her you asked after her."

"Yes. Do that. Have you ever met my friend Anna?"

Kaitlyn turned then, taking in Ben and me. Her eyes widened when she recognized me. I braced myself in case she bolted, but she stayed put.

"We've never met, no," Ernie said. "But of course I know the Black Widow."

Ben chuckled. "Anna Dawson, Ernie Volchek. Ernie was a pit boss at the Flamingo back in the day."

I stuck a hand out, and Ernie shook it. "Nice to meet you, Ernie. Any friend of Ben's…"

"You too, you too. This is, uh…" He was about to flip over Kaitlyn's résumé to get her name.

Not a real memorable job interview, then, if that indeed had been what Kaitlyn had been doing in the office area.

"Kaitlyn," I said. I stuck my hand out to her after Ernie released it. "You might not remember me, but—"

"Yes, of course I do. Nice to see you again," she said. She seemed a little flustered, but not ready to make a run for it.

I motioned to the paper in Ernie's hand, which I could see, now that I was closer, was indeed a résumé. How I wished I could read well upside down to get her information from it. That was probably another skill I should add to my list.

"Job interview?" I asked, motioning between the two of them.

"Yes," she said, a bit of dejection in her voice. Yep, it hadn't gone well.

"As a dealer?" I asked.

"Yes," Kaitlyn said.

"I've been here about five years now. Head of dealer recruitment and retention," Ernie said, more to Ben than to me.

"Is that right?" Ben said. "Well, good for you, Ernie. It's a wonder I haven't seen you here before now. We have breakfast at the Sourdough most every day."

"Is that so? I don't usually get in until a little later, casino hours, you know how it is."

Ben and I both nodded, knowing well the odd hours casino workers kept, even those in management.

"On interview days, we start early," Ernie added. The realization that she was just one of the first in a long line of applicants deflated Kaitlyn a bit more.

"I don't know if my voice carries any weight," I said to Ernie.

"In what way?" he asked.

"A recommendation, I guess. Reference, I guess you'd call it."

"For a dealer?"

"For Kaitlyn here," I said. She looked at me, her eyes going even larger than when she'd first seen me.

"Your word as a poker player means a great deal," Ernie said.

"Kaitlyn dealt a game I played in a few weeks ago," I said. I felt Ben stiffen next to me. I'd explain it to him later that it was the game he knew about—the one that ended up with Johnny

Aces shot in his car.

"Is that so?" Ernie asked. He looked at Kaitlyn again, as if noticing something about her for the first time.

Well, hell, if my involvement made her stock rise, then so be it. If it helped her land a job, I'd do it.

For Niall.

"Yes. And she was very good. Dealt really well, but kept control of the table equally well. And this was a private game, so it wasn't really her responsibility to do so."

Ernie rubbed his chin and glanced at Kaitlyn's résumé in his hand.

"After the game broke up, I stuck around for a bit, and she and I talked poker. I have to say, I was really impressed with not only her knowledge of the game we'd just played, but also her take on the players."

"Really?"

"Yes, really. So much so that it stuck with me. And you can imagine how many dealers I've played with over time."

"Right, right," Ernie said.

No need to mention to him that I'd only had two dealers in the last several months. Let Ernie think that Kaitlyn had stood out amongst hundreds.

She had, but not necessarily for her dealing skills.

I turned my attention to Kaitlyn. "Listen, if Ernie lets you get away, feel free to use me as a reference in the future. You could be dealing at any poker room on the Strip."

Arizona Charlie's was not on the Strip. It was quite a ways off and catered almost exclusively to locals. It was a good, steady clientele, and when tourism was down, it could weather the storm. But it wasn't as high-end as any place on the Strip. Which caused a bit of a chip on the shoulder for the employees.

My words ground that chip a little deeper into Ernie's shoulder. As I had intended.

"Too soon to think I'd let her get away," Ernie said to me.

Then to Kaitlyn, he added, "I do have more people to see, as I said earlier, but I will be in touch in the next couple of days."

"Thank you very much," Kaitlyn said, perking up. Ernie must not have given her as much hope when the interview had wrapped up. "And thank you, Anna," she said to me.

"Of course. Let me give you my contact info in case you need it for a future reference. Ben, I'll meet you at the Sourdough? Ernie, really nice to meet you."

Ben nodded at Kaitlyn, shook Ernie's hand, and moved his walker toward the restaurant. Ernie nodded to Kaitlyn and me, then returned to his office.

"Wow. I can't thank you enough," Kaitlyn said. "That was so—"

"Enough. Cut it. What do you know about Niall being killed?"

Thirty-Three
❖

SHE LOOKED BEHIND HER. AT FIRST, I THOUGHT IT WAS to make sure nobody heard me address her about a murder. But then I realized it was because she thought I was talking to someone else.

"I'm sorry. What?"

"Niall. Where were you when he was killed? In the motel room? Some other room at the Queen of Hearts?"

She shook her head. "I don't know what you're talking about."

Shit. Playing dumb. This was probably one of those times that Jack was talking about where fear of the law could be a powerful persuader. The flash of a badge and cuffs was a bit more menacing than me standing with my journal in my hand and having to catch up to an octogenarian with a walker.

"Listen, let's get out of the way of the office and talk somewhere quiet," she said. "You have me mixed up with someone."

She could have told me to go to hell and stormed out. I would have had no hold on her to make her talk to me.

Again, a badge would have helped out with that.

She glanced at the door to the office area where Ernie had gone through. She didn't want me to make a scene that might cost her whatever chance at a job my recommendation might have given her.

That was why she didn't leave. I had Ernie's ear, apparently, and I could easily recant my referral.

Holy shit, did I give her the recommendation to make her feel indebted to me? Was I that calculating?

Shaking away that thought, I motioned with my chin toward the book room, nearly empty at this time of morning. A few of the hardcore horse bettors were setting up their area, sipping from coffee cups and opening the racing form for the day.

She led the way, and we sat in two chairs that were used to watch games. We both sat on the edge of the large, comfy chairs so we could face each other and not the many screens, which now only showed *SportsCenter* and its ilk.

"Okay. First. Really, thank you for what you said to Ernie. I've been really hustling to find something permanent, but I don't have solid references because I've been mostly dealing private games."

"And Johnny Aces isn't exactly stellar referral material," I said. Not that I was, but at least I wasn't a loan shark enforcer.

"No, he's not. But I'd be willing to use even him, but I haven't been able to get a hold of him. The game you played in was the last time I got the call from him to deal. I don't know if I did something wrong that night or what. I've reached out to him, but only get voicemail. Do you know if I messed up that night somehow?"

It felt like someone took the jigsaw puzzle I'd been working on for weeks and threw the pieces in the air. Falling back to the table, they'd broken apart, creating a messy combination of right-side up, upside down, and disconnected edge pieces.

"You've been trying to get hold of Johnny Aces?" I asked, trying to make my voice sound normal. I wasn't sure if she was playing me or how far she'd be willing to take it. How far back?

Had Niall killed Johnny and then Kaitlyn killed Niall in the same way to throw off suspicion?

"Yes. Like I said, it's gone to voicemail."

I didn't know if the cops had Johnny's phone in their possession. I could ask Jack, see if he could corroborate Kaitlyn's story somehow. Later. I could do that later. Right now, I'd lay it on the line with Kaitlyn and see if she did the same. And if not, could I trip her up anywhere?

"Johnny's dead," I said. "He died later that night. That morning, actually."

Surprise was evident on her face, but she was not only someone who spent their nights watching poker faces, she was also a player. If she was good, she could conjure up whatever face was expected.

"Wow. That's... Wow. He seemed fine when we left, right? Drunk driver or something?"

"No. Murdered."

Her shoulders slumped and she looked down at the carpet. I studied every movement like she held cards and there was a million dollars in the pot.

She genuinely seemed to be gathering herself.

But out of shock or because she wondered how to play it?

"How? Where? At the Venetian?"

I shook my head even though she was still staring at the floor. "Later. Outside his apartment." I left it at that, not giving any more details.

I knew it wouldn't be as easy as the stuff I watched on TV, with an "Aha! I never told you he was still in his car. How could you have possibly known that if you weren't there?" But you never knew. A PI wannabe could dream.

"Jesus," she whispered. "I figured he was into some sketchy stuff, but murdered?" She looked up then, sat back in the deep chair, and placed her hands in her lap. "This town can eat you up. It's a wonder any of us stay."

She was right. But the town was also sunny and bright, and

in my neck of the woods, the biggest beef was someone breaking HOA rules by putting up colored lights at Christmastime.

That was why I loved Vegas. Seedy underbelly one block. Lovely suburbia two blocks over.

I stayed quiet, waiting to see what tack she chose.

She processed the news about Johnny, but I wondered if she was thinking about her own time in Vegas. And her future.

Finally she turned to me. "So, wait. Who's Niall?"

If I'd started mentally rearranging my puzzle pieces after the upheaval, I stopped. Because I would have bet my entire chip stack that Kaitlyn was not bluffing.

"Niall Hendricks. Your partner."

"Partner of what?"

Well, of that I wasn't really sure. They'd been in separate rooms at the Moonlight Motel. And I wasn't sure how they lined up together with Niall's debts and Kaitlyn dealing for Johnny. "Partner in crime" seemed a bit dramatic to throw out.

"You tell me," I said, again trying to not lead her, but also— yeah, okay—lead her.

"I don't know any Niall Hendricks. No Niall, period."

"Come on, Kaitlyn. I know you two were together in some way."

"I honestly don't know him. I mean, I come into contact with poker players all the time. Could this Niall guy have been one of them? Do you have a picture of him?"

I did have a picture of Niall on my phone, one that Monty had sent me that night weeks ago when I helped get Niall to his parents. So I'd know exactly which twitchy, deadbeat gambler to roofie. There was probably more than one at any fleabag place in Vegas.

After calling up the photo, I held my phone out to Kaitlyn, who sat up and held the other side of my phone. "He looks vaguely familiar. So yeah, he probably played on one of my tables. But do you know how many players I see in a week? I never know any of their names, let alone remember them."

"You remembered me," I pointed out.

"I always remember the good tippers," she said. Yeah, that made sense. I always remembered the good players. "Wait. You said he was dead too? Killed with Johnny? Then I wouldn't have seen this Niall guy lately, right?"

Play along with the playing dumb? Try to trip her up? Or assume she's telling the truth and lay my cards on the table?

I thought of the fact that she was at Charlie's for a job interview. That she'd been trying to get a casino job dealing for a while. She didn't exactly seem like she was trying to lie low until Niall's killer was caught.

Unless she was the killer and trying to throw the scent off with the normalcy of job hunting?

It was like the puzzle pieces were lying half off my table, and the slightest movement of my muddled brain would push them onto not only the floor, but into the abyss.

I was overthinking my overthinking. Best to just play it straight.

"Niall Hendricks was killed a week ago, in the same way Johnny was. He owed money to Johnny. Well, Johnny's employer."

"Carla?"

"Yes. You know Carla?"

Which would make sense, but I swore Carla had said she didn't know Kaitlyn, that she'd left the hiring of dealers up to Johnny, to give him more responsibility.

"No. We never met. Johnny mentioned her a couple of times. I knew that she was the owner, I guess you'd call it, of the games he hired me for."

"Which were how many?"

"Just two. One about three nights before the game you played in. Then the one you were at."

"Okay. Well, Johnny was killed, and then later Niall."

"And why do you think I'm involved with this Niall?"

"The Moonlight Motel," I said.

"What about it?"

"You both were there at the same time."

"That's it?"

When she said it like that, it did seem kind of random. I didn't bother going into the thesis that there are no coincidences when dealing with suspects of a crime.

But was she ever really a suspect? She'd been at the game where Johnny had been the night he'd been killed, but so had all the other players and Monty, Raymond, Carla, and I.

She'd also been at the Moonlight Motel when Niall had been. Only a few doors down.

Were the PI gods fucking with me and actually throwing a true coincidence in the mix?

"Your room was a few down from his," I added, like that confirmed anything.

"Oh. *That's* why he looks familiar. He wasn't a player I dealt; he was at the Moonlight. Yeah, now I remember. I didn't see him a lot, but every now and then in the parking lot, or going in or out of his room. Stuff like that."

"How long did you stay at the Moonlight?" I asked.

"I was there a month."

Did I just catch her in a lie? I knew the date when Cassie and I saw her and Niall at the Moonlight. The day Cassie got into her room to look around on the earring ruse. That night I'd given the Moonlight up to Jack, and the next day, Botz and Faxon had gone to question Niall. They'd picked him up and brought him in, but there was no one in Kaitlyn's room.

Empty. Vacated.

"A month? What date to what date?"

She told me. "I'd prepaid for the month. I was doing better, getting more work. And then your tip put me over to getting a better place, but I'd already paid, so I stayed until that morning, when I moved into an actual apartment." She shuddered slightly, and I thought about all the shitty motels—where you could pay for a month or an hour—she'd stayed in.

"So, we were there the day before you moved out. That's when we saw Niall, and you. Both there. Both people who were involved with Johnny."

"I wouldn't say I was *involved* with Johnny. I worked for him a couple of times. And as I said, I never met Niall. Just nodded to him as we passed."

I digested that, watching her for any tell. Nothing.

"Wait. Who's 'we'?"

"What?" I said.

"You said 'we' were at the Moonlight. Who's we?"

"My partner. My boss, actually. She's a PI. You met her that day. She came to your room."

"Came to my room?"

I nodded, not wanting to give up Cassie's earring method, but I wanted to keep pushing to see if Kaitlyn tripped up. "Yes. She's a private investigator, and we wanted to see if you had any signs in your room of your connection to Niall."

"Which didn't exist because there is no connection to him."

I nodded but didn't verbally agree with her. Too soon for that.

"I thought you'd remember me," I said, to which she nodded. "So she knocked on your door. Said she'd lost her earring? Came in to look for it?"

Kaitlyn looked blank. No biting of her lip. No change in breathing. Then the blank look changed to furrowed brow.

"That never happened," she said.

"What?"

"I think I'd remember that."

Well, yes, that was the point of using a distinctive earring. To make it more plausible, yes, but it also made it memorable.

Or should have.

I shook my head and waved a hand in a rewind motion. "She knocked. Said she'd lost an earring. You let her in. She found the earring, even though she hadn't really lost it. It was all to get a look around your room."

Now there was skepticism on Kaitlyn's face. "And what did my room look like?"

She didn't believe me.

Which meant she didn't believe Cassie, since I was repeating verbatim what Cassie had told me.

I thought back to the conversation Cassie and I had at the restaurant in the Red Rock. Was I so enamored with that BLT that I couldn't remember—

"Wait. I have it here," I said, pulling out my journal that I'd tucked into the crack of the chair next to me.

The journal was a gift from Jack, given to me as I began my journey of recovery from compulsive gambling. It was large and had a soft leather cover.

There were no rules for journals, of course, but I guessed most weren't used for notes about ongoing murder investigations.

I fumbled through the pages, suddenly feeling like I was the one being questioned.

"Um. She said there was no sign of Niall anywhere. No men's clothing. That everything was very neat. No disarray that could mean you were deep into..." I shrugged, not finishing the sentence.

"Well, whatever you're thinking, I wasn't into it. Yeah, money was tight, that's why I was in that shithole, but I was working enough to survive while I tried to— Oh! Wait! That was the day before I moved. My room was anything *but* neat and orderly."

"What?" I asked. I looked from her back to my journal where I'd jotted down notes after I met with Cassie. I was positive she'd said Kaitlyn's room looked ordinary.

"I mean, I'm kind of a slob generally. But that day in

particular, I had stuff everywhere while I tried to pack up. Some was coming with me. Some I was trashing. I had meal containers from about a week in there. It was a total shitshow."

I glanced again at my journal, then shut it. I knew there was no "shitshow" note in it.

"I think you have some things mixed up," she said softly. It wasn't because she was trying not to piss off her reference. It was gentle, almost comforting. "I'm happy to help if I can. But I never met Niall. Don't know anything about Johnny being killed. And a woman never came to my room looking for an earring."

I sat back in my chair, my journal slipping out of my fingers, down to wedge between my hip and the upholstery.

What the hell was going on?

"Let's do this. Open a new contact and give me your phone."

Wordlessly, I did as she asked, handing her my phone once I'd unlocked it and opened contacts.

She spoke as she typed. "I'm giving you all my info. Phone, apartment. You can go back and ask Ernie to check it against my résumé if you want." She looked up from the phone and at me. "Though I kind of wish you wouldn't do that. It might set off some red flags for him, and I'd really like this job."

"I won't," I said.

She nodded and continued typing. "By the way, my last name is Randall."

Because I had gone so long without asking or registering Niall's last name, I made a point to say Kaitlyn's out loud. "Randall. Kaitlyn Randall," I said.

A bob of her chin and she handed me back my phone. "I'm not going anywhere, so if I can help clear anything up for you, please reach out."

"Okay. Thanks." She got up to leave, but my legs were lead and I stayed in my chair. Then it hit me. How to trip her up!

"Wait!" I said. She turned and came back the few feet to

me. "I saw you again. After the day at the Moonlight. At The Shops at Crystals. The Aria."

It came to her right away, and a look of embarrassment crossed her face. It was so honest and clear that it made me wonder if she would be capable of hiding all the other stuff I thought she might be.

"Yes. I saw you that day," she said.

"You ditched me," I said.

"Yeah, I did. I was hoping you hadn't seen me."

"I did. I noticed your shoes under the dressing room door."

We both looked down at her feet, which today were clad in professional-looking pumps to go along with her interview pantsuit. No red Chucks today.

"I ditched you because I didn't want you to see me shopping at Dolce & Gabbana."

"Why not?"

More embarrassment. "Because I didn't want you to think I was blowing your huge tip on a pair of shoes or something."

"Oh," I said, my thoughts of Kaitlyn incriminating herself sliding away. "That makes sense, I guess."

"Stupid, I know. I mean, you don't give a shit how I spend that money. After we'd had that good talk, though... I don't know. I just didn't want you to think badly of me."

"I was shopping there too," I pointed out, knowing it wasn't at all the same thing.

Her one raised brow confirmed she didn't think so either.

"And, not that it matters, but I didn't buy anything there that day anyway. Like I said, I put your tip toward a first/last deposit on an apartment. I just like looking and occasionally trying some things on, you know?"

Not being a shopper, I didn't, not really. But I nodded anyway.

"Did you buy anything?" she said. "When I saw you, you had on these boots—"

"I got those," I said, hoping my face wasn't heating at the thought of what Jack had done to me while I'd worn those same boots the night before.

"Good purchase," she said.

"You have no idea."

"Okay. Thanks again for speaking to Ernie." She pointed at my phone, which I still held. "Feel free to reach out. I have nothing to hide."

She left, and I sat for a few more minutes until my stomach growled. As I walked the length of the casino to the Sourdough Café, the puzzle pieces slid along the table in my mind, piling on top of each other. Slowly, they started to slide to different corners. The sky pieces at the top. Edges lining up to be connected. Slowly the picture was coming into focus. Not quite yet, but the pieces were making better sense.

As I got to the entrance of the Sourdough, I saw Raymond entering the casino from the back doors.

Ben and I always parked in the front parking lot as we walked by the book room every morning to pick up the day's odds sheet. The doors in the back of the building, and the smaller parking lot there, were much closer to the Sourdough, but the added exercise was better for Ben. And the odds sheets were important, of course.

I was surprised to see Raymond entering the casino, but gave a small wave to get his attention. He waved back and started heading toward me.

The surprise of Raymond joining us was nothing compared to the jolt I felt when I looked into the restaurant, and saw Frank Botz and Peter Faxon standing behind Ben, Jimmy, and Gus, who sat at our regular table.

Botz and Faxon both had their hands on their hips and were staring directly at me.

I could even see the cuffs that dangled from Faxon's belt.

Were they meant for me?

Thirty-Four

❖❖

YEP, THEY WERE HERE FOR ME. THAT WAS CLEAR WHEN Faxon saw me and a predatory grin crossed his face, which he tried to erase before I saw it. Too late.

That grin did not bode well for me.

Whatever they thought they had—on me or on one of my posse—Ben and the boys didn't need to get involved. I motioned with my chin for Faxon and Botz to leave the Sourdough and come out to the casino floor where I was.

There was disappointment on Faxon's face, but Botz had seen my signal and did a nod. He said something to the boys, and he and Faxon headed to the café entrance. I turned so my back was toward Raymond and did a "stay put" motion with my hand so that Botz and Faxon couldn't see.

A quick peek behind me as the two cops navigated the crowd at the cash register assured me that Raymond was sitting at one of the banks of slot machines, his hoodie pulled up, face down, like the many other slots players intent on only their machine. But he was watching me.

I did the stay-put hand motion again and saw the slightest nod of understanding from under his hoodie.

"What's going on?" I said as the men approached me. "Did you make an arrest on Niall and Johnny?"

It was a dumb question. They wouldn't seek me out just to

tell me that. They'd feel absolutely no obligation to keep me in the loop that way.

"Maybe," Faxon said.

"Maybe you made an arrest?" I asked.

"Let's see how the morning goes," Faxon said, unable to hide his smug grin again.

"Anna, we'd like you to come back to the station again. Some new things have come to light we'd like to talk to you about," Botz said.

"So talk to me about them here," I said. "I came here with Ben. He'll be waiting for me."

"I'm sure one of those other cronies can bring him home. In fact, he should probably get used to life without you as his caretaker," Faxon said, earning a look of disgust from Botz.

I ignored him and turned my attention to Botz. "What's going on?"

"Let's go to the station and talk about it, Anna."

There was a gravity in his voice that made me very nervous. I didn't know what they had—or thought they had—but I knew it wasn't good for me.

If it was Monty, Carla, or Raymond that they suspected, they'd leave me out of it, not wanting to muddy waters.

No, it was obvious they were coming here for me. And they weren't going to leave without me.

"I don't have to go with you, you know."

"That's why we're asking you *politely*," Botz said, pointedly looking at his partner.

His partner. Who was not Jack.

Jack.

"How'd you find me here?" I asked, not wanting to hear the answer.

"Jack Schiller," Faxon quickly told me.

Wow. This went beyond Icebergs. This was leaving me to float on one out to sea.

"Not like that," Botz said, once again shooting a look at Faxon. "He told me once about you and your boys having breakfast here every morning. I thought it was kind of cute. Guess it stuck with me."

Oh. At least Jack was off the hook. Not that I ever really doubted him.

"Does he know you're here?" I asked.

"Why does that matter? He can't step in on this," Faxon said.

"He wouldn't anyway. Not his style. Just wondering if he's aware."

A small shake of the head from Botz. "We haven't seen Jack since we obtained the new information we'd like to speak to you about."

"Like I said, talk to me about it here. I'll even buy you breakfast afterward."

Botz chuckled. Faxon looked ever more pissed off.

The good cop/bad cop moniker could be a good description for the two of them, but not because they played a game of fear building and confidence building with someone.

No. One was simply a good cop. And one was not.

"Tempting as a good breakfast sounds, and smells, this is a conversation best had more privately," Botz said.

"I believe you'd have to have a warrant to *make* me come with you, Frank."

Already my rabbit hole of research was coming in handy.

"Well, a warrant's going to be pretty easy to get now," Faxon said. You could tell he was bursting to tell me what ills awaited me. Like a middle schooler badly keeping a secret about somebody *liking* liking someone.

"Okay, Faxon. You might as well spill it. You're dying to. Let me know what you think it is that I need to explain to you. Then I'll go to the station with you."

"Anna, you should probably—" Botz started.

"Do you still claim that you don't own a gun?" Faxon blurted out.

"Yes," I replied. "I told you I didn't."

"Never had one in your possession?"

"I explained to you both about the one time I did. That was months ago," I said. I'd told them about Saul's gun the first time they questioned me. The one used to kill Danny. But that gun was long gone, thank God.

"That wasn't the right one, anyway," Faxon said.

"Oh, so you've always known what gun you're looking for? Ballistics back and all that?"

I wasn't sure if we were talking about Johnny's or Niall's killing. I knew they'd know what caliber gun they were looking for, but there was so much more that could be determined with ballistics.

"Better. We have recovered the murder weapon," Faxon said.

"For which murder? Johnny or Niall?" I asked Botz.

He wasn't happy that Faxon had said as much as he said, but he answered me. "Both of them."

"So, that should be helpful," I said.

"Very much so," Faxon said. "Especially because there is a clear set of prints still on it."

I knew it couldn't be me, but the glee in Faxon's voice had a shiver running down my spine. "And?" I asked.

"Anna, your prints are all over the gun used to kill both Johnny Kingston and Niall Hendricks," Botz said, gentleness in his voice. Like you'd talk to a mental patient.

"So, are prints capable of being planted on an object?"

"Hard to do on a surface like that," Botz said.

"I'll go with you. We'll get it straightened out."

"Great, thanks," Botz said, surprised. Even Faxon was taken aback.

"It's fine, really. Because, well, I know that it's not possible for my prints to be on that gun the normal way. I haven't even held a—"

"What?" Botz said when I stopped.

I shook my head, thinking quickly.

Shit. How had I not seen it?

"Nothing. I mean, I can't figure it out." Oh, I had figured it out. Now I had to figure out how to get the hell away from these two. "Let me go tell Ben to ride home with Jimmy," I said.

"I'll do that," Botz said. I nodded, and he turned back into the restaurant. "I also need to use the restroom real quickly before we go."

"Oh, hell no," Faxon said.

"You want a mess in your car?" I said. I handed my phone to him, dug my keys out of my pocket, and put them in his palm on top of my phone. "I'm parked out front. There's my keys and phone. I'm just going in there for a second. I'd have to go right by you to get back to the parking lot."

I hitched a thumb over my shoulder, pointing to the restrooms that were right by the back entrance doors. I started to hand him my journal to hold, but he shook his head. It held no flight risk like a phone or car keys would.

"Hurry up," he said.

I walked toward the restrooms. When I turned the corner into the entryway of the ladies' room, I could see Raymond, who was nearly right in front of me at the first bank of slots. Faxon couldn't see me, the doorway blocking his view.

I did a steering-wheel pantomime for Raymond and pointed to the back door. He nodded, pulled his hoodie up more, and exited the casino. Moments later, he pulled right up to the door, and I took a quick peek around the corner of the restroom doorway. Faxon was looking at his phone.

No doubt he'd see me as I exited the restroom, but the doors were only about ten yards away. I thought I could make it.

I dashed out of the restroom entrance and toward the doors.

They were closing behind me when I heard, "Hey!" from behind me.

I kept going. Outside, Faxon's voice was muffled, but I could still hear him yelling after me, his language getting more colorful as I hopped into Raymond's car.

"Drive!" I said, and grabbed my seatbelt as Raymond peeled out of the parking lot. We were almost to the Decatur Street exit by the time Faxon was in the parking lot. I watched from the rearview as he pulled out his gun.

He wouldn't really shoot at me, would he?

I'd never know, because Botz came out of the casino then and said something to Faxon that made him drop the arm that held his gun.

By that time, we were on Decatur and speeding away from Arizona Charlie's.

"Thanks so much. What are you doing here, anyway?" I asked him.

"My class was canceled. I didn't want to go all the way home because I have another class in a couple of hours. Ben told me I was always welcome to join you guys. So I figured why not kill time with breakfast."

"Thank God your class was canceled."

"Are we seriously running from the cops?" Raymond said.

"Looks that way."

"Are you fucking nuts?"

I sighed. "Looks that way."

"Where am I going, anyway? You can't go home. Shit, can we ever go home?"

"Relax, Clyde. I'm just buying a little time to check something out. I'm not really running away from them."

"Well, *Bonnie*, they probably don't see it that way."

"Head toward Rainbow and give me your phone," I said. He got into the right lane, to make a turn at the next light, then nodded to his phone that sat in the cupholder.

I held it out to him, and he unlocked it with his index finger.

I held very few phone numbers in my actual memory, but the one I wanted now was one of them. I dialed the number and prayed he'd pick up a call from what would most likely be an unknown number to him.

"Raymond?" Jack said when he answered. "Are you okay? Is *Anna* okay?"

Later, I would feel warm thinking about the concern in his voice. And also wonder when he and Raymond had exchanged phone numbers, since Jack's contact came up after I typed in the number.

But right now, I said, "Jack. It's me. I need you to do me a favor. Botz thinks I ditched him." A snort from Raymond. "Which technically I did, but I have a good reason. And I was only buying time."

"Anna, what the fuck?"

"Jack, listen. Call Botz. Tell him I'm happy to come in. He can even come and get me. I'm just checking out a hunch and then I'll come with him."

"Anna, this is not how questioning works."

"I know. Unusual circumstances," I said.

I heard a deep sigh on the other end. "They always are with you."

"Ha. Ha. Call Botz. Tell him I'm no threat. No weapons needed this time."

"Weapons? What the actual fuck, Johanna?"

Usually I loved it when he called me by my full name. Right now? Not so much.

"It was Faxon. I'll tell you about it later. Turn right here."

"Are you with Raymond?"

"Yes, but he was unknowingly giving me a ride. Not involved at all."

Simultaneous snorts from both men at that.

"In a couple of minutes, I'm going to text you an address. When you call Frank, tell him it's coming. Give me a fifteen-minute buffer, then send him the address. That's where I'll be. Unarmed and ready to go in with them. And hopefully with the real killer."

"*Un*armed? When were you *armed*?" Jack said, his voice right on the edge. I knew how he felt.

"I wasn't. I mean, I was, but not when— Just call Frank, then text him the address in fifteen minutes."

"Send me the address now," he said.

"I can't; I don't know it. I only know the building when I see it. We'll have to be at it for me to know for sure."

"Anna, this is so messed up."

"I know, but I think I have it all figured out."

"What 'all'?"

"All of it. Who killed Johnny. Who killed Niall. Everything."

"What?"

Before I could answer, the building I was interested in came into view. "There. That one," I said to Raymond, pointing. "Pull into the lot. Park in front. I want Botz to see we're not hiding."

"Anna, where the hell are you?"

"I've got to go, Jack. Call Frank. I'll text you the address right now."

He was yelling more things when I disconnected. Then I went to Messages and sent him the address for the building where we now sat. Then I turned the phone off.

"Where are we?" Raymond asked.

"No time. Stay here," I said.

"Is someone in there? Someone involved in all this?" he asked. He grabbed my arm as I started to reach for the door handle.

"I don't know. I hope so. But probably not."

"I'm not staying here while you go in there not knowing what you'll find."

"The less you're involved, the better," I said.

"You just used me as your escape method. *Now* you don't want to involve me? Fuck that."

He let go of my arm and was quickly out of his side. I scrambled out and handed him his phone as we walked to the front doors of the office building.

I was quiet in the elevator ride up. Raymond seemed to sense that I wasn't ready for any more questions, and stayed silent.

When we arrived at the third floor, we left the elevator and I led the way, turning right down a long hallway.

I knew what I expected to see. It was why it was so urgent to get here right away, to see if maybe I was in time.

But no, I was too late.

I pulled on the outer door, assuming it would be locked. It opened with ease.

Why not? Nothing inside anyway.

No Brenda in the reception area.

No reception area.

Cassie's offices were completely empty. No furniture. No lush greenery. No electronics. Nothing on the walls.

We walked through the deserted reception area into Cassie's office. It was also an empty room.

The only sign of how quickly things had been cleared out was that one of the yellow throw pillows from her couch was on the floor near the door. Probably fell from the couch when it was being moved and nobody went back for it. Or didn't have time to go back.

There was one other thing in the room that caught my eye. It was on the floor where Cassie's desk had been.

Walking nearer, I knew what it was before I bent over to pick it up.

One of the Montblanc pens that had been in a crystal holder on her desk. Raymond joined me where I stood, looking around as if the empty surroundings would offer him some kind of clue.

They wouldn't. There were no clues here.

I handed him the pen. "Here. Now you can start a collection of them."

"What's going on? What is this place? What *was* this place?"

"When you and Ben were watching all those old movies, did you ever see *The Sting*?"

"I don't know. Why?"

I turned back to the empty office and braced for Faxon and Botz's arrival.

"Because I just got stung."

Thirty-Five

❖

"Okay, the cops are going to come through that door thinking I'm a fugitive, so you might want to stand away from me," I said to Raymond, already seeing the cop cars, sirens blaring, coming into the parking lot. Botz and Faxon wouldn't be in one of the cruisers, but they were part of the caravan in an unmarked Ford.

"I heard you on the phone with Jack. You told them where to find you, and that you'd go with them peacefully once they got here."

"Yes, and obviously he got that message to Botz. Did Frank relay it to every cop that's coming up here? I don't know. So better if you stand as far from me as you can."

"Are you fucking nuts? I'm an unarmed Black man. I'm standing *as close to you* as I can. If they want to take me out, they've got to take out the pretty white lady, too."

I couldn't fault his logic. It didn't make me feel any better, though.

I nodded, and we moved to the center of the empty office, widened our legs, and put our hands up, so there would be no misunderstanding with the officers about to join us.

Thankfully, Botz and Faxon were the first ones through the door, no guns drawn. When they saw us, Botz waved in one of the officers, who cuffed me, then another officer came in to do the same to Raymond.

"He's not involved in this, Frank," I said. "He just drove me here. He doesn't even know what this place is."

"This place doesn't look like anything," Faxon said, nodding with his chin for the officer to continue to cuff Raymond.

"What are you charging him with?" I said to Faxon. "You have to charge him to bring him in against his will."

"Aiding and abetting a fugitive," Faxon said. Smug SOB.

"In order for me to be a fugitive, I had to have been wanted for a crime. You specifically told me at the Sourdough that I was just being brought in for questioning. I chose not to do that and left the premises."

"You ran out the fucking back door!" Faxon sputtered.

I ignored Faxon and looked at Botz. "He has nothing to do with this. But if you cuff him and put him through the system, I will stonewall with everything I've got. If you let him go, he'll come with us voluntarily and answer any questions about him driving me here—which, again, is all he did. And I'll let you know why I needed to come here and how this whole thing plays out."

I looked at Faxon as I continued, "Spoiler alert: I'm not the killer."

Botz motioned for the officer to free Raymond, which he did, much to Faxon's chagrin. The cuffs stayed on me, though.

They separated us for the ride to the station, ostensibly so we couldn't get our stories straight. Not that we needed to. I'd told the truth: Raymond didn't know what was going on.

I did, with more and more pieces clicking into place as we drove to the Metro station. I was pretty sure I could clear myself fairly easily, but not until I knew what all had been used to frame me.

Cassie was good. There would be more than the murder weapon with my prints on it.

Marvin was already at the station when we arrived. Jack

must have called him. Bless him.

Once he saw I was okay and that Marvin was with me, Jack made himself scarce. I assumed it was to protect me from any accusation of preferential treatment.

He might have figured out from the address I'd given him that Cassie was involved. Maybe not. I wasn't sure I'd ever told him about going to her office originally. But until I got a chance to talk to him privately, he'd have no way of knowing how deep her involvement went.

Involvement? Shit, more like she was the Master Planner.

Because it all led back to Cassie. From the beginning with Johnny. Before that, even.

My God, the patience she must have had to pull this off.

She'd said patience was a trait all good PIs shared. I'd thought she meant because of all the tedious stakeout type of assignments.

But it helped when pulling off a long-game con, too.

"I need a moment alone with my client before you question her," Marvin told Botz. "Are you booking her now?"

"No, we'll wait on that until after she talks with us," Botz said. Faxon looked at his partner and sighed. He wanted me doing mug shots pronto. But Botz knew the best way to get me to talk would be to leave the specter of booking me hanging above my head. Obviously they already had my prints on file if they matched the gun that had killed Johnny and Niall. I wasn't sure how they'd gotten them, but I wasn't surprised they had them.

I was scared shitless of going "into the system." Not so much because of these murders, which I still thought I could credibly clear up. No, I didn't want to be in the system in case it in some way led back to JoJo's activities.

Which would then lead to Raymond and why he was living with a woman accused of point shaving.

"Okay. We'll be back in ten minutes. You need anything,

Anna? Coffee? Water?" Botz asked.

"Coffee," I said. I never had gotten into the Sourdough between first Kaitlyn and then the cops. God, it was only nine in the morning.

Botz nodded, and he and Faxon left the small interrogation room. Marvin walked up to the camera in the corner of the room, examining it. I didn't know what he was looking for, but he must have been satisfied, because when he turned back to me, he said, "Okay, you can talk freely now. You told them you could clear this up? Is that true?"

I moved to the table and sat down on one side, Marvin moving to sit beside me. "Yes, but here's the thing."

"Ah yes, there's always a thing," Marvin said under his breath as he unpacked a legal pad, a pen, and a small voice recorder from his briefcase before setting it beside the leg of the table.

"You might not want to get too comfortable yet—you might not be my attorney in a few minutes," I said. He stopped cold and looked at me. "Not because I wouldn't want it. But because you might have to recuse yourself."

He straightened and turned toward me. "Go on," he said.

"I will be explaining to the detectives that Cassandra Hall is the woman they're really after. I know you are affiliated with her. Through Vince's will. If she's also your client, then—"

"Ms. Hall is most definitely *not* my client," Marvin said. The tone made me think that Marvin might actually be pleased that Cassandra was about to be thrown to the wolves. Not that she didn't deserve it.

"Okay. So no conflict of any kind? Even with the will stuff?" I asked.

"No conflict. I dealt with Ms. Hall on behalf of Vince Santini only. *He* was my client. Not her." He let out a sigh.

"Your dealings with her? Not great?"

He took a deep breath. It seemed like he was weighing how much to tell me. How much he *could* tell me. Then he did a "what the hell" look and said, "Not great, no. When an estate is settled, there are always delays. Even in the best of circumstances. It's not a situation where a will is read and you walk out with a check. There are appraisals, sales, many things to settle. All of this takes time."

"And Cassandra was not happy about the time it took?"

"To say the least," Marvin said.

That could explain the old 4Runner. It could explain a lot of things.

Or nothing.

"When exactly was the estate settled?" I asked. But I knew. And I also knew why Cassandra didn't push when I'd said no to joining her for the job at Mount Charleston.

There was no job at Mount Charleston.

"Monday," Marvin said, confirming my thoughts. "The bulk was transferred to her account on Monday."

"Was that an offshore or foreign account, do you know?"

He shook his head then turned to his tablet and wrote something down. "I don't, no. But I can have my assistant look into it. If you think it's important."

"I think it will be, yes," I said. "It will probably help establish that she planned this whole thing."

He nodded, wrote a few more things, and then turned back to me. "And you're prepared to make the accusation against her here, now? That is how you want to handle this?"

"Yes," I said.

"Okay. Here's my advice: let them question you first. Don't volunteer anything right away. Let's find out what they have on you. They won't give it all away, hold some back to see what you trip on, but it might give away just how deeply she pulled you in."

"Probably pretty deep," I said. "She was very good."

"She's a very determined woman," he said, writing down a few more things. "Okay, ready?" I nodded. "I'll let the detectives know." He got up from the table and made his way to the door, opening it and speaking to the uniformed officer standing in front.

Botz and Faxon were in the room minutes later, informing me of my rights and that I was being recorded, all of which I agreed to.

"Okay, let's begin," Botz said.

I held my hands up, palms out, giving the universal sign that I had nothing to hide.

"Shuffle up and deal," I said softly as the light on the camera turned red.

Thirty-Six

❖❖

IT WAS INDEED A COLT 1911 THAT THE COPS HAD FOUND with my prints on it, as I knew it would be.

They'd found it in an air vent in a motel room. Among other things in the room were a coffee cup with my prints on it and presumably my DNA, and a blond wig with hair strands in it.

I declined letting them take a DNA swab. Marvin said I could at this point if I still wasn't being charged. Faxon said it made me look more guilty.

I still refused. I thought that might buy me some time to see what else they might have, if anything.

In fact, I was in there for hours before they finally told me about the type of gun and motel room.

Faxon probably thought he could trip me up. Botz let him do most of the talking, sitting in his chair, watching me.

I wondered if Jack had ever told Botz about my tell— whatever it was.

"I was never in that motel room," I said. "Surely you can see this is a frame job. It's way too pat."

"Hiding a gun in an air-conditioning vent isn't pat," Faxon said.

"You found it, didn't you?" I said. "How'd you even know about the motel room? Let me guess, anonymous tip? Come on, guys. You're smarter than this."

"No, we're—" Faxon cut himself off. I didn't even smile at his almost faux pas. I was walking a tightrope here and didn't need to push his fragile ego past the brink.

Botz leaned forward. "So, who would want to frame you, Anna? Who did this to you?"

I turned to Marvin, who nodded. Showtime.

So I told them everything as it pertained to Cassandra. How she blamed me for Vince's death. I wasn't sure when she'd hatched her plan. Had she been following me for a while and took her shot (ha!) when she saw me go into Buddy's? Or had that really been a chance meeting and it all started then and there?

Unless Cassandra left some clues behind, at her home or car or wherever, I'd probably never know for sure. And it was doubtful that she'd left anything behind. She'd covered her tracks pretty well.

Vince. It all came back to me being responsible for Vince Santini falling to his death from his high-rise apartment.

Revenge or money.

This had both.

The gun itself was easy enough to clear up once they told me about it. They told me the serial number had been defaced, but I knew where it had come from, and why my prints were all over it.

I told them of my trips to Buddy's shooting range. They both wrote down that information, and Faxon stepped out at that point to talk to someone. I assumed they'd be hauling Buddy in to question him about chain of custody on his firearms.

Buddy. That one kind of hurt. Not that he was beholden to me or anything. Obviously he was close with Cassie, but still, it hurt.

Or maybe she'd stolen the gun from his place, and he wasn't in on it at all? Seemed unlikely, but I could hope.

"Frank, I was in her car with her, staking out one of her cheating spouse clients. She could have easily gotten my hair from her car to put a strand in the wig you found. Same with the coffee cup. It was one I probably used that day." All true.

And then I remembered the JoJo garb that was still in the trunk of my car from the night I'd helped smuggle Niall to his parents. And the day we traded cars when I followed Niall and Cassie questioned (or didn't) Kaitlyn. Cassie must have taken the wig from the JoJo duffel and put it with the gun. But how to explain why I'd have a wig in the trunk of my car? I let it slide, hoping that at this very moment some cop wasn't at my house carrying out a search warrant and searching through my closet or my car.

I could just imagine how much that would scare Ben.

"She was taking a case in Mount Charleston this past Monday. She invited me to come with her, but I didn't want to leave while…"

"While you were the prime suspect in two homicides?"

"Yeah, I guess. Anyway, she's been out of town since Monday. I'm guessing she's been gone since then, and then called in the tip about the gun in the motel room from wherever she was."

"We'll be getting that information soon. Where the call came from originally."

"It's her, Frank. I'm sure of it." He kept jotting down notes. "Let me lay my cards on the table here," I said, leaning forward. "If it *had* been me, you would never have found a motel room with a bunch of evidence. I would have tossed the gun after killing Johnny and used a different one on Niall, then tossed it too."

"Think about how to pull off a murder a lot, do ya?" Faxon said.

I shrugged. "No. But things like that seem pretty How Not to Get Caught 101, you know? Hanging on to a murder weapon? Not smart."

"What if you had more murders planned?" Faxon said.

"You don't need to answer that," Marvin said.

"No, it's okay, I'll answer that," I said. "If I was going to murder more, I would get another gun. Surely they're easy enough to get in this town. In this *state*."

Sadly, that was true.

"So, why the target practice, Anna? Why start that so recently?" Botz asked. "And why were you in her car with her while she was working a case?"

"I can explain that. But I think getting my journal from Raymond's car will be helpful with that."

Faxon jumped from his chair and went to the door, where a uniformed officer was standing. He whispered something to the officer while I frantically tried to remember how else I could prove my time spent with Cassie was what I said it was. My phone was full of calls and texts to and from her. I assumed Faxon still had my phone. They wouldn't be able to do anything with it unless I unlocked it, which I wouldn't do at this point. Make them get a warrant for that. They could trace calls made and the duration of calls without having my actual phone anyway.

Faxon finished with the officer and sat back down at the table with us. I glanced at the mirrored wall, wondering if Jack was allowed to watch.

Probably not. With the shit this close to the fan, they'd keep him as far away as possible.

Poor Jack. Two homicides. He was finally back at work, and benched again because of me.

"Okay, here's the deal with the gun. I've been *considering*, or at least looking into, *possibly* becoming a private investigator."

I expected them both to laugh, but neither one did. Botz looked curious. Faxon looked horrified.

Both looks were satisfying in their own way.

"So, I talked to Jack about it. You can ask him. And he suggested I needed to learn to shoot a gun. And learn self-defense. So I've been working on that."

"You're going to be a PI?" Faxon said. "Jesus Christ, that's all this town needs."

Not a compliment, but I didn't acknowledge him, just continued telling my tale directly to Botz.

"I hadn't gotten to the self-defense classes yet, but there's a stub in my journal for one that's being offered."

It was then that there was a knock on the door and the officer entered, holding my journal, which he handed to Faxon before closing the door on his way out.

So, either Raymond was still here and gave him the keys to his car, which had to be at the station somehow, or they'd grabbed the journal from Raymond's car at Cassie's office.

Faxon laid the journal on the table, then slid it closer to his side when I reached for it.

"In the front is a slip of paper with the requirements to become a PI. You can see Jack's writing on the bottom of it."

Faxon pulled the sheet out and opened it, placing it on the table between him and Botz. "That's Jack's writing," Botz said to Faxon, pointing to Jack's notes. He looked at me. "Are you serious with this stuff?"

I let out a long breath. Right now, it didn't seem like the brightest of ideas. Clearly I didn't have the right instincts. Sitting in a car doing a stakeout of a murder suspect with the murderer right next to me confirmed I wasn't very good at this.

"Hmm, you might be good at this," Botz said as he flipped through my journal.

"No sense telling you some of that's private, right?" I asked.

Faxon snorted, and Marvin made a deep noise in his throat like he was about to object or something.

"Did you not just offer this up to us as proof that you were investigating Hendricks? As a reason why you wouldn't kill him? And that you were assisted by the woman you're now accusing of two homicides?"

I nodded and waved at them to continue their perusal. Not that they were waiting for my permission.

Botz, bless him, skimmed the stuff I'd written while working with Monty—the compulsive gambling stuff. He stayed more on the pages about Johnny's and Niall's murders. Again, I tried to remember if I'd actually written Cassie's name down anywhere. Something to show we were working together. I knew it wasn't in the bit that I'd just read through with Kaitlyn, about Cassie's non-questioning of her.

At least now I knew why Cassie hadn't bothered questioning Kaitlyn about any of it. She simply didn't care if Kaitlyn was involved with Niall. Didn't matter in the least to her. She knew Kaitlyn hadn't been involved with Johnny's murder.

Because Cassie had shot Johnny herself.

So Kaitlyn and Niall staying in the same motel really was just a coincidence.

Huh. There went that theory. Sometimes there *were* coincidences.

"So you did find Kaitlyn? Talked with her?" Botz asked. I could tell he was on that page because I'd doodled (badly) a pair of Chucks in the margin.

"I did talk with her, yes," I said. I relayed the conversation I'd had with her that morning at Arizona Charlie's.

"And your thoughts on that? On her?"

"Not involved. Didn't know Niall. Only worked with Johnny a couple of times. No motive. In fact, she was trying to get hold of him to work again. He was a paycheck. You keep those alive."

"Didn't know Niall at all?"

"That's what she said, and I believed her about other things, so yeah, I believed her about that. I showed her a picture, and she said he seemed familiar. She placed him at her motel after I told her. Said she'd seen him in the parking lot, vending machines, that type of thing. That's as deep as that connection goes."

"Hell of a coincidence," Botz said. "You being connected to both of them."

I shrugged. "That's what I thought too. But I suppose the gambling crowd, players and dealers, all know the cheap places to stay in this town. I know I did."

"No seedy motel now, though, right?" Faxon said. His face was neutral, but there was a sneer in his voice. Resentment. I could only imagine the shit he probably gave Jack about his sugar-mama girlfriend.

Nah. Maybe once. That was all he'd be able to get in before Jack hit back. Literally.

"In the back is the target from the last time I went to the range. I kept it because I want to track any improvement."

Botz unfolded it and held it up. Light streamed through the holes where I'd shot at the human outline target. Mostly 7s and 8s on the scoring circle. Shoulders, gut, ribs, maybe the heart if the guy moved. There was one less hole than rounds. I'd missed the target completely with that one.

Yeah, room for improvement.

"Where's the last shot?" Faxon said.

"Off target. Way off target," I said. I pointed to the lower corner of the target where Buddy's logo was. "And that is where I shot the Colt 1911. A few times. I'll figure out the exact dates for you. That's the only gun I've shot since Saul died."

Botz and Faxon looked at each other, both obviously thinking about the same thing.

Oh. Oh, right. Not long ago I'd woken up with a dead body. Botz and Faxon had been called to the scene. Not being terribly coherent because I'd been drugged, I couldn't remember anything. It was assumed that I was the shooter. So, even though it had been cleared up, Faxon and Botz were both remembering that morning and thought that I had been brandishing a gun.

Right. That was where they had my fingerprints from. That night. They'd also done a residue test. And probably gathered

DNA, to use for elimination, if not actual evidence.

I shivered, remembering the aftermath of a night that I didn't remember at all.

They left me alone again, Marvin taking a break too. I stayed in the room thinking about Cassandra's plan.

Did she know that her being a PI would be a way to lure me in? Was she even a PI?

There was the information about the federal investigators that she'd gotten for Vince. Yeah, she was probably the real deal. And she'd somehow found out I was looking into becoming a PI. She could have looked over my shoulder literally anytime I was in a public place and my journal was open. Or hacked our search history from the computer at home. It'd probably be easy for someone with her skills.

And that was her in. Getting a weapon with my prints on it must have seemed like hitting two face cards when you've split your aces.

God, I was so stupid. She must have been holding back in those stylish jeans, trying not to laugh at how easily I played into her hand.

The confidence to set up a fake office knowing I'd come a-callin'. Or maybe the office was real and she'd just shut it down on her way out of town?

Out of the country?

When we reconvened, there was fresh coffee brought in and Marvin got rid of his suit coat, slipping it onto the back of his chair. Time seemed to blur.

We all nodded, and the machines were all turned back on. "This is pretty elaborate lengths to go just to frame you," Faxon said.

"I would imagine any frame job would be elaborate. The good ones, anyway." Marvin hid a snort of laughter with a cough. I sighed and leaned forward, putting my arms on the table. "Look, the gun is easily explained away—"

"Not easily," Faxon said.

"Whatever. Easy to me; you guys just have to buy into it. So, the gun is a wash. If it is, then so is the motel room setup. They go together. But more importantly, there is no motive for me to kill Johnny or Niall."

"We have an IOU being processed as evidence that says you have sixty thousand motives."

I scoffed, flicking a wrist for effect. "Why would I okay an IOU and then kill the kid an hour later? Hardly a good return on investment."

"Maybe you followed him to the Queen of Hearts and tried to shake him down there? Couldn't wait until the agreed-upon time for payment."

"Shake him down? You're watching too many cop shows, Faxon."

This time it was both Botz and Marvin who covered up their laughs.

"No, it doesn't make good business sense," I said. "I'm a gambler, yes, but I'm a good businesswoman."

Well, Lor was, anyway.

"No, I was there that night doing exactly what I told you I was when you questioned me the next morning. In fact, this is just a rehash of that morning. Nothing has changed on my end."

"We are now in possession of the gun you used on both Johnny and Niall," Faxon said. "I'd say something's changed on our end."

"I explained the gun. And who planted it. Next?"

Faxon bit his lower lip, which probably stopped him from reaching across the table for my throat. Botz jumped in, leaning in, almost fencing Faxon out. "So, Anna, where we picked you up, why was it so important that you get there before we could take you in? What is that place?"

Faxon sat back, waiting.

"It was Cassandra's office. Or had been. I'm sure it can be

traced to her somehow." As I said it, I had doubts. She was good enough to cover her tracks on that, but did she even bother with that, knowing she was going to disappear?

"Why didn't you just tell us all this in front of the restaurant? Why did you drive to the office?"

I thought about that. "I'm not really sure. I guess I hoped she'd still be there."

"Even more reason to tell us about it. So we could be there to question her, or bring her in."

He was right. But… "I guess…I just wanted to confront her. To let her know I'd figured it out. That I'd solved her puzzle."

"That she'd made you a good investigator?" Botz asked. His voice was gentle, like he knew how stupid that sounded, but it was nonetheless true.

"Yeah. Something like that," I said. "Closure. Whatever."

I sat back in my chair, exhausted.

"So, something I don't understand," Faxon said.

"What's that?" I said.

"This is a lot of work, what you said she did. She'd have to be really motivated to get this all in motion."

"Revenge can be a big motivator. You guys know that better than most people," I said.

"True. True. But we also know that people tend to do things the easy way."

"Right. So?"

"So, this frame job was all out of revenge for Vince Santini dying, right?"

"That's what I believe, yes."

"So why not just kill *you*? If she's going to kill two people anyway, why not just kill you and be done with it? Saves a lot of hassle."

Huh. It was a good question. One for which I had no answer.

Thirty-Seven

❖

AND ON IT WENT. THEY CIRCLED BACK ON THINGS THAT were unclear, and I cleared them up with what I knew. We took bio breaks when we needed, and they brought in food and beverages. Officers would come in and whisper things to Faxon or Botz, and they'd leave for a while. When they came back, they'd go off on a new tangent.

I stuck to my story. Because it was the truth. I couldn't answer why Cassie had gone to great lengths to frame me when she could have just killed me.

"Maybe she wanted me to suffer? To spend my life behind bars for something I didn't do?"

Botz thought on this and then said, "So why not kill Carla Rossetti and frame you for it? She was with you when Vince died. That'd be killing the proverbial two birds. Bringing Johnny and Niall into it all just because you were in contact with both seems odd."

I didn't have an answer for that either.

Botz was the secret weapon I had over Cassie. She had to have guessed Jack would never be allowed near my case, but she didn't know about Botz and that he had a fondness for me. At least, I thought he did. Regardless, he held my thoughts on a murder case in pretty high estimation, having seen me figure out one or two of them in the past. He would take my exhortations of a frame job seriously.

Faxon, not so much.

Around midnight, I gave Marvin a look that said I had nothing left, and he nodded. We'd found out all they were going to give us. And I'd told them all I knew. All that could happen now was to find Cassie.

Or for them to charge me.

"Charge my client or let her go. This has gone on long enough."

They gave me my phone and keys back. I asked for the journal. It was clear they didn't want to, but Marvin spouted something legal at them and they capitulated. I didn't know what I was paying Marvin, but he was definitely worth it.

He and I walked to the elevators in silence, waiting until we had arrived in the lobby and exited the building.

"Thanks again, Marvin."

"Of course. Do you need a ride home?"

"That's okay. They gave me my phone back; I can call an Uber."

"Are you sure? Let me wait with you, anyway."

"I'm standing in front of the police station. I think I'll be okay. Thanks, Marvin."

He nodded and set off toward the parking deck around the side of the building. I powered on my phone, deeply breathing in the midnight air. Heaven, after so many hours in a small room with three other people.

And a lot of my own sweat, though I tried to hide it.

I expected to see a ton of texts and missed calls, but there was only one text each from Jack and Raymond. Jack must have gotten to Ben and Lor and calmed them down.

I read Raymond's first, thinking I might need more time for Jack's.

I'm parked nearby. Text when they let you out.

The time stamp was an hour ago. I didn't know if he just

figured it was a good time to come and wait, or if Jack had somehow tipped him off about my questioning wrapping up.

And how would Jack know?

I looked back into the lobby of the station, looking for Jack's face, but he wasn't there. I texted Raymond that I was out front, and he responded he was on his way and would be there in minutes.

It made me think about those cell phone lots they have by airports. Sadly, it would probably make sense to have one of those near police stations.

I turned back toward the street and kept an eye out for Raymond. Finally, I took a deep breath and read Jack's text.

Very large Iceberg.

RAYMOND PICKED ME UP in my Porsche. I got into the passenger seat. "Home?" he asked.

"Home," I said. "Wait. A drive-thru first. Anywhere. A burger of any kind."

"They didn't feed you this whole time?"

I lifted one shoulder. "From a vending machine. I need grease and cheese."

"Done," he said, getting into the left-hand turn lane. "So the scoop with Jack is he's staying at his apartment tonight. Said it'd be better if you two didn't talk tonight. Both for your case and for him as a cop. But also, that if you *needed* him, then fuck all that and call him."

I smiled faintly as he pulled into a Jack in the Box. I leaned across him to yell my order at the speaker. When I was done, he brought his hand up and kind of hugged my head.

"You okay?" he said softly.

I almost started crying. Okay, maybe I did a little bit. Or maybe Raymond had spilled some water strategically down the front of his shirt.

Either way, his shirt was damp as I put my face on his chest and feebly nodded. "Yeah, I'm okay. Or I will be." He patted my head, then released me. He ordered for himself, and after we gathered it at the window, he drove to a spot in the parking lot and cut the engine. He grabbed the bag of food, nodded for me to get our drinks, and got out of the car, walking to the picnic table in the grassy median of the Jack in the Box's lot.

We settled in and took bites and drinks, mmm-ing as both hit our systems.

When we finished, I started to get up to go back to the car, but Raymond stopped me by grabbing my arm.

"Before we get back in the car… On the off chance that it's bugged or some shit like that."

"Yeah?" I said.

"Tell me where the hell we were today when the cops showed up."

"It's a long story," I said.

"I got all night," Raymond said.

So I told him all about it. When I'd finished, he said, "That's some fucked-up shit."

"Tell me about it," I said.

He stood and made his way back to the car. I followed him. He motioned if I wanted the keys, but I shook my head and got back into the passenger seat.

He got behind the wheel. "Home?" he asked.

"Home," I said.

Thirty-Eight

❖❖

IT WAS THREE IN THE MORNING WHEN WE FINALLY GOT home. I knew I wouldn't be able to sleep, so I went into the TV room.

I didn't want to crawl into a bed without Jack and think about the reason he was staying at his apartment.

Raymond joined me, and I told him to head to bed, but he just waved my decree away and sat down in the recliner next to mine.

"Hey, do you still have that envelope that Vince left for you? The one you got at Marvin's office?" I asked.

"Yeah, of course. Why?"

"Would you mind if I looked at it? Now that I know it was Cassie who gathered the information, I don't know, maybe something different would jump out at me."

He left his seat and strode from the room, back in five minutes, changed into sweats, and handed me the brown envelope.

It reminded me of the envelope that Cassie had handed Greta Gunnell. An office supply standard for PIs—the classic brown envelope.

I tossed a throw blanket to Raymond, and he reclined and covered himself, grabbing a remote and turning on one of the several televisions mounted to the wall.

It was still too early for *College GameDay* even with the time difference, but there was some other pregame show on, and he stayed on ESPN, lowering the volume to just barely audible.

I looked through the information on the two feds who had been investigating Raymond all those months ago for point shaving. I wasn't interested in the actual substance of the report as much as seeing if there was anything innately Cassie written between the lines.

At the point when she'd done the report, she had no reason to want to frame me for murder. Wouldn't have even known who I was. Vince was still alive, trying to get insurance in case the whole Raymond/JoJo connection blew back on him. But he'd kept me out of it. At least in his instructions to Cassie. It wasn't until Vince died that she'd turned her attention to revenge.

And to me.

Even though it was Carla who had ultimately pushed Vince to his death, Cassie blamed me for it.

She wasn't entirely wrong.

Seeing nothing in the report that screamed, "I'm capable of killing two innocent men if it means that bitch Anna goes to prison for life," I put it back into its envelope and slid it to the side table next to me. I then reclined myself and pulled a blanket over me.

Raymond took one of the other remotes and dimmed the lights so they were barely on. I was glad he had mastered the remotes. I'd lived here for a lot longer than he had, and I still turned off a TV when trying for the lights.

We sat in silence, neither one wanting to keep the other awake.

An hour later, it was obvious neither of us would be sleeping anytime soon. I knew I wouldn't until I heard from Botz.

"Hey," Raymond said.

"Yeah?"

He didn't turn my way, and I didn't turn to him. We both

sat in mostly dark, staring at the TV screen in front of us, hearing but not listening to a segment about the lack of depth in the Big East conference.

"That night? When Johnny was killed?"

"Yeah?" I braced myself.

"So, that night, after I left the Venetian, you know I didn't come straight home."

"Right," I said. I'd met him in the hallway to our bedrooms, just getting in after I'd already gotten home.

"I was parked at Albertsons. On the phone. I'd gotten a call, which I didn't want to take here."

I let that sit for a moment. "Okay," I said.

"That night after dinner, when you and the boys were talking about your networks. Building them up, staying in touch. Remember that conversation?"

"I do," I said. I also remembered Raymond being very into his phone during that evening. I hadn't thought much about it at the time.

"Well, the night Johnny was killed, a friend reached out to me."

"Right. The basketball player at Ohio State. And he mentioned some of the football players were partying."

"Yeah, him. The football guys partying came out of the conversation, but he reached out to me for something else. He'd been drinking, so I didn't make a big deal of what he said, but he's contacted me since."

"He wants to know about point shaving," I guessed. I couldn't see Raymond, but I assumed he was nodding.

Months ago, Raymond had mentioned something about knowing so many other college players because of the youth basketball camps and AAU. His network was probably as deep and geographically diverse as Jimmy's was. Just a lot younger.

"Tips about football players partying is one thing. Shit, even stuff like his teammate is only going to play the first half because of a sore ankle is...is..."

"Legit tips. Not point shaving," I finished for him.

"Right. This is a whole different ball game. This is some serious shit."

"Oh, I know," I said. "And I know you know. It's life-altering stuff." I raised a hand around the room we now sat in. A little different than his apartment in Dubuque, where he should have been preparing for his senior season.

"But the flip side is this guy is poor. I mean *poor*. You saw where I came from?"

"Yes," I said. It had been in the very dangerous Englewood neighborhood of Chicago. But Mahalia had provided a warm, loving home for her children. It just happened to be in the middle of the U.S.'s murder capital.

"Where he's from makes my place look like the Taj Mahal."

Oof. Not good.

"Listen, you don't need to make the case to me about universities and coaches making money off players," I said. "And some of the universities are dirty as hell and their players are getting perks and cash, while other programs—like yours—are clean and their players suffer for being on the up and up. It's a system rigged for everybody but the players, and it bugs the hell out of me."

"I know. Friend to the little guy, that's you."

"Fuck off," I said, and he laughed.

"So, I'm torn. Do I bankroll my guy to help him? Or am I doing more harm than good?"

"Geez, Raymond, I don't know. I doubt pretty much all of my life decisions daily. I'm working with Monty on all of that, so I'm hardly the person to ask for advice."

"That's exactly why I'm asking you," he said.

Time passed and I still wasn't sure what to say.

Raymond finally said, "Let me put it this way. If it was you and me, and I came to you to bankroll me, lay some money down for me, what would you do?"

"That's exactly what happened," I said, though I didn't need to. He knew. And that was exactly why he'd phrased it the way he had. "And I blocked you out. Got rid of the number you had for me."

"Because you thought you were protecting me," he said.

"That's what I told myself."

"It wasn't true?" he asked.

"It was true," I said. "But then you went out on your own."

"And got caught."

"So you're thinking your Buckeye would do that? He'd be desperate enough to go out on his own to find a bettor?"

I could hear Raymond shifting in his recliner, the soft leather making a squishing sound. "I don't know. Maybe. Not sure I'm willing to take that chance, you know? I like this guy. Know him from early days."

"Then I think you answered your own question."

"Yeah, I think I did. Season doesn't start for a couple of months. Maybe the idea will die off for him by then," he said.

"Yeah, maybe," I said.

We both knew that wouldn't happen.

AT EIGHT WE HEARD LOR in the kitchen getting our Saturday bagel spread out. We both helped her bring it all out to the sideboard in the dining room where we had breakfast on Saturdays.

"Hannah, dear, Jack called me this morning to make sure you were okay," Ben said. "What should I tell him?"

"You can tell him that I'm fine, Ben. Tell him I'll call him later this afternoon. I think things might be cleared up by then." Hopefully the cops would be able to corroborate my explanation of Cassandra's frame job.

His brown eyes looked worried, but cleared some when I delivered that news. "Oh, good. I like it best when Jack is staying here."

"You and me both," I said.

Jimmy came just before nine and piled a plate high before taking it into the TV room, where the first college games on Eastern time would soon be kicking off.

Raymond and Ben joined him, and Lor and I sat together in the dining room while I filled her in on everything.

"Holy shit," she said when I'd finished.

"That about sums it up," I said.

"What do you think Vince was to her? That she'd be so *driven* to make you pay?"

I tore a piece of bagel off and popped it into my mouth. "Who knows? Obviously it went beyond employer/employee. Was it romantic? Is that part of it? I really don't know. I might do more to avenge a friend than an ex, you know?"

"Totally," she agreed. "If he even was her ex."

"Right. If not, I guess the couple of dates he and I went on—if you could call them that—might have given her more motivation. But I don't think Vince would have done that."

I waited for her to give me a "poor, naïve Jo" look, but she nodded. "Yeah, I don't think so, either." She'd met Vince when he came over to see me.

This town made you size people up quickly. Didn't always mean you were right.

Lorelei looked at her watch. "So, your day is open?"

"Yeah, I guess. I mean, I can't leave town or anything. And I want to stay close to my phone in case Frank calls, but yeah. What do you need?"

"You and I are going to the kitchen to make rugelach. Or try to, anyway."

It would keep my mind off things while the detectives went and detected.

"Perfect," I said. "You're the best, Lor."

"Damn straight. And I think it important to point out that *I* have never framed you for murder."

I chuckled and pushed in my chair. As I left the dining room, I heard her say, just loud enough for me to hear, "Yet."

Before heading to the kitchen, I stopped by the TV room to check in on the boys. Ben asked if there was any news, and I told him no, but not to worry. "Just a matter of time before I'm officially cleared."

"Oh, thank God," Ben said. Jimmy just nodded, not taking his eyes off one of the games on the various televisions.

Raymond was studying me, and I gave a small shrug, telling him that what I'd told Ben was hopefully true.

He nodded, and I was reminded of finding them all in this room a few nights ago when the discussion of Black hair was being had.

"I think twists would look good on you," I said to Raymond. "When your hair is long enough."

"Yeah?" he said.

"Yeah," I said.

He thought on that and returned his attention to the game.

The night of the hair discussion had ended with Jack following me to my bedroom. Today I walked to the kitchen to bake while Jack was probably just waking up in his little apartment.

A lot could change in two days.

Thirty-Nine

❖❖

I WOULD NEVER BE A GREAT CHEF. OR EVEN A CRAPPY one. But I did enjoy spending a few hours with Lor in the kitchen. Every once in a while, I'd sit at the table and repeat a version of "I can't believe I was so dumb."

"You have to let yourself off the hook. She was very good."

"I mean, how many stupid superhero movies did I watch with Jack and Casey this summer? The mentor is *always* the bad guy."

"I wouldn't exactly call her your *mentor*," Lorelei said, with just a touch of pettiness in her voice. I thought that maybe another shopping trip was in our future.

Maybe I'd have another pair of boots to show Jack. If he ever came home.

All those lovely clothes I'd bought in an attempt to look more professional. To look like Cassandra Hall. What an idiot. They would probably sit unworn in my closet, right next to JoJo's clothes.

The kitchen was warm and the scent of cinnamon was delicious. The rugelach that Lor had rolled looked a lot more symmetrical than the ones I'd done, but I knew they'd all taste the same. Early on, I'd wanted to make an Albertsons run and cheat with a couple of tubes of crescent roll dough, but Lor wouldn't hear of it. A good thing, too, because hers (ours!) were wonderfully flaky.

I brought a plate of them into the TV room for the boys, careful not to turn my attention to all the games. The rugelach was tempting enough.

When I re-entered the kitchen, Lor had a dozen or so of the pastries in a pretty cookie tin and was placing the lid on it. Handing the tin to me, she said, "Here. Take a ride to the Strip and give these to your guy there. Keep him happy. Strengthen your network bonds."

I grunted. "Why bother? It's obvious I'm not cut out for this. Might as well let the whole network thing crumble."

Much like when I'd wanted to go with Pillsbury, Lor was having none of it. "You don't know what you're going to do yet. And you're not going to decide anything while this is all so raw. If not to solidify Al in your cabal or whatever, at least take him these as a thank you for the heads-up about Niall's whereabouts."

She made sense, so I took the tin of treats and headed for the door.

"And to get you out of the house for a while," she said softly.

"I heard that," I said from the hallway.

"You were meant to!"

I went to my office to grab my jacket that I'd thrown on the back of my chair during one of my epic police procedural internet rabbit holes. Passing by my cigar box, I opened it, not remembering where things stood after the game where Niall wrote me the IOU. Had I given my stake to Lor to hide/invest/spend?

My chest felt heavy as I remembered that night, and realizing that I'd probably led Cassie right to Niall's door. Served him up on a platter.

There were two rolls of cash in the box, each bound by a rubber band. I could estimate how much money was in each by the size of the roll. There was a roll that likely had three thousand dollars and one that was more like seven or eight. I reached for the smaller one, but my hand veered at the last second and plucked the larger. I stuffed it in my jacket pocket before I let myself think too much on why I thought I'd need a stake when I was simply delivering Jewish delicacies to a friend.

While I set the tin on the passenger seat next to me in my car, my phone went off. Botz.

"Hi, Frank," I said. I truly believed that I would be cleared. The frame job was so obvious, or at least to me. But my voice came out nervous anyway, and I had to clear my throat a couple of times.

"An employee at Buddy's gun range broke. He was paid to give Cassie the gun you used the first time you were at the range. It was a different Colt 1911 that you used the subsequent visits."

She must have doubled back to Buddy's to get the gun after she and I went to the Koffee Klatch the first time. Relief coursed through my body, and I slumped down into the driver's seat. "That's good. That's really good. Wait. An employee? Not Buddy, though, right?"

"Not Buddy himself, no. He checked out okay. It was a lower-level guy. Guy named Craig Waters. The guy who cleans the guns after they've been used."

Or didn't clean them, in this instance.

I didn't know why, but it made me happy to know it wasn't Buddy who had sold Cassie a future murder weapon with my prints. He was a curmudgeon for sure, but it was pretty clear that I had a major soft spot for old curmudgeons.

"The office we picked you up in yesterday looks like a dead end. Shell company of some sort rented it out two months ago. There's still a month left on the lease. We've contacted the management company to get footage from their security cameras at the entrance to see if Cassandra Hall is on them. Her coming and going to her office is in no way incriminating, but it backs up that part of your story. We're also going back through her whereabouts during the murders. She's in the wind, though. You were right: looks like she had about a week's head start. But she had been planning her departure—and you taking the fall—for a while."

"Since Vince died," I said. "I don't think you're going to find her, Frank."

"No? Why?"

"She'll either never be found or she'll be somewhere where it won't matter if she is."

"Like a non-extradition situation," he said. It wasn't a question.

"Yeah. She's too good for any other outcome."

"If she was that good, you'd be in a cell right now."

That was true. Although… "I don't know. She would have known I'd put it together with Buddy's. So either she didn't think you'd believe me at all, or that the employee would hold up his story. Or…"

"Or?"

"Or it didn't really matter. She got what she wanted—me in an interrogation room proclaiming my innocence to a cop who doesn't believe me."

Botz didn't bother pointing out that it was Faxon I was talking about and not him. Botz's belief in me was why we were on the phone right now instead of me asking my cellmate if they wanted the top or bottom bunk. Instead of boots that Jack would like, I should be buying a new cartoon necktie for Botz.

"As of now, Cassandra Hall is wanted for the murders of Johnny Kingston and Niall Hendricks."

"That's great, Frank. Thanks for— Wait. Did you say Johnny's last name was Kingston?"

"Yes. Why? Does that name mean anything to you?"

"No. It's just… Your last name is *King*ston but you get aces tattooed on your neck and go with the nickname Johnny Aces? Seems like a missed opportunity."

Botz chuckled, and the sound made me think that this

whole terrible nightmare was likely over. Over for me, anyway.

"Jack there with you?"

"No. He spent the night at his apartment. We haven't been in contact except through Ben and Raymond to let him know I was done being questioned and that I'm home and okay."

"That's probably the smartest move you two have made."

I didn't let on that Jack hadn't consulted me about that decision.

"Okay, Anna. I'll be in touch."

"Got it. Thanks again, Frank." We hung up.

On the drive to the Aria, it all played in my mind again. Cassie's master plan. Poor Niall as collateral damage. Niall's mother blaming me for her son's death. The anticlimactic ending of having Frank Botz tell me over the phone that I was free to move about the country.

It itched—the feeling of emptiness. Done, but not over. Solved, but the killer still free.

Fucking Cassandra Hall.

AL WAS TICKLED TO GET the tin of rugelach. I'd even gone to the fancy coffee place before stopping into the poker room.

"My God, this is wonderful," Al said between mouthfuls. "Almost as good as Rachael's."

"I can't take any credit. I helped, but it was mostly my friend Lorelei who made them."

"Well, thank her for me."

"You bet."

He took a drink of coffee while I looked around the packed poker room. It was Saturday afternoon during college football season. People had made their bets, maybe watched the early games, and then some had migrated over here to play poker for the afternoon. I did the thing Monty taught about checking in with myself to see what visceral reaction I was having to being in a crowded poker room and not playing myself.

It was fine. I didn't feel any urge to ask Al for a seat at a table. Not with how my last game ended.

"Hey, did you find your guy? The one who was playing in Shorty's game?"

"I did, yeah, thanks."

"It turn out okay?" Al asked. I sighed and shook my head. Al nodded knowingly. "This damn town," he said quietly.

"You got that right," I said. "Enjoy the rugelach, Al. There's something at the bottom as another thank you."

Al knew how the game was played. "I appreciate that, Anna." We said our goodbyes, and I left the poker room.

I'd put a thousand dollars from my roll in the bottom of the cookie tin. Maybe I should have let it be a surprise for Al, but then I pictured him setting the tin out in the employee break room or something, so I'd given him a heads-up.

In the main floor of the casino, I hesitated. If I turned right, I'd head back to the self-park ramp and my car. Turning left would take me to the book room. Going straight through the casino would come out at The Shops at Crystals. I had enough cash on me to buy some more boots. Several pairs, in fact.

I turned left. Of course I turned left.

I got to the entrance of the book room, right next to an alcove that housed the entrances to restrooms. I took a deep breath, ready to walk into a book with college games starting on the hour and a wad of cash in my pocket.

My phone rang with a FaceTime request. From an unknown number. I thought of the people I'd given my number out to recently for leads on Niall or Kaitlyn.

Niall wouldn't have been seen, obviously, and I no longer cared about Kaitlyn Randall, having her info stored in my own phone.

But then I suddenly knew who was calling me. The book room exploded in a cheer as some team did something very good or very bad. Ducking into the women's room for quiet, I connected with the call. At first, I was blinded by the sunlight and the blue of the ocean. Then Cassie's face entered the picture.

"Still want to be a PI?" she said. "Because you're not very good at it."

Forty

❖❖

"WHERE ARE YOU?" SHE SAID ONCE THE BACKGROUND of the women's room showed up onscreen.

"In a ladies' room at the Aria," I said. "What do you want?"

"You're not recording this, are you?"

I laughed. "I don't even know how to do that." It was true: I barely knew how to do FaceTime except for helping Ben to call his grandson, Casey.

"So, you're in the Aria. Not arrested. I've got to say, I was half expecting a cop to answer this call with your phone in their custody."

If she'd called yesterday at this time, that would have been the case.

"Where are *you*?" I asked.

"Somewhere safe," she said. So, someplace without extradition to the States. Or not, but somewhere she'd never be found. She was good.

And as she'd just pointed out, I was not good at this.

Still, I was at the Aria and not in a jail cell, so I guess there was that.

"I'm cleared," I said.

"Bullshit," she said.

I swung the camera around, showing the sleek, dark wood of the bathroom at the Aria book room. "Does this look like a john at Metro?"

"How are you not in custody? Did you make bail? I didn't think you'd be that liquid."

I probably wasn't that liquid, given my instructions to Lor to keep the money invested or spent, not readily available. So I couldn't gamble it away. I hadn't thought about the need to be liquid enough for bail money. Probably should have.

"No bail. No charges. Cleared."

A dark look passed over her face, but it was gone quickly and the emotionless woman I'd been working with the past few weeks came back.

If I'd looked closer, would I have seen this version of Cassandra Hall earlier? Would I have picked up on it? On something being off? The way I would sitting across a poker table with someone?

But I hadn't, so happy to have found someone to help me along my journey.

Except she'd found me.

"How long has this been in motion?" I said. "Since Vince died? The day of the will reading?"

"That's when I became aware of you, yes. There was no 'plan' per se, until the timing stars aligned with Johnny's name being spoken, seeing you at Buddy's, and then Niall. It was like the perfect storm of vengeance."

"Lucky you," I said.

She snorted, though it was soft and ladylike. Did the fact that Cassandra was polished and professional (and a white, pretty woman) color how I viewed this case? Would I have seen her for who she was sooner if I hadn't wanted to dress like her?

"Are you really cleared?"

I nodded. "Free as a bird. I'm assuming they're checking flight records for you as we speak."

She shrugged. "They're welcome to try."

"For what it's worth, I didn't actually kill Vince," I said.

282 ♠   Mara Jacobs

She waved a hand, a large gold bangle on her wrist gleaming in the sunlight. "Carla. Yes, I know. But she wouldn't have been there in the first place if it weren't for you. You were the catalyst for Vince dying."

"You loved him," I said.

Cassie looked toward the water. She seemed surrounded by it, from what I could see. Like maybe she was on a pier or something. When she faced the phone again, she said, "He was my brother."

Oh, shit. It all made a bit more sense now. "He never—" I stopped myself.

"Mentioned me? I know. He was my foster brother, actually. Grew up together in the system. He protected me. When he could. I got moved around a bit more. Then some other shit happened."

She looked like maybe that would be it, and I wondered about the things she must have been through. And what they'd led her life to become.

She took a deep breath and continued, "We kept in touch a little bit. When he settled out here, I decided to try my luck in Sin City too. He helped me get set up in Vegas. Polished me up a bit, helped me look the part for clients."

I thought of the day with Lor not too far away from where I now stood. I could easily imagine Vince Santini, impeccable dresser, picking out Cassandra's wardrobe. In a creepy way, picking out mine via surrogate.

"The rest is as you know it. I am a PI. I did work some work for Vince, including digging up info to help Raymond if needed. And I had other clients too. We had lives in Vegas. Separate, but still saw each other a lot. He kept me away from people like Paulie and Carla. Still trying to protect me if he could." Her voice was soft, and I thought about the times that Vince—or anyone—was not there to help or protect Cassandra.

Those could be lonely days. I knew them well.

"I'm… I'm sorry for your loss." It seemed like a stupid thing to say given all that had gone down. "I liked Vince, cared for him, even given our history and how things turned out."

"He tried to protect me from myself. Just like he did with you?"

She was fishing. Vince apparently had protected me to the end, not telling even Cassandra about JoJo's adventures.

"Why did you need protection from yourself?" I asked, ignoring the baited hook she'd thrown my way.

"Why does anyone in Vegas need protection?"

"Gambling? You?"

"Don't look so surprised, Anna. You of all people know not to judge a book by its cover."

That was true. Very true.

"I don't know how *you* got out of what you owed when you'd lose. But *I* had a certain set of skills."

It was just as scary when she said it as when Liam Neeson said basically the same thing to the bad guys.

"You'd…kill people," I said. I checked under all the stalls again, as if someone had materialized without walking through the bathroom door.

Still empty. Which was what you wanted when calling out someone for murder.

Multiple murders.

"You make it sound commonplace. Like after every bad bet I'd put a bullet in someone's head."

"But more than just Johnny and Niall," I said.

"More, yes. But long ago. And not many. I told you there were avenues that PIs would be asked to take on occasion. I took a couple when I was desperate."

"So Johnny was a contract hit. It had nothing to do with me at all."

"Not at first. I wasn't even going to take it on. But Vince's estate was taking forever to settle, and I needed money."

"But you got the gun I used from Buddy's before killing Johnny."

Another shrug from her. The wind blew a strand of hair across her face, and she tucked it behind her ear. "I saw an opportunity that day, and I took it. You never know when I might need a gun with your prints on it."

"Kind of like the earring ruse? Just another trick of the trade?"

"Something like that," she said. "And then you walk into a game that Johnny Aces was working. And then you need to find Niall Hendricks. Like I said, perfect storm."

"Niall was a contract too?"

She nodded.

"From who?" I asked.

"Who knows?" she said. "Like I told you, there are discreet ways to pad your income. Emphasis on discreet. It's an exchange of sorts, all done with dummy emails and electronic drop boxes and bank wires. It's not like I ever met anyone."

"Do you think Johnny and Niall were on 'the list' by the same person?" I asked. Carla? I didn't think so. Probably just someone they both owed. Or not even related. Just two guys that got in way over their head and ran out of time.

And Cassandra Hall, or someone like her, earned some extra money taking care of someone else's problems.

The framing of me was just icing on the cake to Cassie.

"Seriously, how did you get off?" she asked.

"You mean where did your airtight frame job leak?"

"I am a professional, after all. I don't like loose ends."

I thought about not telling her anything, but figured it didn't matter. "The guy who sold you the gun at Buddy's talked."

She looked surprised, and then her brain turned it over, figuring out what went wrong. "Son of a bitch. I should have taken that degenerate to the airport myself."

"He was supposed to disappear?" I said. I meant leave Vegas, but maybe I should be more precise in my wording.

"He was blowing town with what I paid him. A large part of my front end for Johnny. He owed people money too. Jesus, who doesn't, right?"

I didn't answer her, but I didn't need to. We both lived in the world of gambling, loan sharks, and debts paid one way or another.

I had thought Cassandra was a spectator to that life, or at least a distant member of the team, sitting on the bench watching the game go by. But no, she was one of the starting lineup.

"So you take the Johnny contract to pay debts, and—"

"Only because Vince's estate took so long to clear. I wasn't ever going to go down that road again. Vince had seen to it. He was protecting me to the end, making sure I could live a life out of this world."

"On some gorgeous island without U.S. extradition," I said.

"He didn't say where I should live, just that he wanted me to get out of this life."

"So he knew. Did you ever…for Vince?"

She shook her head quickly, readjusting the phone in her hand, for a better grip. I did the same with mine, feeling my fingers getting a little slick.

Feeling my back get a little slick, too. Not every day someone confesses to being a sometimes-hitman.

Hitwoman. Yay, feminism!

"No. Never. He would never ask me to. That's what Paulie was for."

"But he knew what you did?"

She looked off toward the view beyond her phone. If it was anything like her background, it was more sparkling seas or sandy beaches. "I don't know. We never talked about it. But he did warn me about being careful. And he'd throw me any legit jobs he could."

"Like investigating Raymond's investigators."

"Exactly," she said.

"And that's the only job concerning me that he had you do?" I wondered if she knew about JoJo but didn't know how to ask.

And maybe she didn't know what to do with the truth if she did know.

"I didn't even know that *you* had anything to do with Raymond Joseph until you showed up at Vince's will reading together. Vince kept you away from his dealings as much as he could."

"Like you," I said.

"Like me," she said. "I guess, in a way, he loved us both."

Not in the same way, but I didn't point that out.

"So, you're going to do this job, the timing and opportunity falls into your lap to frame me for it. But why Niall?"

"Like I said, he was on the list too. The portal, if you will. I'd agreed to it before I even knew of your involvement with him. I was already trying to track him down when you walked into my office wanting me to hire you to help find him."

"Yeah, the offices…"

She ran a hand through her hair, and it neatly fell back into place in the way only a very expensive cut could.

"It was an expense I could have done without, but I needed it in case you called, which you did."

I'd called. And shown up at her office. And done everything else to fall neatly into her trap.

"And Brenda?" I asked.

"Temp I hired for a few weeks. That's the time I had to deal with Johnny and Niall. I figured if you didn't contact me by then I'd just leave the gun somewhere it could be eventually found. But you showed up, all bright-eyed and bushy-tailed, ready to be Miss Private Eye, and thus a bit of payback was born."

"So, if I'd never contacted you about PI hours, you would have just done in Johnny and used a gun with my prints on it?"

She shrugged. "Not very elegant, is it? But that's before I knew of your connection to Johnny and then Niall. Like I said—"

"The perfect storm. And I set it in motion by wanting to learn from you."

"I'd say you did learn from me, wouldn't you?"

I nodded. "Yeah, I guess I did."

"I have to say, though, I did like that office. I usually work out of my apartment. There's really no need for an office with this kind of work. That's a tip I didn't pass on to you."

"Thanks for sharing," I said.

She laughed. "Hey, when did you figure it out? You could only be cleared if Craig had identified me as the one he sold the gun to. Is that when you figured it out?"

I shook my head. "I ran into Kaitlyn, and she said you'd never gone to her room and looked around. The earring trick never happened."

Cassie nodded slowly, letting that sink in. "No, it didn't. That was all so I could get into your car. See if there was something there that was usable. Jackpot on that, by the way."

She was talking about the JoJo stuff. God, I had played into her hand the minute the cards had been dealt.

"Plus, there didn't seem like a need to talk to Kaitlyn. We'd found Niall. I knew his name had been *spoken*. She was a non-factor. And I didn't want her to be able to identify me if things went sideways. What was her connection to Niall, anyway?"

"None. Just someone she'd see around the motel. No connection at all," I said.

"A coincidence that they were both at the Moonlight?"

"Yeah, turns out it was."

"How about that. There really are coincidences. Kind of gives me hope in a sad way."

"Me too," I said.

She took a deep breath, raising her face to the sun, making

her pretty features even more stunning. When she looked back at the phone, there seemed to be a peacefulness to her that I hadn't seen before.

Maybe Cassie had outrun her demons. Niall hadn't. Johnny had not outrun his greed.

We all had them. Some were small and kept us at AA or GREET meetings.

Others had our names being *spoken* and flying to non-extradition countries.

"Where are you?" I asked again, not expecting a straight answer.

She hesitated a moment and then must have figured what the hell. "The Maldives. It is spectacular." She moved her phone around to show me she was on the deck of one of those cottages on the water. Literally right on the water.

"Yeah. Spectacular," I agreed.

"I'm already quite fond of it," she said. "I have no intention of ever leaving." There was a finality in her voice. And just a touch of warning.

"I can't do anything to you. I'm sure you've done your homework about extradition countries."

"I have. But I don't want to be looking over my shoulder while I'm sipping drinks out of a pineapple."

"And why would I have anything to do with that?"

"I'm not sure you would. But let's just say it would be in your best interest to forget that you ever met me."

Ah, if only that were possible. To have the last month back, and never have met Cassandra at Buddy's.

But, according to what she was telling me, Johnny and Niall would still be dead. I just wouldn't be the one whom cops suspected.

My heart panged again at the thought of Niall. And his poor parents.

"Believe me, I do wish I'd never met you," I said. She'd

thrown me a lob, so didn't even crack a smile when I returned it with the correct answer.

"I'm sure you feel that way now. But from someone who knows, the idea of payback can start small. But it grows, it festers. I'm saying don't let those ideas creep into your head."

The warning tone again. She wanted me to say "or what?" but I didn't. Let her do the work.

Irritation crossed her face, and I showed no sign of the sick thrill that it gave me. "Here's the thing, Anna. I actually am a pretty good PI. And I have nothing but time now. Time to do some digging as to why a kid from Chicago—who was being investigated for a point-shaving scheme—is living with a professional gambler in Las Vegas. Seems odd, no?"

"Professional poker player," I said.

She chuckled. "Right. Sorry. Poker player. My bad." The amusement left her face as she continued, "A poker player who has a full-fledged disguise in the trunk of her car. One who was very close to a known loan shark."

"Get to the scary warning part," I said, tiring of her game.

She laughed. "Okay. How's this? Forget you ever met me. Forget about payback. Forget the Maldives. Because I don't think it would take a PI of my talents—and my talents are many—to put together the missing pieces of Anna Dawson."

It wasn't the missing pieces of Anna Dawson she'd find if she went digging. It was JoJo.

And JoJo led back to Raymond.

"Got it," I said. "Point made."

"Good," she said. "Well, listen, it's been a pleasure, but I see they're bringing me my champagne, so I really—"

"You'll die there, you know," I said, playing the only cards I had in my hand. Now knowing Cassandra was a gambler, I had an ace up my sleeve.

"Well, yes, that's the plan. But can you think of a more glorious place in which to grow old?"

"No. You'll never make it there. No action."

"I've had enough action for a lifetime."

"Not 'action' as in rollicking nightlife," I said. But she knew what I meant. Every gambler knew "action." Every gambler wanted, needed, craved action. Skin in the game.

A wager.

And right now I was wagering that I could, if not make Cassandra pay for the killings, at least plant a seed of dissatisfaction. She was surrounded by enough water to make the seed grow over time.

"What? You don't think I can get action anytime I want? On this phone alone I can get to any offshore betting site. Not to mention casinos here. And—"

"It's not the same," I said, putting all I had into seeming sure.

I wasn't.

"Action is action," she said.

"No. It's not. And you know it. You'll be itching to be out of paradise and back on the Strip in a year."

The seed had dropped, and her pause was enough to make me think that it had found fertile soil.

"Just keep out of my way, Anna."

"I won't get in your way, Cassandra. I won't have to. You'll do it on your own."

I disconnected the call before she could say anything more. It felt like the only upper hand that I'd ever have with her.

Getting into her head.

She'd sure gotten into mine.

Forty-One

❖❖

THIS TIME I DIDN'T CALL MONTY AND TELL HIM HOW I was feeling.

Screw feelings. Where did they ever get me? And if I was going to talk about feelings, it would be about the Hummer I was about to experience.

It felt so odd to me to have figured out the bad guy (girl) and not be able to do anything about it. No "Book 'em, Danno" moment or some kind of climatic shootout.

I left the ladies' room and headed to the book. I took my wad of cash and spent it all. Money lines, parlays, over/unders, everything. All of them long shots. I spent the whole stake on college football games that were about to start.

I wasn't looking for long-term investment, just short-term satisfaction.

This was my shootout.

The Aria book room was set up with lots of viewing areas that were like mini living rooms with a couch, love seat, even a coffee table. All of those were filled up with game watchers. But as luck would have it (ha!) someone left one of the lone love seats just as I entered from the betting counter. I quickly plopped down in it and slouched low into the leather. I put my pile of bet slips on the table in front of me and waited for the Hummer to take some of the bad juju away.

Three hours later, I still felt like shit.

I couldn't even tell you if I was winning or losing, I was so tuned out.

"This seat available?"

I looked up to see Jack standing over me, pointing to the empty side of my love seat. I nodded with my chin, and he sat down next to me.

"I talked with Botz," he said. "He gave me the all-clear."

I nodded but didn't say anything.

"And then I talked with Lor, who told me she sent you down here to deliver cookies or something?"

"Rugelach."

Jack pointed to the stack of bet slips in front of me on the table. "Yours?" I nodded. As if giving him some sort of signal, he immediately snagged one of the passing cocktail waitresses. "Bourbon. Double. Neat." She nodded to him and kept going. I dug out a bunch of drink tickets I'd been given when I made my bets.

"On me," I said. He smiled and pulled out a five for a tip, putting it with the drink ticket.

When the waitress came back with his drink, he handed her both the ticket and the five. A feeling of protectiveness came over me, and I sat up and took the drink out of Jack's hand just as he was bringing it to his mouth.

"Tell you what. How about a trade? I get this, and you get those." I nodded to the stack of bet slips.

Amused, but still eyeing the bourbon I now held, Jack took the slips and started going through them, checking out the board for current scores as he did.

"Jesus, what were you on, some suicide mission, making these? You might have just as well given the money to the homeless guys on the corners."

"I'll take no lectures from you today," I said, then brought his glass to my lips and took a noisy sip.

"Not a lecture. Never a lecture. But shit, some of these are just…" He shook his head as he went through them all. He handed them to me, but I shook my head.

"I'm serious. They're yours. Any winners in there are yours. And this is mine." I tipped my glass to him and took a deep drink of the bourbon, feeling the burn.

"The winner. Right. With these long shots, if any of them win, I can put Casey through college."

I laughed. "Jack, you don't have to worry about putting Casey through college. He'll be taken care of."

"I would never ask you to—"

"Not me. Though I would and will if we're still… No, I meant Ben. Casey's grandfather. I know he's planning on doing what he can for Casey, since he couldn't for you."

That shut Jack up, and I continued to sip his drink. Good— let him suffer deep thoughts like I was.

"Wanna talk about it?" he said an hour later when I'd gotten another bourbon, and a water for him.

"Not really," I said.

He nodded and sat back in his seat just as I sat up in mine.

"I mean, what the fuck, right? How could I not have seen what was going on! How did I ever think I could be a PI when I couldn't even see someone trying to frame me for murder?"

"You were too clo—"

"And so, what? I'm not going to be one? Just put that idea away?"

"Not necessarily, you—"

"And if not that, then what? I've stopped gambling. Stopped playing poker. No job. No skills. I think I've proven that pretty thoroughly."

"You have—"

"I mean, I'm only thirty-four! What am I supposed to do with my life now?" I looked at Jack.

"Oh, now I can answer?" he said.

I waved for him to continue, and he let out an exasperated sigh, but then sat up in his seat and faced me.

"I don't know what you're supposed to do. Get married. Have babies. Learn to cook."

I gave him a "fuck off" look, to which he held up his hands in surrender.

"Kidding. I was kidding."

Good. Wait. "About which part?"

The hands of surrender dropped to his thighs. "All of it. None of it. I don't know, Johanna."

"Me neither," I said. I took another sip of bourbon. We watched the game on in front of us. An epic upset was brewing. I'd taken the underdog on the money line. They had to win outright, no points given. Had to beat the defending national champs, away, being a thirty-four-point underdog. And it seemed like it was going to happen.

Looked like Casey would be able to choose Harvard if he wanted.

As I was emptying Jack's second bourbon, he pulled something out of his jacket pocket and handed it to me. It was the size of a ring box, but I knew it wasn't that. We were not in that place.

I opened it up to find a beautiful pair of earrings in a horseshoe shape.

"Distinctive, right? Plus, somebody would be more likely to believe you were desperate to find the earring that matched your necklace." He brought a finger up and placed it on top of my horseshoe pendant. I felt the warmth of his finger through the U. "Look, they even dangle so that the horseshoe is always facing up, the right way."

They were delicate and silver and indeed had a nearly invisible strand of silver running down the center for a drop effect and keeping the U up.

So my luck wouldn't run out.

I saw a splash land on the velvet of the box and realized that it had fallen from my eye. Tears.

"Oh, Christ, it wasn't supposed to make you cry," Jack said. He grabbed for the cocktail napkin under my empty glass and handed it to me.

"I'm not crying," I said as I dabbed at my eyes. "This is really so, so sweet, Jack. Thank you."

He waved my thanks away, but I could tell he knew how much it meant to me.

"So last night, in my apartment?" he said.

"Yeah?" My mind started whirling with where this could go. Had he been drinking? Was he confessing? Or had it felt so good being back in his place that he thought he'd stay?

Honestly, I didn't know which would make me feel worse.

"I started packing up my stuff."

I reached for the napkin again. Once I'd collected myself, I got out of the love seat and held my hand out to Jack.

"Let's go home so I can lick my wounds," I said.

He rose and slung an arm around my shoulder, pulling me close to his side as we walked out of the book room.

"Better yet, I'll lick 'em for you," he whispered in my ear. I looked up into his face, and he leaned in and kissed me. We stood still for a moment, kissing in the middle of the Aria, while people brushed past us.

He tasted of bourbon. No, that was me. I thought it was me. I was pretty sure it was me. I was going to go with me.

I tucked my head into the crook of his shoulder when he broke the kiss and we left the Aria. To go home.

Our home.

Acknowledgments

Readers Holli Bertram, Liz Kelly, Colleen Gleason, and Patti Kearly were invaluable in their feedback. The editing at Twin Tweaks and Editing 720 was, as always, top notch. And a big thank you to my last-look editor, Margo Burrage.

The Anna Dawson Series will continue

Try Mara Jacobs's romantic mystery

BROKEN WINGS

Try Mara Jacobs's *New York Times* bestselling Worth series

Worth The Weight
Worth The Drive
Worth The Fall
Worth The Effort
Totally Worth Christmas
Worth The Price
Worth The Lies
Worth The Flight
Worth The Burn

Find out more at
www.MaraJacobs.com

Mara Jacobs is the *New York Times* and *USA Today* bestselling author of The Worth Series

After graduating from Michigan State University with a degree in advertising, Mara spent several years working at daily newspapers in Advertising sales and production. This certainly prepared her for the world of deadlines!

Mara writes mysteries with romance, thrillers with romance, and romances with...well, you get it.

Forever a Yooper (someone who hails from Michigan's glorious Upper Peninsula), Mara now splits her time between the U.P. and Las Vegas.

You can find out more about Mara's books at
www.marajacobs.com

Mara loves to hear from readers. Contact her at
mara@marajacobs.com